Heather MacQuarrie was born in Belfast, Northern Ireland and now divides her time between her permanent home there and her holiday apartment in Portugal. She is happily married to Ross and together they have two sons and one young granddaughter. Heather recently left a long career in teaching to pursue other interests and concentrate on her writing.

A Voice from the Past is her first novel.

For more information about Heather, or to send her a message, visit her website:

www.heathermacquarrie.com

…or find her on Facebook:

facebook.com/heather.macquarrie.novelist

…or follow her on Twitter:

@h_macq_novelist

A

VOICE

FROM THE

PAST

Matador
9 Priory Business Park
Kibworth Beauchamp
Leicestershire LE8 0RX, UK
Tel: (+44) 116 279 2299
Fax: (+44) 116 279 2277
Email: books@troubador.co.uk
Web: www.troubador.co.uk/matador

ISBN 978 1783060 047

British Library Cataloguing in Publication Data.
A catalogue record for this book is available from the British Library.

Typeset in 12pt Aldine401 BT Roman by Troubador Publishing Ltd, Leicester, UK

Matador is an imprint of Troubador Publishing Ltd

Printed and bound in the UK by TJ International, Padstow, Cornwall

A big thank you to Ross for believing in me and encouraging me to keep going and to finish the book and also to my good friends, Trish and Clare, for reading the draft manuscript and responding with such enthusiasm. Your positive comments and insightful observations were very helpful and much appreciated.

I also wish to acknowledge the professional services provided by Amy and her associates at Troubador Publishing Ltd and the expertise of Aaron and his team at Senderon 'smart marketing'. It has been a pleasure to work with you all.

And last but not least, I would like to thank my family – Jason and Clare – Aaron, Louise and Chloë – and my husband, Ross – for the fine blend of technical/marketing support and relaxation/distraction time which they have provided. Thanks, folks!

Prologue

Their eyes met across the crowded lobby of the hotel, the instant recognition quickly turning to beaming smiles. Thank God to see a friendly face.

"You called for me over the Tannoy?" the elegant young woman said to the receptionist, an enquiring lilt to her voice, hardly able to fathom that her name had indeed been boomed out across the building.

"Mrs Collington? Yes, indeed. I have a message for you from your husband."

She riffled through some papers on her desk and found the note she had scribbled.

"He asked me to tell you that he will not be able to make the party tonight after all, as he has to attend a very important meeting. He added that you should still attend and stay for the night as planned. The room is already booked and paid for. He was very insistent that you should not try to drive home in this filthy weather. I know it's blowing a blizzard out there."

This was rather disconcerting. She *had* been expecting to stay the night and already had the key to her room but she didn't want to go to a party on her own. She hardly knew any of these people. Nevertheless, she politely thanked the receptionist for passing on the message. There was no point in phoning him back if he was in one of those meetings. And the February weather had indeed taken a turn for the worse.

The beaming smile was now right behind her.

"So you married the bastard?" he said, jocularly. "*Mrs Collington?*"

"I did," she answered, proudly extending her left hand so that he could admire her flashy diamond ring and plain platinum wedding band.

"And he has just stood you up!"

He couldn't help grinning from ear to ear.

"There will be a genuine reason for that."

She defended him immediately. And she meant it. He was her soul mate, the love of her life. She trusted him completely.

"He has had a few of these meetings recently, mostly arranged very suddenly, and he always arrives home in a really stressed state afterwards. He's reluctant to talk about it but I'm worried he might be heading for redundancy. His brother has been avoiding me too and they both work for the same company. There's definitely something afoot but hopefully it won't come to that."

"Things are OK between you as a couple then?"

She tossed her head and smiled.

"Sorry to disappoint you, but yes, we are very happy together and madly in love. I hope there are no hard feelings about the way things ended with us."

"Course not! I'm happy for you. I'm in a serious relationship myself now, have a gorgeous girlfriend."

"Really? Well, where is she?"

She looked around, expecting his girlfriend to be somewhere nearby.

"She's not with me tonight," he laughed, "but I can show you a photo."

Immediately he pulled out his brown, leather wallet and opened it at the picture he proudly carried around with him. She glanced at it and agreed that his girlfriend was indeed very pretty.

"I've just come from a conference connected to work," he now explained. "I'm just going to have a bite to eat and then try to get home through this snow before it gets too late and the roads become impassable."

She shook her head:

"Not a good idea. Have you seen it out there?"

They both turned towards the window and watched as the large snowflakes fluttered down into the car park. Windscreens, bonnets and roofs were already covered in a thick, white blanket.

She had a sudden brainwave:

"Why don't you come to the party with me? You can have your bite to eat for free. I'm supposed to have a guest with me anyway."

He resisted at first.

"I can't just gatecrash someone's party!" he said. "What is it for anyway?"

"Boss's daughter. Twenty-first birthday. I don't even know her. You'd be doing me a real favour."

She looked at him and saw he was considering it.

"Just for old times' sake," she pleaded. "You can't turn down free champagne!"

Two hours later, when they had eaten their fill of sausage rolls, canapés and mushroom and salmon vol-au-vents and had both sung the praises of their respective partners until there was nothing more left to say, the free champagne was still flowing.

"You can't drive home now," she said very sensibly, her speech somewhat slurred. "You've had quite a few glasses of that. And it's still snowing."

He had already worked that out for himself.

"I know. I'm just going to see if they have a room available and I'll stay over."

"I'll come with you."

As they entered the lobby, they noticed that the same olive-skinned girl was still behind the reception desk. She looked up and recognised the young woman she had spoken to earlier. She *was* wearing a very striking red dress and her blonde hair was beautifully coiffed into a fashionable bob.

"Hello again, Mrs Collington," the receptionist said with a smile, appraising the handsome, young man by her side. "I'm so glad that your husband was able to get here after all. I hope you both enjoyed the party. Is there anything I can get for you?"

"No, thank you. We're just heading up to bed," she gushed, caught off guard. "Good night."

"Good night, Mrs Collington and good night to you also, Mr Collington."

He mumbled a reply as they almost fell into the elevator, giggling at the assumption the receptionist had made. They *had* enjoyed the evening, though. Dancing together had brought back some happy memories of their time together. The receptionist was not the first person to assume that they were a couple.

"Why on earth did you not correct her instead of going along with her mistake?"

"I don't know but we can't back out now. We'd look stupid. And guilty. And it's not as if we've done anything wrong. Why don't you just share the room with me, right enough?"

He was dubious.

"Are there two beds?"

"Yes. A double and a single."

The lift had arrived at her floor and they staggered out.

"Guess we won't be needing the single," she giggled. "Let's have some fun. What harm can it do? Sure no-one will know. I won't tell and I'm sure you won't."

"Don't be ridiculous. That's the champagne talking!"

"You're right. Sorry. Makes me very light-headed."

"Me too! I definitely feel a bit drunk."

She inserted the key card into the lock and they both stumbled into the room, still laughing about the situation they had inadvertently got themselves into. They almost collapsed onto the sumptuous double bed which immediately beckoned them. And suddenly they were kissing. Their arms were all over each other, husband and girlfriend momentarily forgotten.

"I'll just order another bottle," she said, as she lifted the receiver of the internal telephone and asked for room service…

1989

Chapter 1

Susan stared blindly through the partly open window of her stifling railway carriage, unmoved by the serene beauty of the English countryside which flashed before her brimful eyes on this inaptly cloudless summer's day. Thankful to be alone at last, she allowed the tears, unshed for too long, to slowly trickle down her young cheeks.

It's over, she repeated inwardly. *Thank God it's over at last. If only I could forget that it ever happened.*

But she would not forget. She knew already in her sickened heart that the memory of her dreadful action that very morning would haunt her all her life. Nevertheless her whole body tensed as she closed her eyes firmly and involuntarily clenched both her teeth and her fists, her jaw aching and her sharp fingernails digging into the soft skin of her palms as she kept repeating it:

I have to put this behind me. I just need to block it all from my mind, keep busy, get on with my life. It might take some time but things can only get better from now on.

She sat like that for several minutes, listening sadly to the amplified sound of her own heart beat.

Who am I kidding? With a fresh rush of tears, and even as she resolved to forget the man who had unwittingly brought her so much torment and heartache, she allowed her thoughts to wander back to that fateful day last December, when her happy, carefree world had come crashing to the ground, irreparably shattered by a few simple words:

"I'm sorry, Susan," she heard him say again, "but I've met someone else."

Susan was the only passenger in the carriage. She had deliberately avoided the busier compartments further up the train. There was no-one there to witness the force of her anguish but she still raised both hands to conceal the despair on her pale, drawn countenance as the slow trickle became a sudden lachrymal torrent, hot, fierce and intense. Despite the scorching heat of the afternoon her body shuddered. Would this pain ever cease?

"Oh Jonathan," she breathed aloud. "Why, Jonathan? Why? Why? Why?"

She felt better after her outburst, like a caged bird just released following a long and frantic struggle to escape. She wiped away the tears with the back of her hand, smearing the salty dampness across her face and smudging her already blotched complexion and, as she did so, her mind involuntarily reverted to happier times spent with the man she still loved to distraction. She closed her wearied eyes, gently this time, feeling quite calm now, and she dreamed…

Four years drift into oblivion and Susan is transported back to the long, glorious summer of 85. She smiles to herself as she recalls the day when it all began. She remembers twisting her ankle in a fall and hobbling painfully over the rocky shore towards her bicycle. She hears again that friendly voice:

"Hello there. Need some help?"

She looks up into the handsome, bronzed face of a stranger. He is tall, of strong muscular build, with floppy brown hair and twinkling dark eyes which wear an honest and amiable expression. Susan has always believed the eyes to be a perfect judge of character. She trusts him immediately.

"I've hurt my ankle," she answers shyly. "I don't know whether I'll be able to ride my bike."

She squirms in renewed agony as another twinge of pain shoots through her leg.

"Here, let me help you."

He quickly slips his bare arm around her slender waist.

"Put your weight on me," he says gently.

Painful though it is, Susan's ankle is forgotten as she leans on him and stumbles to the grassy verge beyond the rocks. Nothing but her thin cotton dress separating his flesh from her own, the effect of his touch is electrifying and for those few seconds her heart thumps wildly within her breast.

She reaches the dry grass and sits down, stupefied.

"Thanks," she stammers at last, confused by the feelings he has evoked, feelings which she has never before experienced and which she instinctively knows would be quite uncontrollable, given the slightest encouragement.

But her rescuer behaves very properly, making no attempt to seduce her. Indeed there is no indication that she has evoked in him any of the passionate desire she herself feels or even any interest in her beyond her injured ankle. A true gentleman, he drives her home, helps her into the house, deposits her blue bicycle at the wrought iron gate and takes his leave, expressing a wish that she might soon be recovered.

A strange sense of loneliness engulfs her as his red Volvo drives away. As though reading her mind or even mocking her, a solitary sea-gull swoops quite low overhead and screams piercingly.

Who is he? Where does he live? Will I ever see him again?

She has not even asked him his name…

The scenery had changed now from rural, peaceful, green fields and farmhouses and was less picturesque. Letting her gaze bring it into focus, Susan noticed a small copse here, a spinney or a thicket there, some untidy gardens which backed onto the railway track, separated from it only by a tall fence. For a moment she contemplated the lives of the families who lived there and imagined herself, standing at an upstairs window watching the trains pass by, but it was really only a cursory glance. In reality she paid little attention to her present surroundings, her thoughts still on the events of four years ago. She drifts back into her dream…

More than a week has passed. Mum is answering an unexpected knock at the door.

"Hello. I was just wondering how your daughter is." Then, in way of explanation, "I brought her home last Tuesday when she sprained her ankle."

Before she even has time to respond he laughs and corrects himself:

"Well, I'm assuming that she is your daughter…and that her ankle was sprained! It certainly appeared to be very painful."

Susan's heart skips a beat as she recognises the deep, husky voice. She is aware of her mother exchanging a few pleasantries with him. Quickly she removes her apron and glances in the mirror, smoothing her long, auburn hair with the palm of her hand. Then, taking a deep breath, she emerges from the kitchen, where she has been preparing dinner, and greets him as casually as she can, trying not to betray the emotion which has filled her dreams since first meeting him.

"Hi there," she says with a smile. "It's nice of you to call. I'm fine now, thanks."

"That's good," he replies, and the look in his eyes reveals all she longs to know.

A long and beautiful relationship begins that day. How well she remembers his first kiss that very night. They are standing in the moonlight on the little path in front of the sea-shore, where they have been walking, hidden from the house, where Susan lives with her mother, Kathleen, by a raised hedge of wild gorse which has long since lost the best of its bright yellow flowers for this year. Only a faint rustling of leaves from the nearby bushes and the gentle lapping of the waves onto the beach below disturb the quiet stillness. Jonathan takes her hand, interlocking his fingers around her own. She senses a thrill of pleasure.

"I haven't been able to stop thinking about you all week," he admits.

Susan drops her gaze and says simply:

"I've felt the same way."

Then, releasing her fingers, he takes her face in his hands, holding it like a fragile china ornament, and kisses her tenderly on the lips.

"I think I'm falling in love," he whispers, as she melts into his arms…

The past recedes and Susan finds herself back on that north-bound train. Her eyes are dry now, her pent-up emotion spent. How did it all go so terribly wrong?

In her mind she relived that unhappy night in the run – up to last Christmas. With the colourful fairy lights twinkling so inappropriately in the background, not fit for the occasion, just like today's beautiful weather, she recalled his initial hesitancy to speak and the strange look in his eyes. And then, suddenly, he had come straight out with it:

"I'm sorry, Susan, but I've met someone else."

His words had cut her like a knife.

"Someone else…*someone else*…**someone else!**…"

How that phrase had reverberated and pounded through her tortured mind while Jonathan continued to speak. She was aware of him stammering through some kind of explanation, trying to justify himself, but her mind was numb; she did not grasp what he was saying except that her name was Helen and he loved her.

Susan sighed. At least she had behaved with dignity. She had not broken down and begged him to stay with her though her heart yearned for him. It was true she had shed a tear but he too had been upset; his choice had evidently not been an easy one. But he had made that choice. He had chosen Helen.

For a long time Susan and Jonathan had been very much in love. She remembered thinking that if anything was ever to happen to him she would rather die than go on living without him. But she had been thinking of his health, his safety, not the deliberate withdrawal of his love. Never in her sublime happiness had she imagined that he would leave her for someone else. But he had… and very suddenly. She had not seen him since that night, yet she had thought about him incessantly for she still loved him. How could she forget him, she asked herself now, or stop loving him, when his child had been growing within her womb, a constant reminder of his love, because, regardless of whatever happened afterwards, the child had been conceived in love. Of that she was certain.

The traveller suddenly became aware of the beautiful scenery around her and determined to enjoy the remainder of the journey. She opened the window properly and took a deep breath as the fresh summer air rushed in and filled her compartment. It felt good, invigorating, and coupled with the thought that she was on her way home at last, it instantly dispelled any lingering trace of gloom.

Susan loved her home, a quaint little cottage just a few metres from the sea on the rugged coastline of North Antrim. Home was quiet and peaceful, a haven of contentment and beauty, where she had spent all of her twenty-one years. She loved to lie in bed at night, lulled to sleep by the soft, rippling sound of the sea; but just as musical to her ears was the thunderous roar of a raging storm, when the huge waves would crash onto the rocks below and the wind would howl relentlessly, flipping little pebbles and grains of sand against her window pane. Often she would dress in her warmest clothes and venture out into the storm just to look and to listen, to feel the strength of the wind against her face. She would watch the abandoned fishing boats, tossed about like ninepins, as though trying to break loose from their moorings to be carried out into the great ocean for an adventure of their own.

Home meant a magnificent view of a long, golden strand and the white-crested waves of the rolling Atlantic Ocean, a view to be surpassed by no artist though depicted by many. Yes, Susan loved her home. How glad she was to be returning there at last.

The door of her carriage suddenly opened. Two suitcases were pushed in first, to be quickly followed by their owner, a plump, round-faced, jovial woman about twice Susan's age.

"Hello," said the newcomer, a bit breathlessly from carrying the suitcases. "Mind if I join you?"

"No, of course not," replied Susan, aroused from her reverie.

She had been so absorbed in her thoughts that she had not even realised the train had stopped. Now she noticed that there was quite a bit of activity on the platform around her though they soon moved off again without anyone else entering the compartment. She helped her companion to lift her luggage unto the rack above their heads, then sat down again and took a magazine from her own bag.

"It's very hot," remarked the fat woman.

"Yes, it's lovely."

"Too hot for me!"

She wiped the perspiration from her brow.

The train chugged along, gathering speed again and Susan found herself relaxing to its regular rhythm:

"Faster than fairies, faster than witches,

Bridges and houses, hedges and ditches…"

Vivid memories of not so distant school days came to mind with the words of the old familiar poem. It went something like that anyway. She couldn't remember the exact lyrics. How much water had flowed under the bridge since those innocent and carefree days?

"You're not English, are you?" her travelling companion was saying. "Did I detect a Northern Irish accent?"

"That's right," smiled Susan. "I live on the north coast of Ireland. I'm on my way home there."

"I'm crossing over to Belfast myself tonight," the woman continued. "My sister has invited me over for a holiday. She has a cottage in the Mourne Mountains, somewhere near Newcastle," she said. "I suppose you are on your way home from a holiday."

"Well no, not exactly a holiday," explained Susan, taking a deep breath. "I've been working in London since the beginning of the year. When an old school friend invited me over, I jumped at the chance to see a bit of the country. I'd never been to England before. She helped me find a part-time job in a local restaurant near her flat so I was able to earn enough for my keep and had plenty of time left for sight-seeing. I wasn't needed at home because I work in a small hotel which doesn't do much business out of season."

"But the summer's half over now," her companion said,

confused. "Surely you'll have been needed in your hotel before this."

Susan laughed nervously.

"Probably," she answered. "I'll maybe find myself without a job when I get home but London was just so interesting, I couldn't tear myself away any sooner."

How easy it had become to lie. She was amazed at the ease with which she had told her prepared story to this stranger. She almost believed it herself! It was the same story she had told her mother and her friends yet how it evaded the truth. She did indeed have an old school friend who was now a student in London but they had not met even once during her unhappy exile though they had corresponded at the start:

Dear Janet, she had written,

Can I ask you to do me a huge favour? I don't want to tell you why at the moment but I am leaving home for a while and I have told my mother that I am coming to stay with you. When I do get settled somewhere I intend to send her my real address so that she will be able to contact me but I'll tell her that you have moved there too. That way she won't worry about me being on my own. Please go along with this for me, not only with my mum but also if you should happen to be talking to any of our mutual friends and, above all, do not write to me or phone me at home after the end of this month until I contact you again.

Sorry for being so mysterious and secretive   I'll explain it all some day. I really need your help here, Janet. I know you won't let me down.
All the best with your studies.
Lots of love, Sue.

Janet had sent a prompt reply agreeing to the arrangement, though intrigued and somewhat anxious that her friend should act so out of character, she had pleaded for some kind of explanation. Susan had thanked her for her concern and had reassured her that there was no need to worry. She had managed to avoid her subsequent phone-call, shouting downstairs to her mum that she was just getting into the bath and would ring Janet back. She didn't. Thankfully Janet took the hint and didn't ring again.

Susan had in fact spent the first few months working in a small restaurant, as she had claimed, and she *had* managed a little bit of sight-seeing. She earned enough to pay the rent for the modest flat she had found and to buy essential items of food and fuel but she had lived a very solitary and frugal existence, saving every spare penny for the weeks when she would not be able to work. Then she had had the baby. She shuddered even now to think of the vulgar woman who had delivered it and the devious way in which she had engaged the services of such an individual. She had lived under a false name in London, had professed to be from Scotland, and, when necessary, had invented a whole range of plausible reasons for living alone at such a time. She had even deceived that woman into believing that she was perfectly happy about the birth.

Why would she care anyway, she asked herself bitterly; she had been well paid for her services. Wasn't that all such a woman wanted? As a feeling of disgust pervaded her whole being, she tried to banish such thoughts from her mind. For the past seven months she had lived a lie. She wasn't very proud of herself but it was over at last and she must put it behind her.

"Have you been to Ireland before?" she now asked her fellow traveller.

"Yes, several times, but I have never visited the Newcastle area before. What's it like? Do you know that part of the province?"

Susan was in her element now, describing the country she loved. She thought of the peaceful mountain scenery, the remote thatched cottages, the sheep farms bordered by low, picturesque stone walls…the babbling mountain streams of crystal clear water, the lovely waterfalls, the long, golden beaches and little, sandy coves…the rock pools full of interesting marine life, the colourful fishing boats in the many small harbours…the busy souvenir shops, the carefree atmosphere. Lovingly she described it all in vivid detail, her grey-green eyes dancing with zealous praise.

They spent the rest of the journey chatting about their respective homes and families so that the time passed quickly and Susan felt that, for the first time in seven months, she had really enjoyed herself.

They parted company at the port, where Susan joined the queue of passengers who were waiting to embark for the overnight crossing to Ireland. As soon as she was on board she retired to the privacy of her small cabin, where once again she allowed melancholia to take over her spirits. She tried to think rationally about what she had done, tried to justify her action by reminding herself that she did it all for Jonathan's sake. It would have been so easy to have told him. He would have stood by her. They could have been married by now. Tears welled up in her eyes as she contemplated what might have been. How she would love to be his wife, and could have been, for he surely would not have deserted her, had he known about the baby. But she had not told him. By the time she had realised her condition, he had already left her and was with Helen. She knew that he must love her more. What sort of life would they have had, staying together only for the child. He would have grown to resent her and she could not have borne that. He would have grown to resent his daughter. Yes, it was better this way, better that he never knew, that no-one ever knew.

She closed her eyes and tried to see that lovely house in the quiet suburb some miles outside London, that house with the bright blue, newly-painted gate and the beautifully laid out rose garden, that house where she had seen a little girl laughing. Yes, that was where her daughter would grow up, for that was where she had abandoned her baby early that morning. At last, sobbing bitterly into the pillow, exhaustion overwhelmed her and she fell asleep.

Chapter 2

Kathleen Summers greeted her daughter with outstretched arms and tears of happiness. It was great to have her home again and they held each other close for a few moments.

"Lunch won't be a minute," she said, as soon as they were inside the cottage. "I'm sure you're hungry."

"Starving!" came the reply from the bedroom, where the weary traveller was depositing her grey suitcase. "I haven't had a decent meal for days!"

"I thought you looked a bit pale, especially considering this lovely weather we are having. I hope you haven't been ill."

"Oh no, I'm fine," she answered quickly, as she entered the kitchen and tried to put a spring in her step. "I've just been so busy tidying up and packing that I didn't take the time to cook a proper meal."

Kathleen laughed.

"What about Janet, then? Did she not do *any* of the cooking?"

"Most of the time we each cooked for ourselves," Susan ventured, not picking up on the innuendo. "I worked mainly in the evenings, when she was just finishing her day's studies, so it didn't often suit us to eat together."

"That's strange!" Kathleen looked confused. "I was talking to Isobel just last week and apparently Janet has been raving about your cooking."

"Isobel?"

"Janet's mother."

Susan felt herself blush. Maintaining her bluff was going to be more difficult than she had imagined. She racked her brains for a quick response, then added:

"I did most of the cooking at weekends right enough."

She knew that this didn't really make much sense but thankfully noted that her explanation was accepted without further comment. Her anxious mind couldn't help wondering, however, what else had been said during her mother's conversation with Mrs Swanson.

They sat down to a meal of succulent roast beef and spicy gravy, served with buttered carrots, fresh peas and new potatoes boiled in their jackets, followed by a cool fresh fruit salad coated with thickly whipped cream. The mangoes and nectarines were particularly mouth-watering.

"Talking about cooking, Mum, I've certainly missed yours," Susan said. "This is delicious!"

She glanced lovingly at the familiar objects around her, revelling in her surroundings like a traveller through a desert arriving at a long awaited oasis.

"It's been quiet here without you," remarked Kathleen.

It was not a rebuke but Susan experienced once again the pangs of guilt which had constantly plagued her while she was away. In her mother's eyes, she surmised, an inconsiderate daughter had left her alone for the best part of a year for no good reason, the result of a mere whim.

If only she knew, she now thought to herself. *If only she knew*.

Lunch over and the washing-up done, Susan retired to her own room to unpack. She stood at the window for a few minutes, gazing out dreamily at their neat, little garden and the beloved landscape beyond. Then she turned towards the bed, bathed in sunshine, where her suitcase lay, full of the winter clothes she had worn on her outward journey. She had been very careful to dispose of the few loose-fitting garments she had been obliged to purchase in London. Everything was creased so she laid each article out flat on the bed, hoping that they would not all require to be pressed. Her books were taken out next and neatly replaced on the shelves of the little, wooden bookcase in the corner. Finally, lifting her pink and yellow cosmetic bag and some clean, white face-cloths, she walked across to the large, oak dressing table opposite the window and opened the top drawer.

There, staring up at her, was the face she was trying so hard to forget. He was smiling, smiling at her, for she had been the photographer. She gazed at that face she had loved so dearly, at those eyes which had so often looked lovingly into her own, at those lips which had kissed her so tenderly at first, so passionately as their relationship developed, and had uttered so many beautiful words of endearment, at that thick wavy hair which had brushed against her cheeks as they lay together and made love, their naked bodies entwined in rapture and ecstasy. Her memories, conjured up so unexpectedly, totally overwhelmed her so that, acting on a sudden and powerful impulse, she dropped the cosmetic bag and face-cloths like a hot coal, snatched up the photograph from the open drawer, and tore it into shreds.

Immediately regretting her action, Susan threw herself down on the bed and burst into almost hysterical sobbing. She was lying there still, crying as though her heart would break, when her mother entered the room a few minutes later to see if she needed anything. Kathleen was initially alarmed and momentarily bewildered by the change of mood and the very distressed state of her daughter but quickly noticed the fragments she was frantically trying to piece together and realised what had happened.

"I thought you would have got over him by now," she said gently, sitting down beside her and putting a comforting arm around her. "You must try to forget him, Susan. You'll soon find some-one else."

She hesitated, then added:

"He's getting married next month, according to news I heard in town."

Kathleen knew that this information, though not unexpected, would be hurtful to her daughter, but had decided that there was no point in trying to keep it from her. Shielding her from the truth might encourage her to harbour false hopes.

Married? Already?

"I'm sorry," she answered haltingly through her tears, trying to put that thought to the back of her mind. "I'll be all right. Just give me a minute. It's just that I didn't mean to tear the photograph. It would have been nice to keep it.

As a memento. After all it was three whole years. He was everything to me for three whole years, Mum. I didn't mean to rip the picture."

She continued trying to piece together the tiny fragments, but in vain. It was ruined.

Kathleen got up from the bed and slipped out of the room, returning a moment later with another picture, almost an exact replica of the first, one which she herself had removed from view and hidden in her own room lest it evoke painful memories. She handed it to her daughter.

"Be careful with this one," she said. "I don't think I have any others."

Throwing her arms round her mother's neck and hugging her tightly, Susan gratefully took the photograph, expressing what was in her heart without uttering another word. Kathleen gently squeezed her hand and told her that she would forget him in time.

Susan shook her head. "No, I won't forget him, I'll never forget him," she refuted firmly. "I don't want to forget him."

Kathleen looked apprehensive.

Reading the older woman's mind, Susan added:

"Don't worry, Mum. I'm not going to make a fool of myself and go chasing after him. I just know that the time we spent together will always be important to me and influence my life in a big way, though I may never see him again."

How prophetic those words were to be proven, not only in the simple sense Susan intended when she spoke them, but also in a more complex way she would never, in her wildest dreams, have imagined.

Left alone again, she dreamily recalled the good times, in the end commending herself for the action she had taken. There had been no fuss, no bitter arguments, no ugly rows, nothing to mar the happy memories. She had avoided hurting her dear mother, a deeply religious person whose simple faith was bound by a rigid moral code which she had broken. She had done the right thing.

Her spirits lifted, she decided to take a walk along the familiar beach she loved so well. Having changed into a fresh, cotton frock and a pair of light sandals, she set out, towel and swimsuit under her arm. How beautiful the rippling waves were, glistening in the sunlight. How cool and refreshing, how cleansing the water felt and how her body tingled after her bathe. Children were building sand castles, digging big holes in the sand and generally squealing with delight. Here and there games of beach football, cricket and tennis were in progress. Heads bobbed up and down as people swam in the calm, clear water. Everything was just as she remembered it. It was good to be home!

Chapter 3

It was seven o'clock in the evening. Susan breathed a long sigh of relief when Kathleen closed the door behind her and walked down the narrow, garden path and out the front gate. A regular and loyal attendee at the local church , she was on her way to one of her weekly functions, having given in eventually to her daughter's protests over her suggestion that she stay at home on the account of it being Susan's first night back home. A series of awkward questions had arisen at the tea-table and Susan had been rather evasive in her replies, lest she should contradict anything else that Mrs Swanson might have related concerning her supposed sojourn with Janet.

She really should contact Janet and explain what had been going on or at least offer some kind of plausible story. Their mothers could meet again any time soon and she could still be found out, even now. With these thoughts in her head, Susan fetched some paper and a blue ballpoint pen and seated herself at the table. She reflected for some minutes. Janet deserved to know the truth. She had been a truly loyal friend over these difficult months. She clicked the end of the pen and the words began to flow:

Dear Janet,

Thank you so much for being so discreet and helping me through these past months. I'm back home now so you can pretend I have moved out! I want to explain things to you but I must ask you to keep my secret and burn this letter once you have read it. No-one else knows the truth.

As you know, Jonathan and I stopped seeing each other just before last Christmas. He is with some-one else now. All I know about her is her name – Helen. I don't really want to know anything else about her. My mum has heard that they are getting married soon. I am trying not to think about that but it's very hard! Anyway, just two or three weeks after he left me I found out that I was pregnant. You mustn't breathe a word about this, Janet – I know I can trust you. I didn't tell Jonathan. I did consider it but in the end I kept thinking about him growing to despise me and the baby for coming between him and this other girl he loved. I couldn't bear that so I did what I thought was best and went away before anyone could guess what had happened. Everyone thought I just needed a change of scenery for a while to get over the break-up. Well, I had the baby and arranged for it to be adopted, so that episode in my life is finished and no-one knows about it but you.

Please don't think too badly of me and don't blame Jonathan either. I'm sure he would have done the honourable thing if he had known what had happened but, as I said, I don't think that would have been for the best.

Well, Janet, I hope you are still enjoying your studies and have been successful in your exams. I'm glad you enjoyed my cooking!! I nearly got into hot water over that because I said we didn't often eat together without realising that my mum had been talking to yours!!! It's just as well Mum didn't say anything about you moving to a new flat! I didn't think they would even have recognised each other.

Thanks again for being such a brick. I haven't decided yet what to do now that I'm home but I think I might try for university myself. I'd like to try teaching as a career. I really will come to see you next time I'm in London.

Your very grateful friend,
Sue.

As she addressed the envelope and slipped the letter inside, Susan felt that a great burden had been lifted from her mind. It was comforting to know that some-one would soon know her true story, or most of it. She had not had the courage to admit that she had left her little girl asleep on a cold doorstep rather than go through the legalities of adoption. Keeping the tears at bay this time, she visualised again that house where she had left the nameless child. What would they have done with her daughter? In her naivety at the time she had imagined her growing up there and playing in that lovely garden, a sister for the little girl she had seen on a previous occasion. Now she realised how improbable that was. The baby would most likely have been handed over to the police, or to a local hospital, and would later be institutionalised in an orphanage. Anything could happen to her baby. For all she knew she could have died before anyone found her. No, she was beginning to panic. She must stay calm. Had she not rung the door bell before she fled from the scene? Yes, of course she had. Some-one would have been with the child within minutes of her departure. It all seemed so long ago now. But it happened yesterday, early yesterday morning.

"It will be in today's newspapers!"

The thought came as a sudden shock so that she uttered the words aloud and wondered whether she should delay posting her letter, lest Janet should read the reports and connect the two stories.

No, get it over with. Time to start afresh and get on with my life.

Ten minutes later she had found a stamp and was on her way to the post box.

The sun had set and the beach was now deserted, all the day-trippers having gone home. Typical of the constantly changing Northern Irish weather, quite a strong breeze was now coming from the sea, blowing Susan's long, auburn hair away from her face and making her light skirt flap like the wings of a great bird. Rough waves were rolling in from the Atlantic, breaking on the offshore rocks in clouds of spray. The taste of salt and the smell of seaweed in the air were sensations that she loved and which she remembered with nostalgia. How often she had walked along this path, hand in hand with Jonathan, feeling light-hearted and happy. Then Helen had replaced her in his affections. Strangely she felt sad about that, rather than envious or hostile.

She posted the letter and headed back home, reaching the door of the cottage just as the first large drops of rain began to fall and the wind became more blustery, hurling little grains of sand into her eyes and mouth. She shivered as an intense loneliness gripped her heart. She had stood so many times in that very same spot, wrapped in the warm embrace of her lover, while they tenderly kissed goodnight.

"Goodnight, Jonathan," she whispered into the darkness. "Goodnight, my darling, wherever you are."

1994

Chapter 4

"Twenty-six years old! Where have the years gone?" Susan placed the birthday card from her mother on top of the TV in the small but comfortable living-room of her ground-floor flat and opened another, thicker envelope. Even with a postmark showing it had come all the way from Australia, the card had still arrived on the correct day. Amazing! It was from her old friend, Janet Swanson and, along with birthday wishes, contained a short letter and some photographs depicting Janet's new life with her partner, Greg. Greg was in the same line of work as Janet and they were presently co-operating on a new project which would hopefully result in them setting up their own IT consultancy company. They also lived together in a fabulous two-storey house with a huge garden surrounding their own private swimming pool and barbecue area. Susan had been invited to visit and she certainly intended to do so. She may live a long distance away, but Janet remained her very best friend in the world. One more envelope contained a card from Linda, who lived in the flat upstairs. There were no bills and no junk mail, just the three birthday cards, so she arrived at work that Friday morning glowing with a high feelgood factor and mentally planning a possible trip to Australia in the near future.

Susan had only been in this job for a few months but already she loved it. She taught a class of lively ten-year-olds with diverse personalities and abilities. She loved stretching the knowledge and skills of the brighter children and watching their minds develop but gained equal satisfaction from witnessing the little steps of progress made by those with limited ability or emotional problems.

And then, of course, there was Chris.

Chris taught the other class of ten-year-olds in the same school, a situation which necessitated a good deal of consultation.

"Hi there," he had greeted her on her first day, shaking her hand and looking straight at her with a friendly smile, "I'm Christopher Lovell. Don't hesitate to ask me for anything you need. My room is right next to yours." He hadn't let go of her hand yet. She wasn't complaining.

"Thanks," Susan had replied, already thinking how pleasant it would be working alongside him.

"I mean it. Anything at all."

Reluctantly he ended the handshake but they continued to look at each other with interest. The chemistry between them was fairly obvious.

Very soon Susan and Chris were firm friends. He contrived situations on a daily basis to seek out her company, coming into her room on the pretext of needing to borrow some equipment he did not really require or to ask her advice about some problem with which he had been coping competently for years. She knew that he was taking special notice of her but somehow she could not bring herself to discourage him as she had done with others over the past five years, during which time she had been somewhat afraid of encountering intimacy and had kept all male friendships on a very casual level. Suddenly she was happy again and she was not going to destroy that long-awaited happiness, not yet anyway.

The change in their relationship took place on the afternoon of her birthday. Susan had stayed behind after class to finish marking some exercise books, hoping to leave herself clear for the weekend. Thinking that everyone else had gone, she was startled by a sudden noise and, looking up, found Chris hovering, apparently without aim, around the door of her room.

"Oh, it's you, Chris," she said relieved. "You startled me! It's not like you to work overtime on a Friday."

He made no response so she read the last composition, awarded it a B+, indicating a number of minor spelling and grammatical errors. She added an encouraging remark and placed the book on top of the pile. Chris was now standing by her desk.

"I'm sorry," she said, confused. "Did you want to see me about something?"

"Yes."

He hesitated.

"Happy birthday. I heard someone mention in the staff-room that it was your birthday."

"That's right. Thanks."

Still he didn't move. He started fiddling with the pens on her desk.

"Doing anything special to celebrate?"

She didn't even have time to answer before he continued:

"What I really mean is, well, I was wondering whether you would like to come to the pictures with me tomorrow night?"

Susan's heart began racing. This was what she had been waiting for, hoping for. She was amused by his shyness in this situation. He had gone quite red in the face.

"That would be great," she said, smiling.

Immediately he relaxed, obviously relieved that his offer had not been rejected.

"Right. Good. I'll pick you up around seven."

He stopped fiddling with the pens, turned round, and was gone before she could even ask what film was showing.

Susan felt good. Never again would Chris just be a colleague. Today he was a man, a very sexy man, asking her for a date. She was so excited, so full of anticipation, so anxious to enjoy the whole experience, that she went straight from school to the best dress shop she knew and celebrated by treating herself to a new and very expensive frock…and then a pair of shoes…and a bag to match. It wasn't that she had lived a life of utter seclusion and celibacy for five years. There had been friendships and relationships but nothing serious. She just felt different about this. Something had drawn her to Chris from that very first handshake when they were formally introduced. This could be the fresh start she so badly needed.

When Chris arrived at the flat on Saturday night and told her that she looked lovely, Susan was sure that her impulsive spending spree had been worth every penny. They went to see a great film called *Forrest Gump* and then had a few drinks at a bar in town. As they chatted about the film and exchanged smiles, their hands tentatively found each other and soon became interlocked. It was perfect. Susan felt relaxed in his company. She found herself imagining his kiss and hoping…

It was a cold, frosty night but there was a delicious sensation of warmth as they strolled up to her door, hand in hand.

"I've enjoyed tonight, Chris. Thank you."

"My pleasure," he replied. "Same time next week?"

"Fine."

He gave her a light kiss on the cheek, just brushing her lips, not really living up to the passionate one she had imagined, but it was a start… and he wanted to see her again. She closed her eyes and revelled in warm, comforting thoughts.

It was indeed the beginning of a regular Saturday date and each week they became closer, more intimate. Occasionally they met on other evenings during the week as well. They went to gigs at the local bars, films, bowling, skating, swimming. She went to watch his football matches. They took long walks together with his dog, Bouncer, a lively springer spaniel. Susan laughed more than she had done in years. Chris was full of vitality and fun. But he could be serious too. He no longer kissed her lightly on the cheek, but tenderly, full on the lips, as he held her body close to his own, evoking feelings that she had not experienced since those far off days with Jonathan. One thing, however, was a little disconcerting; Chris did not vocalise his feelings, never spoke of love. Certainly she had fallen in love with him.

Very gradually, Susan began to develop a guilt complex. How was she to tell Chris that she once loved another man and had given birth to his baby? Her conscience troubled her in bed at night and she would lie awake for hours, going over and over in her mind her various options. No-one but Janet knew anything about her past life and she would never betray her so why not just ignore it? What Chris did not know could not hurt him. Every night the same thought came to her but every night she reproached herself for thinking it. Had she not resolved to have no more deceit in her life? But it was so hard; she had not been in love when she made that decision. She had not known what she might lose in telling the truth. Now she became withdrawn, avoiding the man she loved as much as possible, putting off the inevitable. She knew she had to tell him but that the moment of truth could bring to an end the wonderful relationship they shared.

"I hope you don't mind if I stay home tomorrow," she told him one Friday, "but I don't really feel like going to the gig."

He looked surprised.

"Never mind," he said kindly. "We can just sit in and watch television."

She hesitated and bit her lip.

"I'd rather be alone for a while," she said at last. "I have a lot on my mind just now."

Chris was taken aback by her rebuff. Hurt and angry he turned away, hiding the emotion which welled up within him. But Susan had seen the hurt in his eyes. Remorse gripped her heart, causing her to backtrack. She followed him into his room while his class filed in behind her.

"I'm sorry," she said softly. "Please do come over tomorrow. I'd like to talk things over with you."

Somehow she managed to put the awful reality of what she needed to say to him to the back of her mind and concentrate on the creative design session she had planned for the afternoon. Surrounded by assorted pieces of balsa wood, sandpaper, glue guns, rolls of sticky tape, packs of dowel rods, rubber bands, plastic wheels and twenty excited children, her mind was soon on other things.

Chris came to her flat on Saturday night, but still angry with her, his mood was sour and Susan decided it was not a suitable time for her confession. As she was unable, therefore, to give a satisfactory explanation for her behaviour of yesterday and just palmed it off as worry over some health issues her mother was experiencing, the evening was a disaster and he left early. They did not actually quarrel but it was the first time he had left her without a kiss.

For several days afterwards Chris totally ignored her, except in professional matters where common courtesy prevailed. She too avoided him for though she acknowledged that the whole situation was her fault, she did not know how to remedy it. Things drifted along with an awkward silence until the middle of the following week, when Chris called unexpectedly at her flat. Bouncer greeted her gleefully, straining on his lead and jumping up to lick her hand.

"I just want to know where I stand," Chris said simply. "Do you want to see me again or not?"

"Of course I do," she answered without hesitation, thankful for the chance of a reprieve. "I'm sorry about last week."

He smiled. Susan gave Bouncer a big hug and tickled his tummy when he rolled over at her feet. The dog salivated with pleasure.

"Women!" Chris muttered. "And I thought I understood you!"

Their relationship was resumed, but realising that she still had something on her mind and often seemed somewhat dejected, Chris came to Susan's room one Friday morning, soon after their reconciliation with a scheme for cheering her up:

"How would you like to spend the weekend at home with your mother?" he asked. "My brother is willing to lend me his car so we could drive up and surprise her. I know you've been a bit worried about her recently…and I think we could both do with a bit of fresh sea air!"

Chris was saving up to buy his own car but hadn't decided yet which model he preferred and kept putting it off.

"Oh Chris, that would be wonderful," she replied, truly delighted with the idea.

"Right, that's settled then. I'll call for you about eight o'clock in the morning and we'll come back on Sunday evening."

That evening, as Susan prepared an overnight case, her feelings fluctuated from intense happiness and excitement to anxiety and guilt. She loved Chris with all her heart and the thought of a whole weekend with him was wonderful but still her secret remained untold. All night she tossed and turned, sleeping only fitfully, so that when daylight began to creep into the room, her head ached with indecision. Her troubled conscience told her that her opportunity had arisen and she could delay her avowal no longer yet her impassioned heart implored her not to mar the joy that this weekend could bring.

At last the blue Ford Escort drew up outside the flat and Chris appeared on the doorstep, dressed casually in a red cashmere sweater and a pair of blue denim jeans.

"Ready Darling?" he asked, kissing her affectionately. "We've certainly chosen a good weekend. Just look at that blue sky! I can hardly wait to breathe in that fresh sea air. And I'm looking forward to meeting your mother. Does she like flowers? I hope so for I have picked her some daffodils and tulips from Dad's garden. They're just at their best at the moment."

"That was thoughtful of you, Chris. She loves daffodils."

He moved forward to pick up her pink and lilac spotty bag which was sitting in the hallway but she, having finally made up her mind as soon as he used the word 'darling', stopped him and suggested that they have some coffee before the journey.

"Why, certainly, if you want to," replied Chris, "although I've just finished my breakfast. I thought you would want to set off straight away."

Noticing her hesitation and nervous state, he added:

"Is something wrong? You're very quiet. Perhaps you don't want to go after all. It's easily enough cancelled. Your mother isn't expecting you so she won't even be disappointed. Maybe I shouldn't have sprung this on you so suddenly but I thought you would like the idea."

Still searching for the right words, Susan said nothing.

Gently taking her by the hand, Chris led her to the beige cord sofa and they sat down.

"Tell me whether you want to go or not," he said plainly.

Susan took a deep breath.

"There's nothing I'd like more, Chris," she answered, shaking now with trepidation, "but there's something I have to tell you first."

He looked puzzled.

"Why do you want to spend the weekend with me?" she asked in a very small voice.

At once his look of bewilderment faded and his face hardened.

"Oh so that's it!" he snapped angrily. "You don't trust me. Have I ever given you grounds to doubt me? Have I ever laid a finger on you? Haven't I always treated you honourably yet when I ask you to spend a weekend with me you suddenly think I'm some kind of sex fiend! Would any man who just wanted you for sex suggest taking you to your mother's! Unbelievable!"

"Chris," she interrupted his rage, managing with difficulty to fight back the tears; "you misunderstand me. The thought never entered my head, I swear it. I only wanted you to tell me why you want to be with me, why you like my company, to tell me that you…that you…"

"That I love you?" Why had he never said it before?

"Of course I do," he said embarrassed, realising his mistake and becoming calm again. "I do love you, Susan," and as though he needed to prove it, he kissed her tenderly on the lips and apologised for his outburst.

"But I thought you said that *you* had something to tell *me*."

"I have, but I couldn't talk about love before you did. It wouldn't be right," she said clumsily, having had some idea in the back of her mind that perhaps, after all, he only wished to remain a casual friend, in which case there would have been no need to tell him anything.

"I love you…I love you…I love you. There, I've said it at last. I've wanted to for weeks, Susan. I don't really know what stopped me."

"Oh Chris, I love you too."

She paused and then faltered:

"But what I have to tell you is… you're not…you're not the first man I've loved, Chris. I once loved someone else…, a long time ago…, and I… and I… I…"

She took a very deep breath and closed her eyes:

"I had a baby."

There was a strained silence for some moments before Chris, his face ashen, said scornfully:

"A baby? *A baby?* Well, no wonder you didn't want me to come home with you!"

He stood up and glared at her.

"I suppose your… your **bastard**," he spat the word at

her, "is being cared for by your mother. You could hardly have passed it off as her own when your father has been dead for nearly twenty years!"

"No, Chris, it's not like that at all. I had the baby adopted and my mother doesn't even know about it. I'm only telling you because you have said that you love me and I don't want to keep you in the dark any longer."

"**Any longer**!" he screamed. "Why on earth didn't you tell me this before?"

"I'm sorry. I wanted to but I wasn't sure how you really felt about me. It's not the sort of thing to tell a casual acquaintance. My best friends don't even know. It was only when you suggested this trip that I was certain you must be serious about me and that I should therefore tell you."

She hesitated, then added:

"Can you ever forgive me, Chris?"

"How can you ask me that right now? I've never had a greater shock in my life! You've certainly put paid to our weekend together."

With these words he flung open the door so hard that it banged against the wall in the narrow hallway, leaving a sizeable dent in the cream-coloured paintwork, and then bounced back and was left swinging on its hinges. He ran down the path, got into the car, and slamming the door shut, he drove off at great speed.

Chapter 5

The clock ticked solemnly on the mantelpiece and Susan, still seated on the sofa, where Chris had professed his love for her just minutes before, felt more lonesome than at any time in her life. An image of Jonathan flashed through her mind and for the first time ever she inwardly cursed his memory. The past was his fault as much as her own yet he was happily married now and had probably long since forgotten her, while she was doomed to a life of either loneliness or deception. But her anger with him was short-lived for she had fond memories of her relationship with Jonathan and she knew that it was unfair to blame him for something he knew nothing about. The moment passed. No, it was not his fault; fate had simply treated her cruelly.

She relived the scene with Chris. At least her conscience was clear now. But how was she to face him again on Monday? She couldn't begin to imagine the difficulties they would face trying to maintain a professional working relationship after this. She thought of his loving smile and his warm embrace. Would she really never experience that again? Lying back against the soft apricot-coloured chenille cushion, she closed her eyes, which were wet with unshed tears, and exhausted from insomnia and mental anguish, she fell asleep.

A hand caressing her forehead awoke her some two hours later and she jumped up, alarmed. She had not locked the door.

It was Chris.

"Forgive me, Susan," he began. "I shouldn't have lost my temper. I just wasn't prepared for news of that kind and I must admit it upset me very much, but after I left you and thought it over I realised how hard it must have been for you, how much courage it must have taken for you to confide in me. There is no reason why I should expect you to tell me everything. We're not even engaged or anything. It was just such a shock."

Not yet fully awake, she stared at him and blinked. Was she dreaming? All of a sudden she was in his arms again and he was kissing her. It was no dream. No, Chris was really there, kissing her and asking *her* for forgiveness. With a surge of happiness she held him close and returned his kiss passionately, her heart pounding against his.

"Will you tell me the whole story some time or is it too painful?" he asked gently.

"I'd like to," she replied and then added hesitantly:

"Can you still love me, Chris?"

He too hesitated.

"My feelings are all mixed up just now," he said at last. "We'll talk about it later."

They were both silent for a few moments, each lost in their own thoughts. Then Chris spoke again:

"Let's not waste any more time. Are you coming to the coast or not?"

He still wanted them to go away together! Susan could hardly believe it. Renewed hope and joy were kindled within her breast, overshadowing for the moment his reluctance to give a direct answer to her question. She went to the bathroom to freshen up and ten minutes later they were on their way.

When Chris turned on the radio Bryan Adams was half-way through his latest single, *Please Forgive Me*. How appropriate! The irony was not lost on either of them. They negotiated the streets of Belfast making slow and laborious progress at first but at last they left the city behind and found themselves travelling through peaceful countryside. Being only April it was still cool but the sun shone brilliantly through the windows of the car, so that Susan felt herself dozing from time to time. They passed fields where cows grazed contentedly, others where little lambs skipped along in the wake of their mothers, bleating. Primroses were in bloom along by the hedge-rows and, at intervals, they saw multitudes of wild daffodils in various shades of yellow, orange and white.

"I wandered lonely as a cloud, that floats on high, o'er vale and hill…"

Susan couldn't help bringing to mind one of her very favourite poems. She knew it off by heart, all four verses. She was reciting it to herself, inwardly, while Chris drove along silently and pensively, absorbed in his own thoughts, his face expressionless.

For a while Susan revelled in the peace and quiet and enjoyed the music. Bon Jovi was now singing one of her favourites, *Always*. Gradually, however, she became uneasy with the prolonged lack of conversation. She glanced at Chris. There was no clue to his state of mind. Longing to know what he was thinking, she became anxious and restless but then, very suddenly, the silence was broken:

"How long ago was it, Susan?"

"Six years."

Silence reigned again for some minutes while he digested this information.

"What was his name?"

"Jonathan. Jonathan Ashby."

"And you say you loved him? He must have been a real bastard to abandon you in that condition or did he at least wait until after the birth?"

"Don't say that, Chris. Please. He never knew about the baby. Never. Even now, he doesn't know. He met someone else he loved more than me and told me all about her. We had already parted when I realised my condition."

"Well either it took you a very long time to discover you were pregnant," he retorted contemptuously, "or he didn't waste much time between sleeping with you and falling hopelessly in love with someone else!"

That hurt. It had been very sudden. How could she blame Chris for thinking the worst?

"And the baby?" he continued, frowning. "What did you say you did with it?"

Susan took a deep breath and felt a huge lump form in her throat. This she had never told anyone, not even

Janet, but she was determined now to tell Chris the whole truth.

"I told you I'd had it adopted…but that wasn't quite true. I actually left her on a doorstep and rang the bell so that she would be discovered right away."

Chris was visibly shocked. He stopped the car along the roadside and stared at her in total disbelief.

"But how could you do such a thing, Susan? How could you be so heartless and cruel? I was telling my parents, just last week, what a kind and loving person you are, how good you are with the children in school. Yet now you are telling me that you recklessly abandoned your own child, your very own flesh and blood, to a life of insecurity. Why on earth didn't you do it legally? I just can't believe it. It's too dreadful to comprehend."

Susan was silent. She wanted to fight back, to explain how circumstances had caused her to act as she had done but she dared not. This was the first time she had told anyone this part of her history and he was obviously disgusted, appalled at what she had done. Somehow, having never previously spoken of the incident, she had repressed its memory, but now it came flooding back to her in all its horror. She felt guilty, not so much for what she had done originally, but more for her total lack of feeling for that child during the five, nearly six years of her life, if indeed she were still alive. Chris was right. She was heartless. She had constantly felt guilty about having had a child, for the fact that it had happened could not be denied, yet she had never thought about that little girl, never wondered what she looked like or where she lived, never even given her a name. No wonder Chris was horrified.

The car was in motion again. Nothing more was said until they were almost at Susan's home and she had to give precise directions. At last they arrived. As he parked outside the cottage, Chris squeezed her hand and said:

"Let's forget it, Susan, for the moment. We're here to enjoy ourselves."

Within seconds of their arrival, Kathleen Summers, startled at first by the sight of an unfamiliar car, had recognised her daughter and was running down the path to greet her.

Chapter 6

"Susan! What a lovely surprise!" Kathleen was overjoyed at the unexpected arrival of her only daughter.

"Hi Mum." She gave her a hug. "I'd like you to meet Chris Lovell, a good friend and colleague of mine. It was his idea to come for the weekend."

Chris shook her hand politely.

"I'd heard so much about the place," he said, "that I couldn't wait to see it for myself and I must admit it's as beautiful as Susan said. What a tremendous view!"

He admired the panoramic vista, taking in the beach and the rocky headlands.

"I hope you don't mind me inviting myself, Mrs Summers, but I got the chance of the car for a few days and I just thought it would be a good idea."

"It's Kathleen, Chris, and you're very welcome. I'm glad to meet you at last. Susan has mentioned you a lot in her phone calls."

Susan blushed uneasily but then, noticing that Chris seemed to be pleased that she had spoken about him, she smiled and relaxed. Surely the worst was over.

"I brought you some flowers from the garden," Chris was saying, carefully lifting them from the back seat.

Kathleen thanked him and immediately set off to find a suitable vase and to arrange the blooms.

Chris and Susan followed her into the cottage with the few belongings they had brought for their brief visit.

"Why didn't you let me know you were coming," Kathleen's voice came from the kitchen, "and I would have prepared a hot meal?"

"It was a very last minute arrangement, Mum," Susan answered. "Anyway we thought it would be a pleasant surprise for us just to turn up, unannounced."

"It certainly is."

"It must be lonely for you here during the winter," put in Chris, as he joined her in the kitchen. "You're fairly isolated."

"It can be, sometimes," she answered pensively, then adding:

"However, that makes a surprise like this all the better."

Standing back to satisfy herself that her floral display was artistic, she smiled at Chris, thanked him again, and began to bustle about arranging the bedrooms.

"I'm so glad you have found yourself such an agreeable young man," Kathleen said to Susan, when they found themselves alone for a moment. "I like him already."

"Mum!" Susan exclaimed in an undertone, lest Chris should overhear them. "He's just a good friend."

"But you are very fond of him, aren't you? I can see that."

She smiled in acknowledgement of her mother's perceptive observation just as Chris appeared at the threshold.

"I don't want you to go to any trouble on my account, Mrs Summers... I mean Kathleen. I can sleep on the sofa."

"Indeed you will not, Chris! What sort of a welcome would that be? No, you take Susan's room and she can share with me."

Everything was soon arranged. Within an hour a delicious meal had been prepared and they were seated at the familiar wooden table. They chatted happily, Kathleen relating local news and gossip and Susan and Chris telling amusing stories about things which had happened in school.

The brightness of the morning had faded. Gradually the sky became heavy and overcast until eventually it began to rain and once it started, there was no let up. They spent the afternoon indoors in lively conversation. Chris was able to put his considerable DIY skills to good use and repair Kathleen's faulty washing machine.

"You will definitely be invited back!" she joked, delighted with the smooth running of the appliance. "That's been getting on my nerves for ages. It was so noisy!"

Early in the evening Kathleen tactfully retired to her room, leaving the two young people to have some quality time alone. As they sat quietly by the warm fire, Chris became uncharacteristically reserved and Susan began to fear that he was not going to forgive her for her past indiscretion, that in telling him her secret, she had, after all, thrown away her chance of happiness. Why was he sitting alone in the big armchair, staring blindly into the fire? It was some time before she plucked up the courage to speak:

"Chris, why are you so silent? Please don't ignore me like this. You have good reason to despise me but I can't bear to be ignored. You seemed happy earlier in the day… Talk to me…. Please."

"I have enjoyed the day, Darling, truly I have…, and I have enjoyed meeting your mum. She has certainly been very hospitable and she's so lively and cheerful considering the length of time she has lived alone in this remote place. I mean it's very nice for a visit but I couldn't imagine living here myself. When was it you said your father died?"

"Not long after I was born. I never really knew him."

She contemplated for a moment the life her mother had become so accustomed to. She had plenty of friends but no-one special had ever taken her dad's place. She had been a widow for a long time.

"It is very lonely here. I always feel a bit guilty when I come home for not being here more often. But Mum seems to be happy…and I loved living here when I was younger."

The ice broken, Chris now moved to the sofa and sat beside her but still his stance remained somewhat reserved.

"Do you despise me?" persisted Susan.

At first he did not respond. Then suddenly he turned to face her and caught hold of her arms, just below the shoulder, pinning them to her sides.

"Susan, I can't get him out of my mind," he hissed in a low voice, gripping her still tighter. "It's him I despise, not you. Of course I don't despise you. I love you. My heart aches when I think of what he did to you. You must help me to get him out of my mind."

She looked searchingly into his troubled eyes.

"What do you mean?" she asked. "There's nothing I'd like more than to forget what happened."

"But you must help *me* to forget it."

He strengthened his grip still further, as though he was going to shake her violently. For a moment she was scared. He was hurting her arms.

"All this time we've been together, I've been taking things slowly, waiting for the right moment, not wanting to offend you. But you have experienced things I knew nothing about with someone else. I thought I was the man in your life! I can't bear to think about it. You have to cancel out that memory for me…and the sooner, the better. Our love cannot survive if you don't do it with me. You must love me the way you loved him, better than you ever loved him. Tomorrow. Come to me tomorrow morning. You said your mother always attends church. Well I don't, and you can make some excuse for not accompanying her and come to me instead. Believe me, Susan, that's the only way I'll ever manage to forget what passed between you and this Ashby fellow."

As he finished speaking, he finally released his grip on her arms but worse was to come. Working himself into a sudden frenzy of jealousy and desire, he pulled open the buttons of her yellow blouse and thrust his hand in under the thin cotton to caress the soft roundness of her breasts. Susan's heart pounded as she sat shocked and motionless, letting his hot, firm hand travel over her flesh. In another situation she could have enjoyed it, she could have relished it. But was this an expression of love or simply revenge?

She did not know. Was his love to be conditional on her obeying him and succumbing to his sexual desires? Was this what he had had in mind all along? Maybe that was why he so quickly jumped to the wrong conclusion earlier on. Was she losing all her self-respect in permitting this to continue? Or was he right? Did she owe it to him as a means of cancelling out her mistake of the past?

Sick at heart and deeply hurt by his manner, she tried to withdraw his hand but he held her all the more firmly, the fingers of his other hand now running frantically through her hair. The memory of a passionate scene with Jonathan suddenly flashed through her mind and she recalled how tender and beautiful it had been with him. They had loved willingly but Chris was forcing her against her will, taking unfair advantage of her vulnerability. Could she really love a man like this? She thought again about what he had said about cancelling out the past. Maybe it would be different next time, more loving, more gentle.

Managing at last to shake herself free, she silently re-buttoned her blouse and smoothed her dishevelled hair. Hot tears were stinging her eyes but she managed to stop them from rolling down her flushed cheeks until Chris had retired to his room, having first reminded her of what she 'must' do in the morning. Now she let the tears flow. They rolled down her face and into her mouth, the salt on her tongue making her feel nauseous. What was she to do? Chris was not the gentleman she had taken him for. Had she been too quick in revealing her secret to him? Would he keep quiet about it if they were to part? Did she now want their relationship to end? She had been so happy. She had been in love. Was she now to face the world alone again with yet another painful memory to add to her collection?

Switching off the lights, Susan went to bed, only to find that her mother was unfortunately still awake and under the delusion that she and Chris had just passed a loving and romantic hour together. Conversation was difficult so Susan, feigning a headache, managed to stop the older woman's prattling and soon the latter fell asleep. Susan herself lay awake for most of the night, unable to come to a decision about Chris. For the second night in a row, it was almost dawn when she finally slept.

Chapter 7

Susan sleepily opened one eye and glanced at the small clock on the bedside table. It was almost nine o'clock. Kathleen was still in the bed beside her. Making light-hearted conversation was unbearably difficult but Susan persevered for a short time, not wanting her mother to become suspicious that anything was amiss. To escape from the bedroom she offered to prepare breakfast. Close to tears she considered her dilemma. What he wanted was not so dreadful. It was really quite natural. But the way he had demanded it had hurt her deeply. Still unresolved as to what course of action to take, she began to busy herself in the kitchen. The clatter of crockery as she laid the table and the appetising aroma of bacon and eggs frying soon stirred Chris. Within a few minutes he was washed and dressed, entering the kitchen at the very same moment as Kathleen emerged from her bedroom. There had been no time to speak alone.

"That smells good, Susan. It's been a long time since anyone made me my breakfast." She turned to their visitor:

"I hope you slept well, Chris."

"Like a log," he answered. "I was very comfortable."

"Will you join me at church this morning?" Kathleen made the enquiry cheerfully.

"Sorry, but I never go to church," replied Chris truthfully. "I gave that up years ago."

"But that's terrible, Chris! I'd feel guilty for the rest of the week if I missed the service on Sunday morning, unless I had a very good reason."

"Well, I think you're very wise to go then but it used to have a totally different effect on me. I used to become really angry having to sit there and listen in silence to a dogmatic sermon, especially when the preacher was one of those fire and brimstone types who try to get their message across by shouting at the congregation. I often felt like standing up and yelling back when I disagreed with something that had been said."

Kathleen looked annoyed.

"It's not for you or me to disagree with God's word," she said.

"One man's interpretation of God's word," he corrected her, "if indeed there is a God."

Anxious to avert a religious argument, Susan remarked that it was a lovely morning which provided a good opportunity after yesterday's rain for her to show Chris some of the local scenery and for them both to enjoy some fresh sea air. Chris immediately assented enthusiastically, so much so that Susan wondered if he really did want to take a walk. As she passed him some toast, however, a few moments later, she caught his eye and saw in his determined look that his satisfaction stemmed solely from her plausible excuse for not joining her mother at church.

Kathleen insisted on walking the short distance to church, as usual. As the door closed behind her, Chris took Susan by the hand and led her into the bedroom.

"Susan," he said softly, "Susan, darling, I haven't slept a wink all night, thinking about this morning. I love you very much."

He kissed her. She noticed that his expression had softened. He sat down on the edge of the bed.

"I'm so sorry about last night," he continued. "I was rough and selfish. I don't know what came over me. I just felt this desperate urge to love you physically, to make you forget that you ever loved anyone else, to claim you as my own. It was wrong of me to force you, to demand that you stay home this morning. I know it was wrong and I'm so sorry but, …" he paused and sighed, "but I still feel the same. I can't help it. I still want to feel your skin against mine, to share with you what he did… and more. How can I feel that we belong together if you won't allow it? Just this once?"

He enclosed her within his strong arms and kissed her lovingly, his tenderness having returned. She buried her head in his warm chest and reflected. He had apologised. He still loved her. What he wanted was only natural and, if she were honest, did she not desire it as much as he? The manly scent of his body was intoxicating, the warmth of his embrace comforting and inviting. She looked into his troubled eyes and saw the overwhelming love radiating from them.

"I do allow it, Chris. I want it too," she whispered imploringly. Immediately the tension between them dissipated and was gone like frost on a spring morning melting in warm sunlight.

Somehow their clothes were discarded as if on auto-pilot and they glided into the bed, their bodies finding each other straight away and relaxing into each others' curves. They made love and kissed long and passionately.

"I love you, Susan," Chris whispered in her ear. "I want to spend the rest of my life with you."

"Oh Chris," she breathed happily, "do you really mean it?"

"I love you. I want to be with you." He nibbled her ear. " Let's get married." He hoisted himself up on his elbow and looked straight into her eyes which were brimful with ecstatic passion. "Will you marry me, Susan?"

"Yes!" There was not a moment's hesitation.

He rolled over and clasped her body close to his own. Once more she yielded to him and their bodies blended together as one. It was such a blissful sensation. Susan had not dared to believe she would ever experience such happiness again. With hearts full of joy, they dozed, breathing in the warm air full of salt and seaweed, which wafted in through the open sash window.

Sometime later footsteps could be heard coming up the path. Realising all of a sudden how the morning had flown, Susan leapt out of bed and scrambled into her clothes.

"Tell her I'm changing my shoes after our walk," chuckled Chris, amused by her state of panic. "I'll be with you in a minute."

Smoothing her hair with her fingers as she raced for the door, she paused and turned to face her lover: "I love you," she said, blowing him a kiss. "But hurry up!"

In the kitchen she grabbed a potato and a knife and

pretended to be preparing the dinner. She peeled a second, then a third potato. Luckily her mother had gone straight to her room to hang up her coat in the wardrobe so that Susan was feeling calmer when she appeared.

"Did you have a good walk?" Kathleen enquired. "It's certainly brought the colour to your cheeks."

"Yes, thanks. Chris is just changing his shoes. He didn't want to walk any sand into the carpet. How was the service?"

"Lovely. It's a pity you didn't come along. People are always asking me about you."

"We'll come with you the next time," said Chris cheerfully, as he joined them. "That's a promise. I'm sorry if I offended you earlier on. I've probably just had a few bad experiences, encountered the wrong people."

She smiled at him. He had rather offended her but she liked the fact that he had apologised and she was glad there was to be a next time. She had a good feeling about Chris.

"Don't make it too long," she said. "It's lovely having you both here."

"We'll be back the first time Alan can lend me the car again," replied Chris, "or as soon as I get one of my own."

Susan looked up from her potatoes and caught his eye. She looked radiant as she returned his smile. Kathleen, noticing the exchange of loving glances, also smiled knowingly.

"Why don't you bring your dog next time," she said. "I know Susan is very fond of him. He would love the beach."

"Well, if you wouldn't mind having him here that would be great. Thanks. I might just do that." Chris was delighted that Bouncer would be welcome.

Humming one of her favourite hymns which was still in her head from the service, Kathleen went into the living room to lay the table, returning a few moments later to find the two young lovers kissing. She tried to slip out again unnoticed but Chris had spotted her.

"Kathleen," he said, "we've decided to tell you right away. I have asked Susan to marry me and she has accepted my proposal."

Kathleen was over the moon. She embraced them both warmly.

"I knew something was afoot!" she said. "This is brilliant news!"

There was great rejoicing for the rest of the day and it was a very happy couple who journeyed back to Belfast that evening.

Arriving about nine o'clock at Susan's flat, they went in to have a light supper and to discuss their plans but ended up once more in the bedroom. Neither of them had intended for it to happen but, having once sampled the joys of a sexual relationship, they now discovered that there could be no going back to their previous platonic state. Desire for each other simply radiated from their whole beings, so that, when such an opportunity arose, it was the only natural thing to do.

"I promised Alan that I'd return the car tonight," Chris mumbled reluctantly after some time.

"Not yet," murmured Susan, softly.

"It's getting late."

"Wouldn't it do in the morning?"

"Oh Susan, don't tempt me."

He looked at her and smiled:

"You know something? I think your friend Ashby really did me a favour. We could have drifted on for months as we were. I wouldn't have dared to touch you a few days ago. It was only jealousy that brought our relationship to a head, showed me what I really wanted and gave me the courage, the right to ask for it. Just think about what we would have been missing."

He kissed her and held her naked body close to his own. Susan's heart could have burst with happiness. Last night's awkwardness was forgotten. At last, at long last, her past was truly behind her, where it belonged.

It was six o'clock on Monday morning when Christopher drove the borrowed car into Alan and Doreen's driveway and slipped the keys through their letter box.

2009

Chapter 8

Neal opened one eye and glanced at the clock on his bedside table. He could just see it amidst the papers, books, coffee cups, loose change and other assorted debris which cluttered the dusty, walnut surface. He must have a good tidy-up and cleaning session today. He really was not one who could live in squalor. He liked things to be neat and tidy, fresh and clean. He squinted at the green, digital display. Half-past eight. Time to get up, things to do. Maybe today will be the day. They can't keep him waiting for ever. He jumped out of bed and turned on the radio and his computer. Immediately the air was filled with the sound of the Arctic Monkeys and *Cornerstone*, obscuring the sound of the laptop whirring into action. Neal started to sing along as he entered the bathroom, pressed the shower button and felt the warm water splash all over his body, refreshing his handsome, boyish face and his young, supple limbs. The start of a new day always excited him. He was a positive person with an optimistic outlook on life, always ready for a new challenge. Out of the shower now, he shaved and added a touch of Armani *mania*, just enough for a hint of manly fragrance, not too intense. He brushed his teeth and glanced at himself in the mirror, while gently rubbing a little gel through his long fair hair. He appraised himself and was generally satisfied. It wasn't vanity but he did take care about his appearance and general presentation. A quick spray of deodorant and he was back in his bedroom to check whether the expected email had come through.

"Yes!"

He clicked it open and quickly scanned the content. He had got the job and they were willing to consider the flexible working hours he had requested so that he could continue with his university research at the same time.

"Brilliant!"

Recently qualified with a degree in psychology, Neal was still undecided which branch of the subject he would like to specialise in for the optimum career move and was attempting to keep his options open. Getting any kind of employment was difficult in the current economic climate and he had been frustrated by several unsuccessful interviews. Now an opportunity had arisen which had ticked all the right boxes. The pay was not bad at all, the hours were largely up to himself to choose, and the company was close to the neighbourhood where Charlotte lived. He could hardly wait to tell her.

Charlotte. He still could not think of the way they met without a chuckle. He had been shopping in Sainsbury's at the same time that Charlotte had been there with her twin sister, Melanie. Somehow their trolleys had got mixed up. Neal had reached the check-out before either of them had been aware of the switch and had started to unload his goods unto the conveyor belt. He lifted the items out one at a time and set them down for the check-out girl to scan... ketchup, marmalade, bread, milk, fruit juice, yoghurt, beer, crisps, biscuits, toilet rolls, washing-up liquid. Then he came to his *Daily Mail*. Suddenly, underneath the newspaper he encountered items that he had not in fact chosen. First there was a tube of toothpaste, not his usual brand. A mistake easily made, he told himself. It will probably be fine. Then he picked out a couple of *Dove* deodorants, definitely from a very feminine range. How could he have got that so wrong? He quickly scanned his eyes over the items remaining in his trolley and realised that none of them were his. There was girly, mango shampoo, conditioner, face cream, even a pack of tampons! In amongst the unwanted items he also spotted a small purple handbag.

"I'm sorry," he told the check-out assistant, feeling his face go very red, "but there seems to be some mistake here. This is not my shopping!"

He handed her the handbag and waited patiently while she rang for her supervisor who checked the bag and made an announcement over the Tannoy system. Within seconds they noticed the commotion at another check-out about four aisles away. Charlotte and Melanie had just lifted their copy of the *Daily Mail* onto the conveyor belt, only to discover that it had been concealing several male body products and two packets of condoms!

There had been embarrassed faces all round but the erroneous items had been quickly exchanged and Melanie had been so relieved to get her handbag back, even though she had only just realised that it was missing. Neal had come face to face with the two girls in the car park afterwards and they had laughed about the situation until their sides ached! He had been immediately drawn to Charlotte, noticing how her friendly, brown eyes twinkled and danced, set within her perfectly formed oval face which was framed with long, wavy auburn hair. Her lithe and athletic-looking body was casually clad in blue denim jeans and a pink linen blouse with sleeves rolled up to the elbow. She wore a plain gold bracelet on one wrist, a pretty Gucci watch on the other. Neal took a quick glance at her left hand. No wedding or engagement ring. Good! She was beautiful and he was entranced. They had ended up exchanging telephone numbers although he could see that Charlotte had been a bit wary of those condoms lurking in his otherwise innocent-looking trolley of groceries. What on earth had possessed him to buy those today of all days? He had only lifted them as a precaution, handy to have, just in case. He wasn't actually intending to use them in the near future, wasn't even in a current relationship. How embarrassing!

When he thought about it afterwards, Neal remembered that he had perused the magazines for some moments after placing the newspaper in his trolley. They weren't in their usual place due to some renovation work being carried out in the store and had been squeezed into quite a small space at the end of the toiletries aisle. The girls must also have been distracted at the same time. Since they had both lifted the same newspaper, the two trolleys would have looked identical so it had been easy to walk off with the wrong one. He realised now how engrossed he must have been in that photography magazine as he hadn't even noticed the girls. Melanie too was strikingly pretty but Charlotte was gorgeous. He couldn't get her out of his mind. Did they say they were twins? Obviously fraternal rather than identical.

Neal had phoned Charlotte the very day after the supermarket mix-up and they had gone out that night for a drink. Since then they had become good friends. He had not seen her, however, for about three weeks now because he had moved back home to his own flat in Yorkshire, whilst awaiting examination results and travelling to various job interviews around the country. Uppermost in his thoughts now was the fact that he would soon see Charlotte again because he had just secured a part-time place on a post-graduate course in a college just outside Cambridge and Charlotte had a part-time job at one of the university libraries. Furthermore he had now been offered a job close to where she lives in Hertfordshire!

Fully dressed now, Neal excitedly dialled Charlotte's number. His call was answered almost immediately.

"Hello. Is Charlotte at home, please?" he asked cheerfully.

"I'm afraid you've just missed her." This came from a deep, mature man's voice at the other end of the line. Neal could sense a lively, bustling atmosphere in the background. He could hear the sound of cutlery and crockery in use and several female voices chatting over breakfast. The radio was tuned to the same station as his own, which was now playing *I'm Yours* by Jason Mraz.

"She left for work a few minutes ago. You must be Colin. Can I give her a message?"

Neal's exuberance faded and a lump came into his throat.

"No, thank you. Just tell her Neal phoned."

"Neal?"

"Yes, Neal Ashby."

He replaced the receiver, feeling sick at heart. It was quite obvious that Mr Jamison had never even heard of him and who on earth was Colin? He reached into his pocket and took out his mobile, quickly locating Charlotte's name and number on the screen. Then he stopped himself. It would be better to speak to her in person.

He sat down on his bed and thought over his relationship with Charlotte. She had become an important part of his life but did she know that? He realised that he had allowed things to drift along very casually. He had not told her that she was very special to him, that he was, in fact, in love with her. She had appeared to be so happy when they were together that he had just assumed she felt the same way about him and would wait patiently for his return.

But why should she wait? He asked himself the question, knowing that he had taken too much for granted. *I haven't even told her how I feel!*

Hoping desperately that he would not be too late, he resolved to see her without delay. He also needed to find more suitable lodgings for the new term. Impatient and restless, he set off at once. That cleaning session would have to wait. He could have kicked himself for his stupidity in letting the girl he loved slip out of his grasp. Hopefully things had not gone too far with this guy Colin, because the thought of Charlotte in the arms of another man was hard to bear.

Neal arrived at the library late in the afternoon, only to find that Charlotte had finished work early and had already gone home. He was tempted to follow her but did not want to appear foolish in front of her family, whom he had never met, if indeed she had begun a relationship with someone else. Resolving to confront her the next day, he reluctantly transferred his thoughts to the other matter in hand and made his way to the accommodation officer.

Having first lodged a complaint about his previous room, which had been cold and damp and badly in need of numerous repairs, he looked through the list of accommodation available for the new term.

"This one was added to our list just this morning," said the girl in the office, pointing to an address at the bottom of the page. "I went to check it out myself and it's a really lovely room. The landlady is a school teacher, a widow I think."

"Thanks," said Neal, taking a note of the address. "I'll go and see it for myself. I'm actually working in educational research so a school teacher would be ideal. I'll be needing access to a school population from time to time. Do you have a note of the lady's name?"

The girl entered something into her computer, then consulted another document and found the name. "Mrs S Lovell," she said.

Chapter 9

Susan had settled down very contentedly in her new home and was looking forward to the beginning of the new term at the school where she had secured a post as Deputy Head, because then she would become better acquainted with people and hopefully make some more new friends. While still desperately lonely at times, she was attempting to be positive. Chris would not have wanted her to grieve for ever. Having two spare rooms at her disposal and being in such close proximity to the university, she had decided to take a student lodger and keep one of the rooms free for visitors, especially for her niece, Alannah, who had promised to pay her an early visit. She had furnished the rooms accordingly and now waited anxiously for some response to her advertisement, wondering how she would adapt to having a total stranger living in the house. She was watching a gardening programme on her recently purchased wide-screen television when the door bell rang. A little nervously, she rose to answer it.

"Mrs Lovell?"

"Yes, that's right."

"I'm a student at the university. I've come to enquire about the room you have to let."

Susan was very impressed with the young man who stood on her doorstep. He was very handsome and, though casually dressed, had a smart, clean appearance. A crop of blond, curly hair surrounded his tanned face, still quite boyish, and his bright blue eyes shone with honesty and a twinkle she felt sure no young girl would be able to resist. She invited him in to see the room, hoping that he would take it, for she already had a feeling that she would like him.

She preceded him up the stairs and into the room she had prepared. A double bed stood in the centre of the shiny, laminated floor. To one side of it was a writing desk and bookshelves, to the other side an extensive range of built-in drawers, cupboards and wardrobes. In front of the bed was a large vanity shelf and mirror. A couple of blue shaggy rugs were scattered across the floor and matching blue and cream striped curtains hung by the large bay window. Susan watched as the young man surveyed the room, open-mouthed.

"It's perfect," he said at last, hardly able to believe his eyes. "I'll take it if you'll have me. I'm Neal Ashby, by the way."

"I'll be happy to have you, Neal," she replied, starting at the once familiar name. They went downstairs to arrange the details.

"Ashby," she repeated, as she wrote it down. "You wouldn't be George Ashby's son, would you?"

She hoped her bluff was not too obvious.

"No," replied Neal, taking the bait nicely. "My father's name is Jonathan."

She had not really expected that. Susan turned away quickly to hide her face, as colour flushed into her cheeks and emotion surged up involuntarily in her heart, bringing sudden tears to her eyes. Could this really be Jonathan's son, coming to live in her house? To compose herself she went to the kitchen and made some coffee.

Neal looked around the living-room and marvelled, comparing it to his former lodgings. He could not believe his luck.

"You certainly keep your house in great order, Mrs Lovell," he said, when she returned with the tray. "You should see the rooms some students have to live in!"

"Oh, I haven't lived here for long," she answered modestly. Then laughing, she added:

"Of course that doesn't mean that I don't intend to try to keep it like this!"

"I thought you weren't from these parts," surmised Neal. "Are you from Scotland?"

"No, Ireland. The Northern Irish accent is often confused with the Scottish. I moved here from Belfast just six months ago."

"That's interesting," continued her prospective lodger. "My parents are both from Northern Ireland, County Antrim. In fact I was born there myself but we moved away about two years afterwards and I really don't remember it at all. Dad's sister still lives there, Auntie Belle."

Susan remembered Jonathan's sister, Annabel, very well. She was quite a few years older than him and ran a small boarding house on the coast, took in visitors for bed and breakfast. She had a great reputation in the area for friendly hospitality, cleanliness, and the best Ulster fry for miles around. Everybody called her Belle. In the kitchen Susan had decided that the similarity in names was a sheer coincidence but now she was convinced that she was indeed speaking to the son of her former lover, of whom she had heard nothing for so many years. How strange that he, of all people, had turned up on her doorstep!

"Have you any brothers or sisters?" she asked, trying hard to make her conversation sound like the casual talk she would have with any new young acquaintance. Her relationship with Jonathan had been too intimate for her to reveal the connection to his son.

"A younger sister," he replied, "Suzannah."

Susan started at the name, a variation of her own. Could there conceivably be any significance in that? Of course not. She must not become paranoid. They both sipped their coffee and nibbled their chocolate biscuits silently for a time.

"What are you reading at the university?" Susan asked after a while, not wanting to show unnatural interest in his family lest she arouse suspicion.

"Educational psychology," he told her. "I'm actually doing research into the causes of underachievement in school, *under*achievement as distinct from straightforward *low* achievement, in other words linking standardised scores to potential ability."

"I'll be interested in the results of your research," she said. "I'm a teacher myself."

"Yes, so I believe."

She looked surprised.

"The accommodation officer mentioned it," he explained.

His coffee finished, Neal prepared to take his leave.

"I'll be in touch when I've got things organised," he said amicably. "I'll let you know the exact date to expect me."

"Are you travelling all the way home tonight?"

Susan recalled the address he had given her and suddenly realised how late it was to be starting such a journey.

"No, I've some-one to see here tomorrow. I'll crash with a friend for tonight."

On hearing this, Susan insisted that he stay where he was.

"The room is yours now," she argued. "You might as well use it."

It didn't take too much persuasion for Neal to agree to this and very soon he was settled in his new home from home, still marvelling over his extreme good fortune.

Susan lay in bed that night, unable to sleep, wondering about the strange circumstance that had led Jonathan's son to her door. He was sleeping now in the next room, the son of a man she had once loved dearly, a man with whom she had spent three wonderful years of her youth. Jonathan's memory had been repressed during the ten happy years she had spent with Chris but the events of the last few hours had brought the memories flooding back. On a sudden impulse she slipped out of bed, opened the top drawer of her bedside table, drew out a little white box from the back of the drawer, and slowly opened it. It contained two items, a silver chain bracelet from which hung the two initial letters, S and J, and an old, somewhat faded photograph. Sitting down on the edge of the bed, she gazed at the handsome, smiling face of Jonathan. She wondered if he had changed much over the years, whether she would still know him. Neal was not really like him, she decided. He must take after his mother. She never did get to see what Helen looked like. She brought the photograph up to her lips and tenderly kissed it before replacing it in its box, where it had remained hidden all through her marriage. Then, fastening the bracelet around her wrist, she slipped back into bed and drifted into a reverie of the day when Jonathan had given it to her...

They have been playing tennis on the beach, the hot sun streaming down on them and lapping up their strength. At length, too exhausted to continue, they wander off, hand in hand, into the sand dunes to find a quiet, private spot to relax. The sound of the waves recedes and the heat grows more and more intense as they leave the sea breeze behind. They finally choose a place to spread the rug they have brought and lie down. What a glorious day it has been. Not a breath stirs the air and the cerulean blueness of the firmament is broken only by a few wispy white clouds, high above their heads. They are so completely alone they might have been in another world. Susan remembers lying there, her young limbs soaking up the sun, the distant sound of laughter and merriment on the beach very occasionally reaching her ears, carried there on a soft, warm breeze. This is heaven. The man she loves lies beside her, his gentle breathing and her own the only sounds that disturb the quiet stillness.

Several moments pass in total silence. Presently there is a rustling sound and Susan opens her eyes to find Jonathan rummaging in the pockets of his discarded jeans. He now wears nothing but a pair of blue swimming shorts.

"I have a present for you," he says, handing her a little package, wrapped in pink tissue paper and encased in a black velvet pouch.

Susan unwraps the present, the bracelet she is now wearing once again.

"It's beautiful," she says. "Thank you. What's the occasion?"

"You are beautiful," he replies and tenderly kisses her. "That's the only reason I need to buy you a gift."

Susan remembers vividly, as though it were yesterday, what happened next. His strong hands fasten the delicate silver chain around her wrist and then slowly travel up her bare arms. Tentatively he places one hand on the bodice of her cotton frock and feels the firm roundness of her breast beneath it. She begins to breathe more quickly. Closing her eyes, she allows him, almost wills him to undo her buttons and remove the dress. Her heart thumps wildly as she feels him roll over on top of her and bury his face in the soft, white flesh of her bosom. There, under the glare of the sun, they make love for the first time, a beautiful experience which will be repeated only a handful of times before Jonathan begins to bestow his love elsewhere…

And now, here was his son, sleeping under her very own roof! Suddenly Susan was back in the present and feeling very guilty for letting her thoughts run wild. Once again she slipped out of bed to look at a photograph but this time it was not hidden away in a box. On the contrary it was prominently displayed in a silver frame on her dressing table, a portrait of her late husband, who had been so tragically killed in that horrific road accident three years ago. As she looked at it lovingly, she found herself wondering and asking herself which of the two men she had loved more. She was alarmed to discover that it was a question she dared not answer.

Chapter 10

Neal scanned the reception area of the library block where Charlotte worked and spotted her immediately, looking elegant as usual in a bright green blouse, and wearing a simple gold chain around her neck. She was seated behind her desk, which was laden with recently returned books and manuscripts, and was busily entering some data into a computer. She smiled radiantly as he walked over and confronted her.

"Neal! I wasn't expecting you back so soon. Any news about that job yet?"

"Yes," he answered without expression. "I got it. Looks like I'll be moving down here for a while."

"Oh, congratulations! That's brilliant!"

"Is it?"

The sarcastic tone of his voice took Charlotte by surprise.

"I thought that was what you wanted," she faltered hesitantly, her smile transformed into a look of uncertainty. "You talked about nothing else a few weeks ago."

"In other words you were bored listening to me," he retorted coldly.

"I didn't mean anything of the sort." She was angry with him for the unfair accusation.

Neal made no reply. He was aware that he was not handling the situation very well. He nodded to a couple of friends who had just come in.

"Hi Neal," one of them called over. "You flunked your exams too?"

"No, I passed. I'm not here to work."

"Oh yes, I remember. Your bird works here." He shot a glance at Charlotte, who had moved off to attend to someone at the desk. "I'm here to study for resits."

"That's hard luck."

"Me too," added his mate, who looked as if he had just crawled out of bed. "Shouldn't have gone to all those parties a few weeks back."

Neal suddenly brightened. At least that was one problem he did not have to deal with.

Realising that he would not be likely to win Charlotte back if he continued with this sour attitude, he managed a smile as he moved across to speak to her again.

"Charlotte," he said more gently, "we need to talk. Have you a break coming up soon?"

"Not until lunchtime," she answered, puzzled by his uncharacteristic manner.

'We need to talk' usually means 'I'm dumping you'. Surely not. She hadn't seen that coming.

"I'll be free at twelve o'clock."

Neal looked at his Rolex watch, a present from his maternal grandfather; it was only a quarter past ten. Reluctantly he agreed to come back at twelve and spent the rest of the morning strolling around aimlessly, unable to settle his mind on anything else.

As the appointed time grew near, he returned to the library and waited anxiously for Charlotte to come out. She appeared just after twelve.

"What's up?" she asked immediately.

She was now as worried and stressed as he was.

He appraised her lovely face with its smooth, creamy skin, her dark brown eyes, her soft, chestnut curls which shone and bounced as she approached him and he wanted her more than ever. He decided to come straight out with it.

"Who is Colin?"

"Pardon?"

"Who is Colin?"

"Colin? Colin who?"

She was cool. Neal was impressed. There was not a hint of recognition, not even a blush.

"That is what I am asking you. Who is Colin?"

"I don't know anyone called Colin. What are you talking about?"

"Your father implied that you have a boyfriend called Colin."

"My father?"

"Yes, your father!" There was exasperation in his tone now. "For God's sake stop repeating everything I say. Why can't you just tell me the truth?"

"I am telling you the truth. I don't know anyone called Colin."

Neal was beginning to believe her.

"I phoned your house yesterday," he said more calmly,

"and your father said you had just left for work. He then said that I must be Colin and did I want to leave a message."

Charlotte's face broke into an amused smile.

"He must have thought you asked for Mel," she explained. She has a boyfriend called Colin."

"Mel?"

"Melanie."

Neal was not convinced.

"I thought you said you didn't know anyone called Colin," he said.

"I don't. I've never met him. I didn't even think of him when you started interrogating me."

She started to laugh at the mixture of relief and embarrassment in his expression.

"Were you really so jealous?" She took great pleasure in knowing that he was.

"Yes, I was!" he admitted. There was no point in denying it now and making an even bigger fool of himself. "So you haven't been out with anyone else after all?"

"Of course not. Not since I met you."

"Oh Charlotte," he said quietly, "I thought I'd lost you and it made me realise how much I love you."

Charlotte had longed for him to say those three words. She felt a flutter in her heart. He wasn't dumping her at all, quite the opposite!

"I love you too, Neal," she said.

Happily they joined hands and made their way to a local snack bar for a quick lunch. Over coffee and chilli chicken paninis, Neal told Charlotte all about his new lodgings where he had spent the night. He intended moving in within the next few weeks as he wanted to start planning his thesis right away, maybe even earlier depending on the start date for his new job.

"Don't forget I'll be away for a week," she reminded him. "We leave next Saturday."

The holiday with two girlfriends had been booked some months ago. He *had* forgotten, and now that their relationship had reached a new level, he was reluctant to see her go.

"I wish you weren't going," he said wistfully.

"Don't worry. It's only for a week."

"Promise you won't forget me."

"Don't be silly. I'll text or phone you every day."

"But what about the men? Three young girls on their own with all those red-blooded continentals about the place? Are you just going to ignore them?"

"I'll not be unfaithful to you."

"What does that mean? You won't talk to strange men at all or you won't go as far as actually sleeping with them?"

Charlotte was furious with him for even thinking it and the romantic atmosphere was broken.

"You're the one who buys contraceptives as part of the weekly shop, not me," she retorted, loudly. "You have a nerve!"

Was she never going to let him live that down?

Grabbing her handbag, Charlotte said she had to get back to work and stormed out, the swinging bag somehow knocking over her unfinished cup of coffee on the way. The brown, lukewarm liquid poured along the table and off the edge unto Neal's knee.

"Shit!"

"Serves you right!"

She didn't even glance back at him and ignored the startled looks of other students, to many of whom hers was a familiar face. The dark-haired guy in a blue and grey checked shirt and his spiky-haired companion in a red polo shirt at the next table looked amused.

"He says he loves me!" she muttered to herself. "A bit of respect wouldn't go amiss."

Her temper gradually cooled throughout the afternoon though her feelings towards Neal remained ambivalent. He was waiting for her outside when she finished work for the day.

"Did you have to create such a scene?" Neal asked. "It was very embarrassing."

"Good. You deserved it," she retorted. "Actually I didn't create any scene, *you* did."

Neal laughed and said:

"You look even nicer when you're angry!"

She glared at him. No sign of forgiveness.

"All right, I'm sorry. I shouldn't have said what I did but I can't help being jealous. I want you all to myself."

"It's got nothing to do with jealousy. You implied that I would go sleeping around with strangers just because I'm going on holiday with other single girls. You obviously don't know me very well."

"I didn't mean it. I said I'm sorry. Come and have a drink with me. I have to be getting back soon."

Over a glass of Chardonnay for Charlotte and a pint of real ale for Neal they soon forgot their quarrel and once again expressed their love for each other.

"It's been a strange day," Neal admitted, "and that made me irritable."

Then he thought about his success over the accommodation issue.

"Mind you, I think I am going to be happy with my new room. The atmosphere at breakfast this morning was weird. It was like being in the home of an aunt or at least a good family friend, rather than a landlady I have only just met. I can't quite explain it but she was so friendly and really made me feel at home."

Charlotte chuckled.

"Just think," she said, "I actually helped you to get that room. If you hadn't come rushing all the way here to find out what I was up to with 'Colin', you would probably have been too late. Some-one else would have snapped it up."

"So I have your father to thank for that? I must remember to tell him!"

Neal suddenly made a decision:

"Charlotte, I'm not going to wait for term to start, or the new job for that matter. I am going to move in right away. By the time you come home from Portugal, I'll be here in Cambridge and we can see each other every day."

"I was hoping you would do that." Charlotte smiled at him radiantly. "It's turned out to be a great day, after all."

Neal kissed her and she responded with passion. Some-one behind them started to giggle, a guy in a blue and grey checked shirt.

"Hope you've done your weekly shop, mate!" he said with a smirk.

Chapter 11

"Don't lose that recipe for sangria! We'll make some the next sunny day we have."

"We'll have to get a karaoke machine and have a big beach-themed party."

"Great idea! See you next week and we'll get it organised. Ate logo!"

Neal, and Emma's dad, Nigel, exchanged amused smiles.

"They'll soon come back down to earth," Nigel said with a chuckle, as Emma and Lianne climbed into the back of his silver BMW and he stacked their luggage in the boot.

Charlotte was delighted that Neal had come to pick her up. She had missed him so much but had still enjoyed the week in the sun.

"This time yesterday we were still relaxing by the pool," she sighed, as he placed the key in the ignition and the engine of his yellow Porsche Cayman began to purr. There was something to be said for having rich grandparents! Neal had accepted a few special gifts from them over the years but he was determined to make his own way in the world. He was not going to be a sponge. Charlotte respected him for that but she did get some pleasure from experiencing the reaction of friends when they saw her in the Cayman. It was sheer luxury.

"I moved into my digs last night," Neal said. "No more long journeys home."

"What will you do with your flat?" Charlotte enquired. "Are you just going to leave it empty?"

"For the moment, yes. I'll be using it some weekends. Maybe you'll come with me?"

She didn't reply. It was a very tempting idea but she wasn't totally sure whether she was ready for that. She had never yet gone beyond the kissing stage with a man.

Neal registered her silence. He had already figured that it would be her first time. He wasn't going to push her too soon.

The constant late nights and the frustration over the delayed flight were catching up with her. Charlotte closed her tired eyes and dozed. Instantly she was back on that sandy beach in her skimpy red bikini and lying under a yellow and pink parasol, taking a short break from the intensity of the midday heat and sipping cool iced water that they had brought from the freezer in their apartment. Now she was splashing about in the crystal clear water and frolicking in the waves, giggling at the antics of Pedro and Carlos who were hurling their football further and further out to sea and then chasing after it with such gusto, as though their lives depended on winning the race. They were both excellent swimmers. Emma had certainly hit it off with Carlos. She wondered whether they really would keep in touch as they had promised. Holiday romances didn't often survive. Pedro and Lianne had got on pretty well too. She had felt like such a gooseberry at times! She conjured up again that cerulean sky! They hadn't seen a single cloud all week. Her thoughts drifted to the lively square where they had sipped pina coladas and caipirinhas in the evenings, whilst listening to the diverse sounds coming simultaneously from a multitude of street artists all belting out the same songs over and over again, but not in unison of course, and then there were the karaoke bars. They had all had a go at that. What a laugh that had been. But, hey, she never knew Lianne was such a good singer. She had brought the house down with rapturous applause and admiring wolf-whistles to her rendition of *Love Shack*. Pedro had joined in with the duet parts and had sounded so funny with his Portuguese accent. They may have been in Portugal but English was definitely the spoken language. They had hardly used their phrase books at all. It was so, so hot, even at night. She saw again the bright pink bougainvillea draped across their apartment block, the flowering mimosa trees and the abundance of red and yellow hibiscus shrubs in the garden, sheltering beneath tall palms. It was another world.

"Do you want to go straight home or shall we go for a drive and have a bite to eat?" Neal's voice just got through to her, as if in a distant haze. She tried to shake herself awake.

"That would be lovely." Much as she would have liked to go home and freshen up, she wanted Neal all to herself after the week away, not in a house full of her large family. "I *am* quite hungry," she added.

He took a left turn off the main road and veered into the countryside, winding through narrow lanes and passing several small hamlets and villages. It would have been very pretty if it hadn't just started to rain. The sky was grey and overcast.

"Where are we going?"

"One of my favourite country pubs is along here. A friend of dad's owns it. They do great food."

They were hardly through the door when Neal was recognised by the jovial round-faced landlord, Jack, and given an enormous wide-mouthed smile and a hearty handshake. Neal introduced Charlotte. It was still early in the evening so the pub was not yet busy. They sat down on a green leather sofa in the corner and ordered a bottle of red wine, while they perused the menu. Neal left it to Jack to recommend one. He served them himself.

"So how are Jonny and Helen? It's a while since they've been down this way."

"They're fine, thanks. I won't see so much of them myself for a while as I'm living near Cambridge for the moment. I'm in digs there."

Jack addressed himself to Charlotte:

"This guy's dad was my best friend when we were growing up back in Ulster. We had some good times together. A lot of laughs!"

He laughed now, just thinking about it, and then related some schoolboy pranks they had got up to and some memorable fishing expeditions.

"You know, Neal, it's a small world," Jack continued. "Your dad and I were at school with a bloke called Ian

Swanson. He happened to drop in here for a drink recently and we got talking. He was just back from visiting his sister in Australia. Had a great time, he said. But while he was there,… your dad will be interested in this – make sure you remember to tell him…, while he was there he came across this woman who also lived near us back home. Kathleen Summers was her name. Your dad had a thing going with her daughter back then. I'm sure he won't mind me telling you that. Nice girl she was too. Lovely girl."

He paused and looked contemplative, as though remembering something. "But very prim and proper Kathleen was in those days, very jejune in a beguiling sort of way, and very religious. Well, tell your dad she's out there now, living like a hippie, shacked up with Ian's sister's neighbour! Can't remember his name."

Neal laughed.

"I'll tell him to give you a ring. You can fill him in with all the details. I'd never remember all those names."

"It's great to see you, lad. You should come in more often. I'll send Tina over to take your order."

Jack went back through the bar and into his small office. Charlotte took out her digital camera and started to show Neal some of the photographs she had taken. They were mostly of Emma or Lianne surrounded by sun, sea and sand or restaurant shots with fancy cocktails full of sparklers and other colourful gimmicks.

"Did you not think to ask them to take some of you?" laughed Neal. "Maybe they'll be able to give you copies from their own cameras."

"They'll have loads of me. I'll get them to email them to me."

Tina dutifully arrived to take their order. Charlotte chose roast chicken and home-cut fries in a basket and Neal ordered a chilli beef stir fry. They sipped their wine while they waited for their meals to arrive.

"The menu is simple but everything is fresh and cooked to order," observed Neal.

"Well, there is certainly a good smell coming from the kitchen," agreed Charlotte. "You seem to know Jack pretty well," she added. "He's very friendly."

"I've known him all my life. He's great. Suzy and I used to call him Uncle Jack but we're not really related. I'm not sure Mum was so keen on him."

Charlotte excused herself and went to the ladies' to freshen up. As she passed the bar she couldn't help overhearing Jack's voice. He was evidently speaking on the telephone.

"He's with a really pretty girl called Charlotte," he was saying. "Reminds me of someone but I can't think who it is. I told him about your visit down under and about you meeting Kathleen Summers, told him to tell Jonny. It got me thinking. Why don't we all get together for a few pints? Just the lads. I've nothing against your missus, Ian; she seemed very nice that day you were in. But I can't stand that Helen. I never did like her. Jonny was much happier when he was with the Summers girl. Pity it didn't work out…"

Charlotte slipped past and into the toilets without being seen. *Seems the dislike between Helen and Jack is mutual,* she thought to herself, but decided not to tell Neal what she had overheard. At least she had been described as 'really pretty'. She didn't feel it after a day's travelling but now did her best to at least make herself look presentable, combing her hair and applying some moisturiser and lip gloss. Jack was still on the phone as she passed the bar on her way back to their fairly secluded nook in the corner.

"Money's not everything," she heard him say. "I wouldn't have given up someone like Susan Summers for all the money in the world. I think he was mad and I'm not saying anything behind his back. I've told him often enough."

Interesting!

The food was delicious and Charlotte drank most of the wine since Neal was driving. They finished off with a cup of freshly-ground coffee. Much as she had enjoyed her holiday, the warm, cosy atmosphere of this friendly pub and the sensation of Neal's manly, sensuous body next to her was already making her forget Portugal. They said goodbye to Jack and headed out to the car. It was still raining with a light drizzle.

"I'm so glad you're home," smiled Neal, throwing both arms around her and holding her close. "I love you, Charlotte."

"Mmm," she drank in his fragrance and felt the beat of his heart against her own through his blue and white checked shirt and her pink, summer blouse, the slight hint of stubble on his face against her soft cheek. She loved that characteristically slanted smile. Her lips found his and they kissed.

"I love you too," she breathed.

"So would you recommend the Algarve then?"

"Depends what kind of holiday you are looking for."

"I'm thinking of a honeymoon," he whispered in her ear, and he kissed her again.

Chapter 12

"When am I going to meet Charlotte?" Susan Lovell asked her 'adopted son' one morning. They were sitting together at the breakfast table enjoying coffee and croissants with apricot jam. They had been together for some months now and, as usual, he could hardly manage five minutes without mentioning her name.

"Remember, Neal," she said, "while you are living here this is your home and you are welcome to bring any of your friends in. I want you to feel that you can do anything here that you would do in your own house."

"That's very generous," smiled Neal, who had never ceased to marvel at the motherly attention he received. "I'll bring Charlotte in for supper some night this week."

"Oh good, that will be nice. Any night except tomorrow," she continued, "as I'm having a group of friends in from school. Actually I was thinking that you might like to join us. They might be able to help you with your thesis."

Neal was certainly on the lookout for first-hand information from local teachers to compare and contrast with his book and internet research so he thanked her for the invitation and said that he would be delighted to join the party. He would bring Charlotte in some other evening.

They arrived about eight o'clock the following evening, a curious assortment of characters from the young and frivolous Pearl Keating, who kept giggling and ogling Neal hungrily, devouring his every word, to the prim and elderly Miss Murchison, who spoke to him as though he were one of her pupils. Neal was pleased to find two young men amongst the group and was soon in conversation with them about his studies and research as well as other mutual interests and hobbies. They both went outside with him to admire his car properly and came back in after a spin round the block, raving about it. On hearing that Neal was particularly interested in examining the effect of a child's date of birth on his subsequent educational achievement, Richard Walkington disclosed that he himself had done some research in that field and that he still had a great deal of literature on the subject, to which he said Neal would be welcome.

"Call round tomorrow evening," he suggested, writing down the address, "and I'll go through it with you."

Presently the supper trolley was wheeled in laden with an assortment of savoury and sweet snacks and Neal was led into a more general conversation. Topics ranged from keep fit and floral art classes to recipes, washing machines and breast-feeding, for which purpose Pearl Keating had to leave the group early.

"Unbelievable!" Neal muttered to himself, almost choking on his sausage roll when he thought about the way she had been trying to flirt with him all evening and now realising that she was the mother of a very young baby. Presumably she had a loving partner waiting for her at home.

In the end, as invariably happens with school teachers, anecdotes about school took over again. Some of them were certainly amusing and, taking everything into account, Neal quite enjoyed his evening. As he said to Charlotte in the library the next day, it was 'different'.

He had called in to say that he would be busy that evening but wanted her to come the following night to meet his landlady and have supper with them. There was a hectic atmosphere in the library so they did not have a chance for a prolonged conversation but Charlotte was agreeable to the arrangement. She still thought it was a bit strange, Neal being so friendly with his landlady. She hadn't even met Neal's actual family yet. But then they were much further away. And Neal did seem to be very fond of this Lovell woman. She didn't mind giving up a few hours of her time if it was important to him.

As arranged, Neal drove to Richard Walkington's house at about nine o'clock to see whether Richard's books would be of any use to him in his own studies. A pretty young girl opened the door. She was very thin with long, straight, jet-black hair. She looked only about eighteen years old but, as Susan had mentioned that Richard was married, Neal realised that she must be his wife.

"Is Richard at home?" he asked her.

"You must be Neal."

"Yes, that's right. He's expecting me."

"Come on in. I'm Stephanie."

Neal was already inside, having a drink, before he realised that Richard had been obliged to go out to deal with an urgent family matter.

"He asked me to apologise," she said, "and to give you the papers if he's not back in time. I'll just go and get them."

Neal glanced around the tastefully furnished lounge of their modern bungalow while she was gone. He looked forward to settling down in a place like this with Charlotte. He heard the phone ring and Stephanie's muffled voice answering it.

"That was Richard," she explained some minutes later, bringing an armful of papers into the room and depositing them on the coffee table by the window. "He says he'll not be home for a couple of hours yet. He's sitting at A & E with his mother. He doesn't think it's anything serious but you can never be too careful."

"Never mind," said Neal, rising to take his leave. "I'll call again another day. I hope his mum will be OK."

"There's another box of books for you," she replied hurriedly, "but I can't reach it."

"Sure there's plenty here to keep me busy for the time being. I'll get it from Richard next time."

She looked anxious about something.

"But the best books are in it," she persisted. "It's just in here, on top of a cupboard."

She walked out of the room and headed towards another door.

Neal followed her into the room and climbed up onto a chair to fetch the box. It was difficult to reach and heavy to move but he managed to get it down and turned to go out.

He had not noticed Stephanie closing the door. Now he realised for the first time that he was in her bedroom, the curtains were drawn, the door was closed, and Stephanie was standing in front of it, absolutely naked.

"Put your clothes on," he said calmly, averting his gaze and feeling anything *but* calm.

The flimsy, red dress she had been wearing was lying at her feet. There was no sign of any underwear. She must have removed that the first time she left him in the lounge, as soon as she received her husband's phone-call. Neal waited for her to move. He could not open the door until she did.

"Let me out, please," he said patiently.

Still she did not move.

At last he looked up and the sadness in her pretty face touched him. The nakedness of her body frustrated and aroused him.

"Richard doesn't love me any more," she whimpered pathetically.

Something snapped in Neal's brain. He set down the heavy box he was holding and began to undress. Then throwing her down on the bed, he took her roughly, just as she wanted. Not a word was spoken between them. When it was over, he dressed again quickly, lifted the box, and ran from the room. Stephanie was still lying on the bed.

"He's never here on Mondays or Fridays," she called after him.

Chapter 13

Charlotte came for supper as arranged and was an immediate hit with Susan who, for the past few months, had lavished on Neal all the care and affection which she had once felt for his father. A special bond having been formed between them, she was delighted that Jonathan's son had chosen someone she approved of. All three chatted amicably until supper was over, when Susan tactfully retired to her room, leaving the two young people together. She wanted some time alone anyway, to reflect. Today was her wedding anniversary.

"I've eaten far too much!" said Neal, rubbing his stomach.

"Me too," agreed Charlotte. "She had gone to so much trouble, I didn't like to refuse anything. That ginger and lime chicken was delicious."

Charlotte took a sip of her wine.

"I might as well have this last glass," she said, "since you have to drive me home. I know it's only forty minutes or so but you have already had a large glass."

"No problem." He wasn't going to argue. It was closer

to an hour and a half considering he had to come back again. He didn't drink and drive anyway, even on short journeys, had always been very sensible in that respect.

"She's very nice," Charlotte now commented. "Has she any family of her own?"

"No. I think that must be why she's so good to me. Her husband died very young. Car crash."

"That's sad. It's such a pity because she seems like the motherly type."

Neal snuggled up close to her and kissed her.

"Just like you," he whispered. "Just think, we could be parents some day."

Charlotte's mind explored that thought with a mixture of excitement and trepidation."

The Coldplay CD that had been playing in the background came to an end and Neal got up to change it. He selected U2's Greatest Hits and sat down again, putting his arm round her.

"Don't you have a half-day tomorrow?"

"Yes."

"I'll be free from two o'clock onwards," he muttered suggestively, "and Mrs Lovell doesn't get home until after five."

An afternoon with Neal in his own bed? Her heart missed a beat as she tried to cope with the conflicting wishes of her body and her mind. Something was holding her back.

"No," she said at length.

Though not really surprised, Neal was disappointed.

"Oh Charlotte. Why not? *Please*."

"No." This time her answer was spontaneous.

Still hoping for a change of mind, Neal was persistent.

"You won't need to worry about anything," he said. "I'll take the necessary precautions. It *is* the twenty-first century, you know. We're not living in the Dark Ages. It's only natural to have sex, when you're in love, like we are."

"I said no."

Tears welled up in her eyes and immediately Neal felt ashamed of himself.

"Forgive me," he whispered. "I got carried away. I'm sorry."

He didn't ask again.

On the way home to Charlotte's house, they discussed their future plans for becoming engaged. They had talked about marriage for several months now. Why wait any longer? It was what they both wanted.

"That's what we'll do tomorrow," Neal said, as he kissed her goodnight. "We'll go shopping for a ring!"

★ ★ ★

They would have been out celebrating, having a nice romantic meal somewhere posh, just the two of them. That was how they had marked all their anniversaries when they were together, ten of them in total. Instead, Susan sat alone in her bedroom with her memories. She was glad Neal had brought his girlfriend in for supper. Organising things in the kitchen had kept her busy, helped to take her mind off the date and its relevance in her life. She seemed like a lovely girl. She was pleased for Neal.

It was still relatively early. Susan had wanted to give the young couple some time to themselves but she didn't really want to go to bed yet and she didn't feel like reading. She knew she would have some difficulty getting to sleep tonight. She lifted the framed photograph of her late husband from the dressing table and looked at it with poignancy. Why did bad things always happen to her? What had she done to deserve such heartache?

Christopher's death had been a horrendous experience. He had been driving to Alan and Doreen's house to deliver a birthday present for their daughter, Alannah. It was her tenth birthday that day. The crash had happened not far from their home. Doreen had actually heard the impact but didn't know Chris was involved until some time later when the police came to her door. The brakes had failed on a huge articulated lorry. He hadn't stood a chance. The driver of the lorry was also killed. Susan had tried to move on with her life, not let her thoughts dwell on the events of that day, but certain days were more difficult than others, birthdays for example, Christmas, New Year, Valentines' Day, the date he died, wedding anniversaries, like today. At least he had survived until after midnight, hadn't actually died on Alannah's birthday. It shouldn't make any difference but somehow it did. She kissed the photograph in her hand and whispered:

"Happy anniversary, Darling."

What a stupid thing to say, she thought to herself, but she couldn't help it. She looked again at the picture, this time holding it close against her heart and mumbling:

"I miss you, Chris. I miss you so much."

She put the photograph back, close to the bed. She might just want it under her pillow tonight.

Susan was aware of the music downstairs stopping, heard the front door close. Neal was leaving Charlotte home. She really was on her own now. She undressed and got into bed but lay awake for a long time, thinking over the good times she had spent with Chris, determined not to focus solely on his untimely end. She remembered the holiday in Australia. They had brought Kathleen with them, her rather narrow-minded and very religious, widowed mother. She hadn't seen her since! Kathleen had fallen, hook, line and sinker, for Brandon Peasbody, an apple farmer who rode about the place, bareback, with his long hair blowing in the wind or sometimes scrunched into a ponytail, and was as open-minded and humanistic as they come. What a transformation! Brandon was twelve years younger than her mother but that didn't seem to matter to either of them. They lived together now and were very happy. She had also caught up with her childhood friend, Janet, and her husband and exchanged stories about their lives since leaving school. That had been a good holiday!

Chris had been very good at his job. His professionalism had earned him the respect of children, parents, colleagues and governors alike and he had secured a new position as head of a brand new school in Belfast, not long before his accident. They had moved into a beautiful, modern bungalow on the outskirts of the city and were in the process of furnishing it. Just the day before the tragedy, they had been out together, choosing a new marble fireplace. It was fitted the week after his funeral.

Alan and Doreen had been a tower of strength. Susan would for ever be grateful to them for the way they took over those funeral arrangements and shielded her from further harm. She had spent a great deal of her time with them over the next two years. As well as Alannah, they now had a little boy. They had named him Christopher in memory of the uncle he never knew.

Chris had loved his dog, Bouncer. They used to take him for walks at the seaside. How he loved running into the water and battling against the waves. The wetter he became, the more he barked with excitement. Those were good days. That dog had got them into some scrapes! The worst incident was probably the time he had bounded excitedly over a picnic rug, where a young family had been preparing to eat, stealing a sausage and trampling all over the sandwiches and cakes. Whilst Chris had been trying to apologise, Bouncer had made matters worse by chasing the youngest child into a nearby river. Susan remembered hauling the little boy to safety. Thank God he hadn't drowned!

If he had had a fault, it was that he was too nice, too soft. Like so many modern teachers, Chris had believed in praising children at every opportunity, making sure they all had positive experiences in abundance, achieving success in their daily endeavours. Susan, on the other hand, believed that such an approach often led to complacency and a lowering of both academic standards and behaviour. If a child is praised for something which did not actually require much effort, what incentive is there to try harder next time and produce something of real value? In her experience, too many children were being classified as having 'special needs' and were being given easy work to keep them 'busy', then rewarded with stars and stickers and other treats or privileges when they completed it correctly. These children sometimes constituted almost half of the class. Many of them did not have 'special needs' but were simply performing below average for a variety of reasons. Without them the concept of 'average' would be meaningless. People are not equal in all respects. Some children simply are more intelligent than others. But these below-average children were being hoodwinked into thinking that were actually doing very well, and in many cases their parents were being hoodwinked with them. Susan did not think it was right to mislead people in this way. It was not preparing them properly for real life, not encouraging them to make that extra effort. She and Chris had often disagreed on this issue. He had believed that the increased self-esteem brought about by continued success would outweigh any negative factors that concerned her. But she could still visualise those stories, poems and pictures that Chris had accepted from pupils as works of art. He had displayed them proudly in his office, sometimes even in their home. Susan had frowned upon the justification of such laxity. She would have handed most of them back with requests for improved presentation or redrafts to eradicate grammatical or spelling errors. Maybe she was just too harsh as a teacher, too traditional, too anxious to achieve perfection.

Even nursery schools were diagnosing children with 'special needs', mainly boys, potential entrepreneurs of the future, whose non-conformist behaviour didn't fit nicely with the expectations of the totally female staff, or the youngest children who were almost a year behind some of their peers. What was simply immaturity due to an accident of birth became a label of weakness while their older classmates were granted labels of assertiveness and intelligence. Subsequent progress often depended on these early labels that were wrongly attached to children. Mud sticks. So does inflated praise. They can both lead to a self-fulfilling prophesy at both ends of the spectrum if not carefully handled. Chris's views had been more in line with her own on this point, especially since his niece, Alannah, had had to contend with teachers thinking she was 'slow'. With a birthday at the end of June, Alannah was in the same class as children who were already walking and playing purposefully with educational toys before she was even born. If she had been born a few days later, she would not have started school for another year and would probably have been considered very advanced and intelligent. Susan was glad that Neal had picked up on this point in his current research. While the very brightest children would no doubt achieve high standards regardless of the system in place and the very weakest would continue to struggle no matter what remedial action is put into action, the vast majority of pupils are affected by such factors. Susan loved her job but it could be so frustrating at times.

Paris, the most romantic city in the world! She had a sudden image of the two of them strolling hand in hand through the Latin Quarter, sipping wine under a parasol at a kerbside bistro on the Boulevard St Michel, queuing up under a clear blue sky to visit the Eiffel Tower, watching the Bateaux Mouches from the bridges over the Seine, having dinner at their hotel in one of the avenues which converge at the Arc de Triomphe. Paris had been their favourite destination for a mini-break and a tear came to her eye now, as she contemplated the fact that she would never experience it again. She didn't want to go back there, not without Chris. Maybe someday it would be different.

Thus her thoughts rambled on in no specific chronological or sensible order, just as they came to her, some happy, some sad, some significant, some frivolous. When she lost Chris she had had a choice to make. She could have given in to depression and wallowed in self-pity or she could be sanguine and go with the words of that old John Denver song her mother used to play, *Today is the first day of the rest of my life.* She had chosen the latter. She still had the odd blip, like tonight. It would be unnatural if she didn't, but generally she had tried to be positive, proactive. She heard Neal come back in and go to the bathroom, then to his room for the night. *Hopefully fate will be kinder to those two*, she thought, as finally she drifted into oblivion.

Chapter 14

As messages of congratulations and engagement presents flooded in to the happy couple, plans were soon being made for the two families to become better acquainted. Neal had already met most members of Charlotte's family on various occasions, when he called to take her out, but now that a more formal welcome to the family had been arranged, he went along somewhat nervously to have dinner with her parents and sisters. They soon put him at ease. They were very natural, putting on no airs or graces. Rusty, the cocker spaniel, gave him a particularly warm welcome, jumping up to lick his hand and then lying down on his back, exposing his tummy for a tickle. Neal obliged willingly. He liked dogs. Mr Jamison apologised profusely for the telephone call which could have ruined their whole relationship.

"Mel was going out with someone called Colin at the time," he explained for the third time, "and it was so early in the morning. I wasn't thinking straight. When you asked for Charley … "

"There's no harm done," laughed Neal. "In fact you did me a favour. If I hadn't come rushing back to see Charlotte that day, I would never have found such good lodgings. Honestly, you should see my room; and my landlady, Mrs Lovell, treats me like a long-lost son!"

"Charley speaks very highly of her," put in Mrs Jamison. "I believe she has no family of her own."

"No, her husband was killed in a car accident. I don't know how long they had been married."

They discussed Susan's tragic circumstances for some minutes until Charlotte and Melanie called them all to the table, at which point the conversation changed to more cheerful topics. All in all it was a very successful evening and not the ordeal Neal had feared. Rusty sat by his feet throughout the meal, dozing contentedly.

"It's about time we had some men in the family," joked Mr Jamison, shaking him warmly by the hand as he left. "Jayne and Dean will beat you to it, I suppose, but the other two don't seem to be interested in settling down yet and Yvonne's only a child of course."

Neal was still trying to get his head round the five girls as he drove home but soon they all faded into insignificance except Charlotte. He repeated her name over and over, wishing that she was in the car with him, coming back to sleep with him. How lonely his bed seemed now that he was in love. How he longed to lie in her arms and feel her body respond and yield to his. He knew he needed to finish his studies and get a steady job before he could go ahead with a wedding. The purchase of the engagement ring had completely exhausted his savings for the time being.

"I can't wait," he told himself, as he lay in bed that

night, frustrated, his passion aroused to an intensity never reached before. "I won't wait."

And as he recalled Stephanie Walkington's parting words, he realised with gratitude that he would not have to wait for long. Today was Thursday.

Once he had decided to go ahead with it, Neal longed for the evening so much that the physical pleasure he anticipated became an obsession. He knew that he should not go but he was unable to go back on his decision. It would be a purely physical affair, he told himself, with no emotional involvement. How could anyone expect him to ignore a girl who threw her naked body in his face, who offered him physical release and asked for nothing in return? How much more easily he would be able to respect Charlotte's wishes and wait until she felt ready for the next step, if he could relieve his frustration elsewhere. As long as she never found out, what harm would be done?

Having thus justified his behaviour, and having made a rather feeble excuse to Charlotte for not seeing her that evening, Neal was very shocked and annoyed when Richard Walkington himself answered his knock at the door.

"I ...I...I just wanted to th...thank you for the books and papers," he stammered awkwardly, caught off his guard. "You weren't in the night I called for them."

"Oh you're welcome to them," replied Richard. "Were they any use to you?"

"Yes, indeed. I was very interested in your findings." Neal did not elaborate. He felt sickened, cheated. He had not given up the chance of seeing his fiancée to spend the evening discussing his work! When Richard offered him a drink, however, he felt he had to accept lest he arouse suspicion. Stephanie joined them in the lounge.

"You've met my wife, of course," said Richard.

"Yes," he answered, and glared at her accusingly.

"Actually," said Richard, himself offering the explanation Neal sought, "it's only by chance that you've found me at home this time. This is normally my night out with the boys, a game of squash and a drink, but my partner had to cry off at the last moment so I decided to give it a miss."

Neal glanced again at Stephanie, this time returning her apologetic smile. It was not her fault. But why did she have to sit there looking so seductive and sexy, her long black hair flowing over a tight-fitting, lacy, black camisole and her shapely, slender legs protruding from a very short blue denim skirt?

"Well, I must be off," he said, finishing his drink and making his escape. "I just happened to be in the area so I called to say thanks. I'll return the books as soon as I'm finished with them."

His plans thwarted, Neal spent a restless weekend, wanting Stephanie more than ever. Monday evening found him once again at her door. He had a contingency plan this time, just in case. He had written down a couple of questions based on Richard's research. They were in his pocket. He didn't need them. Stephanie opened the door and he quickly stepped into the hall. She was wearing a navy blue, sleeveless blouse, the buttons open at the neck, and a pair of tight-fitting cream trousers.

"Would you like a drink first?" she asked him.

"No, thank you." He had already had three.

She led him straight to the bedroom and took off her clothes. Neal quickly scrambled out of his, told her to lie down on the bed, and took her twice in quick succession. As he lay on the bed afterwards, recovering his breath, he could not help wondering what was wrong with her marriage. He wondered whether she treated all strangers like this, whether she had found him particularly appealing, or whether he had just happened to come into her life at a time when she needed someone. He wondered but he did not really care. She was providing him with something he needed and she was doing it willingly.

They had not spoken since he told her to lie down. Now she said:

"I'm sorry about Friday."

"It wasn't your fault. Will he be here this week?"

"No."

Neal was glad.

"Why did you marry him?" he asked after a pause.

"We were in love."

"But not anymore?"

"He doesn't love me. He told me so. He says he wishes he had never married me."

"Why do you stay with him?"

"I don't know. I suppose I still love him."

"Has he another girlfriend?"

She hesitated.

"More likely a boyfriend," she blurted out bitterly.

He hadn't seen that coming. He hadn't picked up on any signs that Richard might be gay.

"Do you still sleep together?" He wasn't sure how to handle this.

"Well, we still share a bed but we don't do anything."

Neal put his clothes on. "May I come again on Friday?" he asked.

She nodded. "Yes, if you want to."

"Do you want me to come?"

"Yes."

He had a sudden urge to take her in his arms and kiss her. She was so vulnerable, so unhappy. But he kept this urge under control, remembering his resolve not to get emotionally involved. One thought of Charlotte and any inappropriate feelings had vaporised in a flash.

"I'll see you on Friday then," he said, and he was gone.

So began Neal's double life. During the week he never gave Stephanie Walkington a passing thought; on Mondays and Fridays he thought about nothing else. Their relationship remained a purely physical one, just as he had intended from the start, so much so that, on occasions, they did not speak at all. He always went straight to the bedroom, took his pleasure, and went straight back to the car, which he parked at various places along the road to avoid his visits being observed or monitored by neighbours. He never kissed her, never stroked her body, rarely chatted to her. During it all his relationship with Charlotte continued as before and he looked forward happily to the day when she would be his wife.

Chapter 15

Susan yawned and closed her eyes again dreamily. It was the mid-term break and she was free for a week. Bliss. She turned on the radio and lay on for another half hour, relaxing to the music and listening to the news. At last she rose and took a refreshing shower, then dressed casually and wandered around at a leisurely pace, making breakfast to the strains of Brandi Carlile singing *The Story*. It made such a pleasant change, not having to rush out to work. When the telephone rang, she left the eggs she was beating and lifted the receiver.

"Mrs Lovell?" inquired a man's voice.

"Yes, speaking."

"Jonathan Ashby here. My son, Neal, tells me you're treating him like a king. May I speak to him for a moment, please? He must have his mobile switched off."

Susan froze. She stared stupefied at the telephone in her hand. Her whole body began to tremble and, though she tried to speak, no words would come. It really was Jonathan, a voice from the past. Her heart pounding, she stood there speechless as the memories came flooding back. The voice was older, more mature, anglicized to some extent, but still familiar. Tears welled up in her eyes and emotions she had long believed to be dead filled her heart. Completely overcome by the unexpectedness of hearing his voice, she replaced the receiver and tried to compose herself, lifting it off the hook again until she felt calm enough to face Neal, who was sitting at the table reading the morning paper, not long back from his jog round the block. When the initial shock had passed, she told him that his father had phoned but that the line had suddenly gone dead.

"I must contact the telephone engineer today," she continued, in an effort to make her story sound convincing. "That's the third time this week that the same thing has happened."

As she spoke, the telephone rang again and Neal answered it himself.

"Yes, there's something wrong with the phone," she heard him say and was relieved to detect no hint of suspicion in his voice.

"Battery's dead," he went on to explain when his father said he had also tried his mobile. "I forgot to put it on charge."

From the rest of the conversation, which she could not help overhearing, Susan understood that Neal's parents were going to pay him a visit so hastily she thought of a plausible excuse for absenting herself.

"They were looking forward to meeting you," said Neal, disappointed that her dental appointment would clash with their arrival the following morning. "I do hope they will get on well with Charlotte."

"I'm sure they will," Susan said encouragingly. "She's a really lovely girl. Anyone would love her."

Susan's relaxed mood had dissipated like melting snow.

Early the following morning she reversed her blue Toyota Yaris out of the driveway and drove around aimlessly for some time, feeling very nostalgic. How lovely it would have been to see Jonathan again, after all these years. She wondered how much he had changed. The picture she had in her mind was still that of a young man of twenty-four with brown wavy hair and a sexy, mischievous grin. He would be in his mid-forties now. Would she even recognise him? Having no genuine reason for being away from home, she allowed herself to drift into a reverie, her thoughts going from Jonathan to Chris and back to Jonathan and suddenly back to that day she had for so long tried to erase from her memory, the day when she had left Jonathan's daughter to the mercy of the world, a daughter he never even knew he had. She had a sudden urge to return to the area where she had abandoned her baby all those years ago, a sudden longing to know what had become of her. A drive of forty-five minutes, an hour at the most, would take her there. She had known it, subconsciously, when she applied for the job in this part of England, yet she had never made the journey, never even considered it. If she were honest with herself she had to acknowledge that she had actively avoided making that journey. It had been somewhere at the back of her mind all the time, maybe just waiting for the right moment. Now she set off in that direction. As she approached the suburb she had selected and saw the familiar landmarks, she began to tremble and perspire all over. Her clammy hands clung to the steering wheel and her heart palpitated wildly.

Suddenly she was there, outside the very house. Amazingly it was just the same, just as she remembered it, though it no longer stood alone in its own large grounds. Now it was part of a modern development, surrounded by other buildings. Nevertheless it was the same house. That was even the same flower-bed she had walked past on that fateful morning! She did not cry. The house still had that peaceful aurora about it that had attracted her to it in the first place. She experienced a strange sensation of contentment as she stared from the security of her car up that path she had once trod. It was many years since she had considered her action and examined her conscience but now she remembered Chris and his appalled reaction when she had confessed her guilt. He had called her heartless as indeed she must have been. It all seemed so pointless now, the intervening years having changed society to such an extent that one-parent families were now taken for granted. An unmarried mother no longer had to hide her face from the world. Convention had gone out of the window. Look at her own mother, for goodness sake, her own mother whom she had been so anxious to protect. She was now living with a man much younger than herself and without a care in the world. She contemplated the complex, sometimes dysfunctional family arrangements experienced by many of her pupils. It was commonplace in today's world for children to have two separate homes, mum in one, dad in the other, and often a tangled web of siblings, half-siblings and step-siblings in the background. Susan could count on her fingers the number of children in her class who actually lived with both their parents and all had the same name. But it wasn't like that when she was growing up, not in the little, provincial seaside town in Ulster where she had lived anyway. Life had been simple back then. Everyone stuck to the rules. It was only when she moved to Belfast that Susan had begun to realise how cocooned she had actually been.

She was jolted back to the present by signs of movement within the house. A figure passed by the window, the front door opened, and a woman, maybe ten years her senior, came out and got into the silver Volvo which was parked in the driveway. Not wanting to arouse suspicion, Susan started up her own engine and drove off, determined that she would not stay away this time for twenty years. Her interest in her own child had been awakened at last.

While Susan was driving about and reminiscing, Neal was entertaining his mother and father prior to meeting Charlotte for lunch.

"You're certainly very comfortable here, son," remarked Jonathan, sipping his coffee.

"Just think of that awful place you stayed in last year," added Helen Ashby and her son laughed.

"There's no comparison," he said. "It's a pity Mrs Lovell had to go out. I really wanted you to meet her. You would like her."

"Well, she certainly keeps a clean house," said Helen approvingly, casting her eye around the room and fingering the furniture for dust. There was none.

As they chatted about family matters, Neal's studies, and his plans for the wedding, Jonathan gradually withdrew from the conversation and became very quiet. Neal noticed this with some concern.

"Is something wrong, Dad?" he asked.

"No, no, nothing. I just have the oddest feeling of having been here before yet I know that I have not. I don't normally get those déjà vu feelings but there's something familiar about this room."

He looked about him, a puzzled expression on his face.

"That picture over the fireplace, Helen... don't we know someone with a very similar one?"

Helen turned her gaze to the picture in question and shook her head.

"I don't think so," she said, "but of course I'm not so interested in art, not the way you are. I wouldn't have noticed it."

"And that ornamental vase in the corner?" continued Jonathan. "I've definitely seen that somewhere before."

"Well, you may be the real aesthete of the family but I *would* have noticed a beautiful item like that," his wife said, going over to the vase in question and fingering it admiringly. "I certainly haven't seen it before, though it's a bit like one the Conways have, similar colourings but a different shape. Maybe that's what you're thinking of."

Helen had a flush of embarrassment and not a little envy as, momentarily, she recalled the vase in question. Elaine Conway had shown it to her during a visit to their home and she had stumbled when her foot caught in the rug and almost knocked it over as she grabbed the small display table for support. At the time she had believed it to be some sort of ersatz imitation of the one she had seen in a catalogue on Elaine's coffee table but in fact it had turned out to be the genuine article and quite priceless. No wonder Elaine had watched her like a hawk for the rest of the visit!

"Yes, you're probably right," agreed Jonathan, though he was anything but satisfied with the explanation and continued to survey the room with a bewildered eye, intrigued by feelings evoked in him by various other small ornaments on the shelves around him, things which obviously meant nothing to Helen, who continued to bombard her son with questions about his fiancée.

Soon it was time to meet her and Jonathan was so impressed with his future daughter-in-law that, for the time being, he forgot his confusion of the morning. They all had a very enjoyable meal together at the new classy restaurant which had just opened nearby, after which Neal promised to bring Charlotte home soon for a weekend so that they could all become better acquainted and so that she would be able to meet Suzannah, who had not been able to accompany them on this occasion.

Alone together at last, Neal and Charlotte hugged each other and exhaled loudly.

"Well, Darling, both our parents seem happy enough so we won't need to call it off," joked Neal.

It was early evening and Susan was not due back until at least ten o'clock, having pretended that she was visiting friends. She wanted to be absolutely sure that Jonathan would be gone before her return. Neal and Charlotte would both have been horrified if they had known that she had ostracised herself from her own home for the whole day on their account without any genuine reason for being anywhere else. But they had just accepted her excuses without question.

"They got on really well together," agreed Charlotte.

They had spent an hour or so at her home during the afternoon. Charlotte, having been coaxed upstairs at last to see Neal's room, was now sitting on the edge of his bed, half fearing and half hoping that he would entice her into it. It was some time now since he had tried to persuade her to go to bed with him. She wondered why he had given up but respected him for his will power. His emotions too were mixed. He did not want to hurt or offend her but how he longed to make love to her and he had a strange feeling about today. Was he wrong or was she giving him mixed signals here? Surely this was a golden opportunity not to be missed.

Neal drew the curtains and sat down beside her. She took a deep breath and gazed lovingly into his eyes. He kissed her, holding her face like a bowl to drink from, his hands tight against her soft curls. Then gently, lowering her body down unto the bed, he began to undo her clothing. She did not resist. Her dress slipped from her shoulders and she closed her eyes, intoxicated by his manly fragrance. Her feelings a confused mixture of excitement and shame, she felt her remaining garments being gently removed and Neal's hands and eyes caressing her whole naked body. Then he was slipping out of his own clothes. As they snuggled in between the cool sheets and clung together, he kissed her tenderly, immediately expelling any lingering feelings of shame. There could be nothing shameful about something that felt so good, so right, so perfect. Yet she was nervous, wasn't sure what to expect. This was her first time with a man. This was all she wanted, she thought, to lie here in his arms, to feel his nakedness against her own, his breath mingling with hers. They didn't need to do anything more. She hoped he wouldn't make any move. She might not like it. She didn't want anything to spoil this. Yet she knew that he wanted more. She would have to let him do it; she could not back out now. She hoped it would not take long.

As he released her from his embrace, her whole body went tense and rigid in anticipation, almost dread. But Neal sensed her nervousness and knew that she was not ready for him. He would be patient. He stroked her body lovingly, feeling the firm roundness of her breasts until they responded to his touch. His hand fluttered softly over her stomach and down towards the smooth silky warmth of that part of her which hitherto had remained quite private. Charlotte's heart missed a beat as his fingers touched her softly and lightly, then sent little quivers through her whole being as they began to probe in the gentlest manner. She moaned, revelling in delicious sensations she had never dreamed possible. He continued to fondle her intimately with an ever so gentle rubbing motion, frustrating her, arousing her desire for him until all the tenseness vanished and her body became supple, lithe, sensuous, receptive. Thrilled by the knowledge of her innocence, her virginity, and by the undisguised pleasure she was experiencing, Neal expertly persisted, ever so slowly, ever so tantalisingly and Charlotte held her breath, trying to prolong the moment. The sensation was unbelievable, almost unbearable. This was heaven, pure heaven. She had never dreamed it could be like this.

As they eventually made love in perfect unison, both Charlotte and Neal were aware of an intense happiness, a feeling of completeness. Afterwards they lay for some time still locked in each other's arms, engulfed by their love for each other. Neil smiled at Charlotte as he admired her beauty, her hair glinting in the evening sun, which shone through a gap in the curtains.

"You're so beautiful," he sighed contentedly.

Charlotte felt as though her heart would burst.

"Oh Neal," she breathed dreamily, "I love you so much."

And words became unnecessary as they kissed long and passionately.

Chapter 16

Susan could not settle after that first nostalgic trip into the past and became obsessed with the idea of discovering what had become of her baby girl. After all this time she could not simply introduce herself and expect to be welcomed but she started to acquaint herself with the area, hoping for snippets of information which might lead her to her daughter. She would drive past the house, wondering how often it had changed hands over the years, whether the present owner would know the whereabouts of previous occupants. She would park her car a little distance away and walk past the house, hoping some day to see a young lady walking about in the garden. Back at home she would search the internet, looking for news reports from that time, but was unable to find any useful information relating to the incident.

It was on one of her walks, about a month after her first visit, that Susan received the greatest shock of her life, to date. She was approaching the designated house when suddenly she heard her name called from across the road and, looking over her shoulder, saw Charlotte coming towards her, carrying a bag of shopping. Neal had brought Charlotte in quite regularly over the past few weeks so that now they were on very friendly terms.

"Hi there, Mrs Lovell," said the younger woman, cheerily. "Imagine meeting you here! You weren't looking for me, where you?"

"Looking for you?" What could she mean?

"I just thought it seems strange, finding you right outside my house. I didn't even realise you knew this area."

"I don't know it very well," Susan answered quickly. "I was just delivering something for a friend and thought I would stretch my legs for a bit before driving home. So you live around here?"

Here, perhaps, was an unexpected source of information. If Charlotte lived in this area, someone in her family might know something about the events of the past. She didn't really know her well enough yet to start asking awkward questions but she was getting there. She would think about it, come up with a subtle way of broaching the subject. It was at least a start. But she was unprepared for Charlotte's answer:

"Yes, right here."

Susan watched aghast, as Neal's girlfriend stopped at the gates of the very house where she had left her newborn baby, *the very same house!*

"Come on in and meet the family. I'm sure you've time for a cup of coffee."

Not fully aware of what she was doing, Susan accepted the invitation and followed Charlotte inside, where she was warmly greeted by Mrs Jamison, while Charlotte busied herself putting fresh water and coffee beans into an impressive looking DeLonghi coffee machine and setting out some chocolate biscuits on a plate.

"This makes a change," she said in a light-hearted manner. "It's usually you entertaining me."

The machine burst into life, reminding Charlotte, as it always did, of the Black-Eyed Peas song, *I've Got a Feeling*. She sang along to it as the aroma of freshly ground coffee began to fill the air.

"What a delightful house," remarked Susan, subtly delving for information but attempting to sound casual. "Have you lived here for long?"

"Ever since I was married," replied Mrs Jamison. "Almost thirty years."

She chattered on about 'Charley' and Neal and how Neal had raved about his excellent digs but Susan was not really listening. Dreadful questions were flashing through her mind. Could Charlotte herself be her very own daughter? If this were the case she was engaged to be married to her own half-brother. No, didn't Neal say she had a twin sister? Thank goodness for that. It can't be her.

As these thoughts flitted through her mind in a whirl of confusion and panic, she heard Charlotte call upstairs that there was some coffee made and, within minutes, four more girls appeared and were introduced by their mother. Susan tried to be sociable as she drank her coffee but she could not take her mind or her eyes off the five sisters. She noticed some photographs on the walls, all of little girls at play. She had no pictorial record of her own daughter's progress as she grew up, no idea what she looked like today or at any stage of her childhood. What a dreadful admission for a mother to have to make.

"Is it someone's birthday?" she enquired at length, noticing some cards on top of the television.

"Yes, Yvonne is eleven today," said Mrs Jamison, and Yvonne herself blushed and smiled shyly.

Susan wished her many happy returns but wished it had been one of the others. Yvonne was the only one she could easily eliminate on the grounds she was obviously far too young. She tried to guess the ages of the other four girls but found that she kept changing her mind. They all looked about the same age, about the right age to be her daughter! She kept telling herself, however, that it was unlikely that any of them was in fact hers. Would a couple with three children of their own be likely to keep another child abandoned on their doorstep? Would they even have been allowed to do so? Of course not. But one thing was certain. If Mrs Jamison had been living there for nearly thirty years, she would at least know what happened to that baby. She just needed to be patient a little longer and the truth was sure to come out.

Back at home that evening, Susan was pensive. What a strange day it had been. Could one of Charlotte's sisters actually be her daughter? Could one of those laughing faces in the photo frames she had seen actually be a glimpse into the past, her past, an image of the little girl she had forsaken, growing up? She couldn't settle herself. Neal was out and she decided to take the opportunity to change his bed clothes and towels. She just needed to keep busy, put the time in. She went upstairs and entered his room. What a brilliant idea it had been to take in a lodger. She congratulated herself yet again on her foresight. Quite apart from the financial gain, she enjoyed the company, especially when it was someone so special, someone who was connected, even though he didn't know it, to a happy time in her past life, and someone who was never any bother whatsoever. His room was immaculate, as usual. She lifted the two white towels from the rail above the radiator and stripped the bed, carrying the sheet, pillow cases and quilt cover down to the utility room, where she put them all straight into the washing machine. She added the washing powder and turned it on. Immediately it whirred into action. She then went to the hot press and fetched the clean replacements.

On entering the room again with a pile of fresh linen, Susan accidentally knocked her elbow against Neal's bookcase and sent some papers fluttering to the floor. She set the bedclothes and towels down on a chair and went to pick them up, hoping that she hadn't disturbed anything important. She set the papers back on top of the bookcase. Hopefully they were still in the right order. As she did so, her gaze landed on a photograph album, lying open on the top shelf. She lifted it out and admired the photograph on the open page. It was a recent one of Neal and Charlotte, taken to celebrate their engagement. They both looked radiant and so handsome. They could have been film stars. Susan turned back a page and found another lovely picture of them both, taken down by the river. Again they both looked very photogenic and the background in this one was also magnificent, depicting a riverside scene with several boats and punters framed by tall willow trees and colourful shrubs. She knew that Neal was very keen on photography himself and spent a lot of time on his computer, developing his pictures using *Photoshop* and *Lightroom*. Whoever had taken these pictures was also pretty good.

Susan sat down on the stripped bed and began to leaf through the album. It was the story of Neal's life to date and included several shots of her beloved Jonathan. She started as she realised who it was and a tear came to her eye but she was fascinated. She couldn't put it down. At last she could see what Helen looked like and that must be Neal's sister, Suzannah. Yes, like many of the shots, the picture was briefly annotated. *Mum and Suzy, 2006,* it said. Helen was quite pretty. Susan turned back another page and saw a shot of a whole family gathered round a dinner table with a celebratory cake in the middle. *Granny's birthday bash, 2005,* it said. There was one of Jonathan's sister, Belle! She hadn't changed that much over the years. She looked back further in the book, skipping a few pages, and there was one of Jonathan, looking more like his old self, in the company of some friends. There was a Christmas tree in the background. Susan looked at the caption: *Dad with Uncle Jack, Christmas 2000.* Susan remembered Jack from their schooldays. So they had kept in touch. She thought back to the turn of the century. She had been thirty-two that year. She and Chris had celebrated the Millennium in Dublin. She had dragged him along to a Boyzone concert at the Point. He wouldn't admit to having enjoyed it but he sang along with the rest of them! It had been the most fantastic experience, one of the best concerts she had ever attended. The atmosphere had been so electric! Susan really missed Chris; they had been so happy together. She was still going backwards through Neal's album. *My new baby sister,* she read beside a shot of a newborn infant, *Suzy and me* beside another one. The earlier ones weren't dated. Neal looked so cute! He must have been about five in that one. There were photos of other friends and relatives, holding either Neal or Suzy or both. *Danny and Joe with me* was the caption beside one of the pictures, maybe before Suzannah was born since Neal was only a baby in that one, *Fishing with Dad and Uncle Jack* beside another one which showed Neal as a very small boy, proudly standing beside his dad, holding a big fishing rod and a huge fish. Susan cried when she saw that one because Jonathan looked exactly as she remembered him. There was another lovely picture of Neal as a baby with either Danny or Joe, Helen's brothers she assumed; she wasn't sure which was which from the one where they were named. Helen was in this one too but there was no caption. It was a particularly nice photograph yet somehow it disturbed her as though there was a sadness lurking behind those happy smiles.

Susan closed the album and reluctantly replaced it on the shelf, where she had found it. How strange that she should have come across this the very same day that she had seen photographs of Charlotte and her sisters growing up. Both families had a lovely record of the various stages in their children's lives, a pictorial memento of important events and occasions. But she had nothing. She knew nothing about her daughter's life. She didn't even know if her daughter was still alive. Sadly she got on with the job of remaking the bed.

★ ★ ★

"It was lovely meeting all your sisters," Susan began, the next time Neal brought his fiancée in for supper. She hoped that her nervousness was not obvious.

"I was trying to decide where you fit in but couldn't make my mind up. You must all be quite close together regarding age."

"Oh, we're a strange family," laughed Charlotte very naturally. "Hasn't Neal told you? We're all adopted or fostered, all five of us."

"Oh, no, he's never mentioned it. I had no idea," gushed Susan, genuinely surprised.

She hesitated, her heart in her mouth, and then added, "Do any of you still have contact with your birth parents?"

"Not much," Charlotte replied and for a moment Susan was worried that she was not going to elaborate.

They all munched their ham and pickle sandwiches and drank their coffee. Neal took a sip of his beer. He was enjoying an episode of *Frasier* and laughing to himself, not really paying attention to the conversation.

"Actually," Charlotte appeared a little embarrassed and hesitated, "...actually Yvonne's parents are both in prison."

"In prison!" The older woman was horrified, yet curious, even though she had already discounted Yvonne as a candidate.

"Yvonne has only been living with us for just over a year."

Despite her curiosity and thirst for information, Susan felt rather uncomfortable at this unexpected revelation.

"I'm sorry, Charlotte," she said. "I didn't mean to pry. This is none of my business."

"No, it's OK. I know you weren't prying. It's not really a secret. Most of our friends know about it."

"What did they do, her parents?"

"I don't know the full details but it was something to do with fraudulent business transactions. All I know is that a lot of money was involved. They both pleaded guilty in the end and got five years each."

"Does Yvonne visit them in prison? How has it affected her?"

"She's been a couple of times but she cried for days afterwards. It was awful."

"She's very philosophical about it all," added Neal, during a commercial break in his programme. "She accepts that her parents have done wrong and have to pay for it. She doesn't try to defend them."

"Except when some nasty bully makes a cutting remark to her at school," put in Charlotte.

"Poor kid," mused Susan. "And it was her birthday that day I called in. That must have been tough for her. I wouldn't have drawn attention to it if I had known."

"She's tougher than you'd think. That was her second birthday with us. She coped with it very well. Thankfully she does not seem to have inherited any of her parents' rapaciousness. I've always found her to be very kind and generous. But she has been damaged, traumatised. I don't know how she'll cope when she goes back home."

Charlotte cut herself a slice of apple tart and raised a forkful to her mouth.

"Mmm, this is delicious," she said appreciatively.

Susan suddenly realised with gratitude that her genuine concern for Yvonne's circumstances had calmed her nerves. She was feeling much more composed.

"Is she the only one who keeps in touch with her natural parents?" she now enquired with a lightness of heart which surprised even herself.

Charlotte took the bait nicely:

"Jayne's parents separated when she was very young and her father eventually remarried and emigrated to New Zealand. By that time Jayne was already living with us off and on because her mother had taken ill and was in and out of hospital a lot. When she died, I remember there was some discussion about whether Jayne should go out to New Zealand or stay here. I was still quite young at the time so I wasn't aware of all the facts and details. Anyway they decided she should stay. She writes to her father and he sends her presents but he has never come back to see her. She doesn't mention him much."

So it wasn't Jayne. Charlotte and Melanie were twins so it wasn't either of them. Susan breathed a sigh of relief. That still left Erin. There was still a chance that she would know the identity of her very own daughter before the night was out. That thought didn't last for long.

"Erin is actually my cousin," Charlotte now revealed, "the daughter of Mum's brother. When he and Auntie

Ruth were both killed in an accident, Mum and Dad took Erin in. She was only six at the time, same as me."

"Your parents must be a remarkable couple," Susan said with genuine admiration. "You are obviously very proud of them."

"Oh yes, they're the only parents I've ever known. They have been wonderful parents to all of us."

"I wonder why they never adopted a boy," put in Neal, who had been listening with one ear. "Imagine having five girls in the house!"

"I don't know," mused Charlotte, "but I've wondered about that too because there have been others as well who stayed with us for shorter periods and they were all girls too. Fiona was my favourite. I cried when she went away. It was years ago but I still think of her as my big sister. Then there were Judy and Kate. All girls. I have a feeling that Mum and Dad never really gave up trying to have a child of their own. I suppose that, if they had had a son to carry on the family name and so on, a boy with their own flesh and blood, they wouldn't have liked him to have had an older adopted brother. Older sisters somehow don't have the same significance. It shouldn't be like that and society is changing but old attitudes die hard. Anyway it's academic. They never did have a son, or a daughter for that matter."

Neal looked pensive but said nothing. Susan began to panic. There had been more girls in that house than she had realised, maybe dozens over the years. Somehow fate had led her to a home where a rejected baby would have been accepted and cared for. As she poured everyone another cup of coffee and passed round the biscuits, she remembered the little girl she had seen playing in the garden that day.

"Are you the eldest?" she asked tentatively.

"There's not much difference in our ages," was the reply. "Fiona was the eldest when we were little, but now, yes, Melanie and I are the eldest and Erin is just a few months younger. We're just like triplets. We were all in the same class at school. The teachers used to think it was really weird!"

"But you and Melanie really are twins? I remember Neal saying you had a twin sister."

She had not yet found her lost baby but at least it wasn't Neal's girlfriend. What a relief!

But Charlotte had not actually answered her question, had neither confirmed nor denied the assumption she had made. Now she set her empty cup down on the table.

"We're not absolutely sure about that," she said, a puzzled yet bemused expression on her face.

"Mum and Dad have always been a bit evasive when we talk about it. It seems so odd that they wanted to or were even allowed to adopt two babies at the same time. They have assured us that we are not actually natural twins. The birth certificates both bear the same date, 4th August 1989, but I sometimes think that they found one of us under a hedge somewhere and just use the same birthday for convenience."

"Charlotte!" Neal exclaimed, aroused from his reverie and shocked by her remark.

"I'm only joking," she laughed. "Maybe we really are twins but they don't want us to know for some reason. I don't even think about it any more. It doesn't really matter."

No-one noticed Susan turning a deathly shade of pale. She excused herself and went straight to her room, where she lay down on the bed and tried to think rationally. They had guessed her baby's age very well indeed; her real birthday was 7th August. She lay there, stunned, until her head ached with confusion and indecision. Looking at the clock she realised that two hours had passed. She changed into her nightie and dressing gown and went back down to the kitchen to take something for her headache. The living-room door was slightly ajar and the low voices told her that Neal and Charlotte were still there, chatting. A Snow Patrol CD was playing in the background. She did not intend to eavesdrop but could not help overhearing their conversation.

"Don't tease me, Charlotte," she heard Neal say. "Will you come tomorrow? I'm longing to make love to you again."

"Are you sure we would be alone?"

"Yes, Mrs Lovell has a function on at school. She won't be home until late. We could have the whole evening together."

Tears streaming down her cheeks, Susan tiptoed back upstairs and got into bed.

"Please, God," she prayed, "let it be Melanie. Don't let them be brother and sister."

And she wondered all night how on earth she was ever going to find out.

Chapter 17

Stephanie Walkington answered Neal's knock and, as usual, led him straight to the bedroom.

"Where were you on Friday?" she asked accusingly, as they undressed.

"With my fiancée."

Stephanie stood still and stared at him, puzzled.

"I didn't know you were engaged," she said.

"So what? You're married!"

"Some marriage! Richard didn't even remember my birthday. He only cares about his boyfriends."

Her voice was full of bitterness when she spoke of her husband.

"When was your birthday?"

"Yesterday."

"I'm sorry. I would have brought you something if I had known."

He didn't really mean it but it seemed the right thing to say.

She was unusually talkative.

"Do you love your fiancée?"

"Yes, very much."

"Then why do you come here?"

Why indeed? Neal did not really want to examine his reasons, was not very proud of himself, but she was waiting for an answer.

"I don't know. Just for a fuck, I suppose."

She flinched, hurt by his words. A guilty conscience had caused him to be uncharacteristically cruel and rude.

"You started it," he reminded her. "If you want to end it, just say so."

"I missed you on Friday," she said piteously. "I was waiting for you."

Neal's thoughts reverted to Friday. He had not paid the slightest heed to the fact that it even was a Friday. There was no question in his mind of comparing the beautiful evening of passion he had spent with Charlotte to the mere physical pleasure he experienced with Stephanie. This had just become a habit and habits can be hard to break.

"My fiancée comes first," he said.

"Did you have sex with her?"

"That is none of your business."

All of a sudden Neal realised that he no longer wanted this relationship to continue; he had to break the habit. He glanced at Stephanie's naked body waiting for him and he felt nothing, no thrill, no urge, no desire. Nevertheless he could not back out now. Somehow he struggled through the whole act, thinking the entire time about how he had betrayed Charlotte's trust. He felt disgusted with himself, ashamed at his actions. What on earth had possessed him? It was bad enough at first when he had needed sexual release and Charlotte had not been ready but recently she had given in and they had enjoyed a wonderful physical relationship. He should not be doing this. When at last it was over, he quickly pulled on his clothes and looked awkwardly at the girl who had been his mistress.

"I won't be back," he said simply.

She opened her mouth to speak but no words came. Her eyes filled up with tears.

"Goodbye, Stephanie. I hope things improve between you and Richard."

Then, for the first time ever, and solely to assuage his guilt, he kissed her gently before walking out of her life. Or so he thought.

Chapter 18

Helen Ashby threw herself into her favourite, crimson, velour armchair and put her feet up on the plush velvet stool, breathing a long sigh of relief. Entertaining a visitor was always tiring and she was glad to have the house to herself for a while. Neal and Charlotte had gone out for the evening with Suzannah and her current boyfriend and Jonathan had been away on business since early morning. She glanced around the spacious room with its elegant furnishings in crimson and gold. There were photograph albums everywhere, piled high on the coffee tables, while the two laptop computers still sat amongst them, long untidy extension cables reaching across the beige carpet, attached to multiple socket holders, some still plugged in to the wall, others lying loose on the floor. There had been great merriment that afternoon as Charlotte viewed the screens and leafed through the albums, looking at snaps and shots of her fiancé at various ages. How she had laughed at him in his school uniform and short back and sides haircut. Charlotte seemed a nice girl.

Picking up one of the albums at random, Helen began to look through it herself. Memories, both happy and sad, came back to her as she regarded the faces of people she had known in the past. There was one of her grandparents, both long since dead. Here was one of Jonathan and herself on their wedding day. Didn't they make a lovely couple! She stopped to look at one of the children, aged about three and seven. How time had flown – Neal engaged to be married and Suzannah also at the dating stage. She could hardly believe it.

Suddenly Helen noticed another photograph lying on the floor underneath the television. Thinking it had fallen out of one of the albums she went over and picked it up. It was one of Suzannah, aged about five, but she could not recall seeing it before. She did not recognise the lakeside surroundings nor could she even remember the green and white frilly dress she was wearing. Feeling bewildered, Helen turned the photograph over for Jonathan almost always recorded some details on the reverse. Sure enough there was something written there but it was in a strange hand and badly smudged. However she managed to decipher it:

'*Charlotte, Aged 4 ½*'

Charlotte? It was not Suzannah at all. This was one of the pictures Charlotte had brought with her!

Amazed, she turned the photograph over and looked again at the little girl's face. She realised now that it was not the face of her own daughter but she had certainly been fooled. How strange that the two girls had been so alike as children.

I must show it to the others, she said to herself, as she set the photograph down on the table.

★ ★ ★

Jonathan had left home early that morning on the pretext of visiting a business client but his true objective was to satisfy his curiosity concerning the identity of Mrs S Lovell. For days after his brief visit to Neal's lodgings he had mused over the familiarity of several objects in the house. He felt sure that they belonged to a house he knew, knew well, yet they appeared to be utterly meaningless to his wife. He considered various business associates whose homes would be known to him and not to Helen but rejected them all. He had not visited any of their houses more than three or four times yet he had a feeling that the ornaments in Mrs Lovell's house belonged to a place where he had once felt very much at home.

Five or six days had passed with a confused haze in the back of his mind. Then suddenly one night he had awoken from a dream and everything had clicked into place. He had been dreaming about a girl he had once known, a girl called Susan Summers. It had been over twenty years ago, before he had married Helen, yet in his dream it seemed like yesterday. He had stumbled upon her one summer's day, hobbling over some rocks on the beach, her ankle sore and swollen from a fall. He had been attracted to her from that first moment when she rested her weight on him, as he helped her to his white Honda Accord, which had been parked nearby. Or was it the red Volvo he had in those days? His memory was playing tricks with him, as it does in a dream. But most of this dream was authentic, a clear window with an uninterrupted view into his distant past. One thing led to another and before long he had been deeply in love with Susan, and she with him. Now he dreamed of the day they had played tennis on the beach under a hot, glaring sun and had later lain together in the privacy of the sand dunes, where they had tenderly made love. Later he had walked with her the short distance to the little cottage where Susan lived with her widowed mother and they had gone in for some refreshments.

At this point Jonathan awoke, feeling guilty for still having feelings of love and desire for another woman besides his wife, for the love he had once shared with Susan had been very much alive in his dream. He remembered now that they had even talked of marriage and that he had wounded her deeply when he left her for Helen. He still remembered the look of disbelief and hurt in her lovely eyes when he told her, but he remembered too the dignity with which she accepted his decision, apparently bearing him no malice. Though he never saw her again, he remembered hearing that she had left the area soon afterwards and he knew in his heart that it was on his account that she had gone from the home she loved so well, albeit temporarily.

Helen was still sleeping peacefully by his side. He looked at her and wondered what had brought Susan into his mind after two decades of married life. Then his thoughts continued where the dream had ended…

… He is inside that cottage now having a cool beer and there, over the fireplace, is the picture of sunflowers and lavender that he had seen in Mrs Lovell's house. There, in the hallway, stands the large ornamental vase that Helen had admired. The glass ornaments and Hummel figurines are neatly arranged along the mantelpiece. Jonathan's imaginary gaze settles on one of them, the figurine of a little boy with a bird on his foot. He remembers buying it himself. *Singing Lessons* it was called. He had given it to Susan's mum for her birthday…

"Good God!" breathed Jonathan, as the truth gradually became clear to him. "Mrs Lovell must be my old girlfriend."

Thanks to his friends, Jack and Ian, he knew that Kathleen Summers, herself, was now living abroad. They had mentioned it recently when they had all met up for a drink. But those were certainly her things he had seen in that house, relics from a very happy time in his youth.

The thought of Neal living in Susan's house had obsessed him ever since so today, while Neal was up in Yorkshire and there would be no danger of meeting him, Jonathan had decided to pay her a surprise visit.

Chapter 19

The door bell rang. Susan glanced up from the Sudoku puzzle she was doing and saw the shape of a man through the glass panel. She was expecting a delivery of some stationery she had ordered but was somewhat surprised that it had come so soon. Feeling pleased about this she got up and opened the door.

"Hello Susan."

The colour drained from her face. This was no mere delivery of stationery items. It was that voice from the past, that lovingly remembered voice that still sent shivers down her spine.

"Jonathan?" she whispered.

She felt as though her feet were fixed to the ground and her tongue had lost the power of speech. She gazed at him, as though in a trance... that same handsome face, those familiar eyes.

"May I come in?" he faltered.

"Of course. I'm sorry. This is so unexpected."

She paused.

"How did you know?"   —

She led him into the lounge where they both sat down. The atmosphere was still very strained.

"I hope you don't mind me coming, Susan," began that familiar voice she loved so well. "I visited Neal here recently and recognised various objects from your mother's cottage, though it took me a while to remember where I had seen them before and put two and two together."

"You have a good memory," smiled Susan.

"I believe she's living abroad now."

Susan looked surprised. How on earth did he know that? Jonathan saw her look of bewilderment and went on to explain.

"You remember my friend, Ian, at school? You were friendly with his sister. Well he was out there, in Australia, recently and met your mum. He mentioned it to Neal. Not that they knew who you were, of course."

Susan smiled.

"Mum loves it out there," she said. "Chris and I went out to visit Janet and we brought her with us. It was supposed to be for a fortnight but she never came back! She fell head over heels in love with this guy, Brandon, and moved in with him. That's why I have so much of her stuff here. She asked me to rent out her cottage for her. I don't think she'll ever come back now."

"Chris?" queried Jonathan. "That was your husband?"

A look of sadness crossed her brow.

"Yes, he's dead now."

"I know. Neal said you were a widow. I'm sorry."

"It was five years ago. He was on his way to his brother's house when a lorry crashed right into his car."

"That must have been dreadful for you, Susan. You had no family?"

"No."

Susan's simple answer belied all the years of heartbreak when she had longed for a child. She had constantly blamed herself, believing it was some kind of divine punishment for abandoning her unwanted child all those years ago yet she knew that Chris had also blamed himself because he was aware of the ease with which she had conceived that unplanned child. Doctors assured them that there was nothing wrong with either of them but it had never happened.

Susan was aware that her answers to Jonathan's questions were short and might come across as unfriendly, even impolite, but she just did not know what to say, could not relax. Here was her opportunity to get assistance in investigating Charlotte's parenthood. His wife need never know. But how could she tell him now that he had fathered a child twenty-one years ago? Why destroy his ignorance of that fact, shatter his happiness, unless it was absolutely necessary? There was still a good chance that Melanie was their child. She resolved to continue her own enquiries first.

"I'm sorry, Susan." Jonathan now said. "I can see that I have upset you by coming here. You have been so good to Neal that I thought maybe it was on my account and that you wouldn't mind seeing me again. I haven't told Helen, of course."

He prepared to take his leave.

"No, don't go, Jonathan. I *am* happy to see you, very happy. It was just a bit of a shock the way you appeared right out of the blue. You haven't upset me at all. Tell me about your work. Are you still working in the world of PR?"

Her decision made, she felt more relaxed and they chatted about their respective jobs, old times, happy memories, mutual acquaintances.

"I'm so sorry about what happened to your husband. Was your marriage happy?" he asked after some time.

"Oh yes, Chris was a wonderful man. I still miss him dreadfully."

She paused a moment and looked wistful.

"We would have liked to have had a family but it just didn't work out that way."

There was a moment's silence before she continued,

"You must be very proud of your son; Neal is a fine young man. You have a daughter too, I believe."

"I do indeed. Would you believe I had you in mind when I chose her name, Suzannah? Actually Neal... Why, what's the matter?"

Tears were rolling down Susan's cheeks and suddenly she was in the arms of her former lover once again, experiencing the same sensations she had felt that first day when he had helped her over the rocks so long ago.

"Did you really name her after me?" she asked, not daring to look him in the face.

"Yes." He wiped her tears away. "You've always had a very special place in my heart. I felt so bad about the way I'd treated you."

"And Helen didn't mind?" That seemed incredulous.

"Oh, I just said it was a name I liked. I'm sure she suspected the real reason but she didn't raise any objection. She said she liked it too."

"She must be a very remarkable woman. Where does she think you are now?"

"Meeting business associates. I don't like to deceive her. It's not something I would normally do but I just had to check that it really was you and it *has* been lovely seeing you again."

"Yes, it has," agreed Susan. "I'm glad that you came."

They talked for another half hour over a drink and then he was gone, just as suddenly as he had appeared. It had been an afternoon of memories Susan would treasure but was it a lost opportunity to disclose what had been kept secret for too long? Or was it better for that secret to remain unspoken for ever? Susan squeezed her eyes shut and prayed earnestly to the God she did not believe in, or did she? If only he would answer.

"Let it be Melanie," her anguished heart cried out. "Please God, let Melanie be my daughter."

And for a fleeting moment she wished that she had not been so noble in the past, wished that she had told Jonathan about his baby from the start, wished that she had stopped him from marrying Helen, kept him for herself, wished that they had raised their own child together, acting as proper, conventional parents. In that same moment she admitted to herself at long last that she loved him still, that she had never ceased to love him.

Then she thought of Neal, whom she loved as a son. Did she really wish he had never been born? She thought of Chris. Would she really forfeit the years she had spent with him. The moment had passed and already she regretted it.

★ ★ ★

"You've had a tiring day, Jonny," said Helen, looking at the clock. "Your dinner won't be a minute."

She bustled about, laying a place for him at the table, while he collapsed onto the sofa and closed his eyes. He *was* tired. He had set out that morning with an air of expectancy and excitement but his visit had proved to be somewhat disappointing. Susan had been so reserved and nervous – not at all the way he remembered her. At times during their conversation he had witnessed the former animation highlighting the natural beauty which she still possessed, but for most of the time she had appeared uncomfortable and preoccupied.

"She's had a hard life," he admitted to himself. "I suppose it was wrong of me to go flaunting my happy marriage and children in her face."

Helen kissed his forehead.

"There you are, Darling, if you have the energy to eat!"

He opened his eyes and smiled. As he ate the tasty meal she had prepared for him he contemplated admitting where he had really been but decided against it lest he should cause her unnecessary pain.

"Do you know who that is?" Helen suddenly asked, showing him Charlotte's photograph.

He glanced at it and shook his head.

"No."

"Doesn't it remind you of anyone?"

He took a closer look and again replied in the negative. Helen lifted one of the albums which were now arranged in a neat pile and leafed through it until she came across a photograph of her own daughter at a similar age. She held the album out in front of him.

"Don't you think it's the image of Suzy?"

"There is a certain similarity," he agreed now, "especially around the eyes. Who is she anyway?"

"Charlotte."

"Charlotte? Why, yes, of course it is. I can see that quite plainly now. She was a very attractive girl even then. Neal has made a good choice. Where are they all this evening?"

"They've gone into town. Suzy wants them to meet Matthew. I'm glad she and Charlotte seemed to get on well. They're not long away."

"We needn't wait up for them then. Let's have an early night."

Helen assented happily and they were soon sound asleep. When Jonathan cuddled up to her seductively some hours later and made exceedingly passionate love to her, she was quite unaware that he was dreaming of another time, another place, another woman.

Chapter 20

Charlotte or Melanie? The question haunted Susan day and night. To think that one of those girls was her very own daughter, the baby she had once been afraid to love and care for, had thoughtlessly disowned and abandoned to the mercy of a cruel world, unaware of the true maternal feelings which lay dormant within her breast, feelings which were to be aroused years later, when she and Chris longed in vain to have a child. During those painful years her daughter had been growing up here in England, a stranger for whom she felt nothing. Given two quite different girls in both looks and personality she could not even recognise her own. One day she imagined she had seen something of herself in Melanie; the next a smile from Charlotte reminded her momentarily of Jonathan. Increasingly she found her concentration slipping at work. In her dealings with her colleagues, the parents, and the children themselves she found herself continually apologising for not having grasped what had been said to her. At night she would wake up in a cold sweat from bad dreams in which girls were engaging in incestuous acts with their brothers.

Neal was awakened one night by a series of delirious cries and screams coming from Susan's room. At first he refrained from intruding on her privacy, realising that it was only a dream, but the cries continued for some time and he became concerned. He ventured into her room and found her flailing about in the bed, sweat pouring from her forehead. Whilst he could not make out much of what she said, he grasped a few disconnected words including 'brother', 'sister' and 'baby'. This was followed by a period of relative calm before she again shouted out:

"She's my baby, my baby, my baby…brother and sister, brother and sister…"

Neal fetched a cold, wet flannel from the bathroom and gently wiped her fevered brow. Slowly her delirium subsided and she opened her eyes, conscious that she was not alone.

"You were having a bad dream," explained Neal sympathetically, believing from the words she had uttered that she was lamenting over her childless state, fantasising about the family she never had.

"Did I say anything?" She seemed suddenly terrified.

"No," lied Neal. "You were making enough noise but I didn't catch any actual words."

She immediately relaxed.

"I'm sorry for wakening you, Neal. You go back to bed now. I'll be fine. And thank you."

He went back to bed but lay awake for some time, wondering what was wrong. Mrs Lovell had been very nervous and strange for some weeks now. There was obviously something worrying her but, whatever it was, it was clear that she did not want to talk about it. In fact she had looked quite frightened when she thought she might have spoken in her sleep, might have accidentally let something slip. Eventually he attributed it to sheer loneliness and, feeling sorry for her, he went back to sleep himself, quite unaware that he would soon be the one facing problems, big problems.

The first bombshell was dropped the following evening while he and Susan were having dinner together. Susan happened to remark that things had been hectic in school because, for various reasons, they were understaffed.

"I ended up teaching two classes for most of the day," she said, "because neither Pamela Wingrove nor Richard Walkington was in. You'll remember Richard, I'm sure. He was here that night you joined us all for supper. I don't think you've met Pamela."

"Yes, he lent me some books afterwards. I must return them soon," Neal answered, embarrassed, hoping that she would not prolong the conversation.

"Oh yes, I'd forgotten that you had been to his house. Did you meet his wife?"

"Yes." He looked at her cautiously.

"What was she like?"

"I …I …I don't really know. She seemed pleasant enough. Very young."

Susan slowly drank a glass of water before continuing.

"I don't normally like to spread gossip," she said, "but rumour has it that Richard was arrested last night over an incident of domestic violence and that his wife is in hospital. Apparently he suspected that she had been having an extra-marital affair."

Neal was glad that he was eating fish, for when he choked on the news he had just received, he was able to blame it on a bone.

"I do hope it's not true," Susan went on. "I rather like Richard."

Neal was still coughing. He took a drink.

"It's hardly the kind of rumour to start without substance," he said, already believing the worst.

He excused himself from the table, refusing anything more to eat, and went straight to his room. He felt awful. What had he done to that poor girl? He remembered with shame the callous way he had treated her, never stopping to think that she was capable of being hurt. No matter how much he loved Charlotte and wanted to forget that he had ever been unfaithful to her, he knew that it was now his duty to go and see Stephanie. Of course she might have had another affair; maybe Richard had caught her in the act. It was a possibility but there was no point in deluding himself, delaying the truth; he was partly if not wholly to blame for Richard's alleged attack. Perhaps his own name was shortly to be dragged through the mud. He hoped not; he was desperate to keep this from Charlotte, from Susan also. How had Richard found out? Well, he would soon know.

An hour later, his date with Charlotte cancelled, Neal stood nervously outside the local hospital, clutching a large box of chocolates. His enquiries at the reception desk led him to Ward 17, which he found by following arrows and signposts as he made his way through a maze of over-heated corridors smelling strongly of antiseptic and disinfectant, and into an elevator which bore a sign claiming it could take a maximum of seven people. There were four other occupants and, even at that, it felt very cramped.

The ward sister was seated in her office.

"I'm looking for Mrs Stephanie Walkington," said Neal.

She gave him a hard, disdainful look and asked coldly, "Are you her husband?"

"Oh no," he assured her. "I believe he is in police custody. I'm a friend."

Now she smiled. "I'm sorry, sir, that is certainly where he belongs."

"How bad are her injuries?"

"We weren't able to save the baby, a little girl," the sister told him. She also has a fractured arm, several stitches in her face and multiple bruises."

Baby? What baby? Alarm bells were sounding in his brain.

"My God," he exclaimed. "I'd no idea it was so bad."

The sister said she was not really in a condition to receive visitors but she took his name and went into a private side ward, saying that she would check whether Mrs Walkington was awake. Neal waited anxiously, wondering now that it was too late to change his mind, whether he should have come. Almost immediately the sister returned.

"You could be just the tonic she needs, Mr Ashby," she said. "Your name produced the first smile I have seen all day. Go on in."

The list of injuries had been bad enough but the shock of seeing her face was dreadful.

"Oh Stephanie!" Neal cried, bending over the bed and taking her small, helpless hand in his own. "He's worse than an animal."

A deep cut ran from her forehead to her right eye which was so badly swollen that she could scarcely open it, another from the corner of her mouth into her cheek.

"He'll be locked up for this, Stephanie."

"No. I told the policewoman this afternoon that I would not be pressing charges. They'll have to let him go. He *is* my husband."

"Are you mad?" Neal was enraged. "Look what he has done to you."

"It was my own fault. I asked for it."

"You'll not go back to him, surely?"

Tears formed in her eyes.

"I don't know," she said. "I've nowhere else to go."

"Where are your parents? They should be here with you."

"I have no parents. They both died when I was in my teens."

"A sister then, a brother, an aunt?"

Stephanie shook her head miserably.

"I have nobody," she said.

"You have me," said Neal softly. "You cannot go back to Richard. We'll work something out."

Neal was filled with shame, realising again how callous he had been. He had been to bed with her but he knew nothing about her, did not even know whether she was financially independent from her husband, whether they would be able to work something out, as he had so rashly promised. He handed her the chocolates, the first gift she had ever received from him.

"Thank you, Neal," she said, "and thank you for coming. How did you know?"

"I heard from my landlady that Richard had beaten you. I don't know any more. Was it because of me, Stephanie? How did he find out?"

He paused, afraid to utter the words. "Whose was the baby?"

"Yours."

Neal felt sick. There was a moment of deathly silence. How had he got himself into such a mess?

"Oh Stephanie, I'm so sorry. I've treated you abominably. Why didn't he come after me instead of taking it out on you?"

Stephanie sighed.

"He doesn't know about you, Neal. I told you it was my own fault. He found out that I was pregnant. He found the test I had used. He just stared at it and then he went mad. He hit me and I fell to the floor. He just kept on hitting me and swearing at me. A neighbour heard me screaming and called the police."

Now Stephanie burst into tears as she relived the horror of the attack. Neal tried to comfort her. A nurse came in carrying a large bouquet. She took one look at the distressed patient and told Neal had he would have to leave.

"No, please let him stay," Stephanie protested. "I'd be crying far more if he wasn't here."

"Just five minutes more then," said the nurse firmly. "These flowers were left at reception for you, Mrs Walkington."

Stephanie gazed in disbelief at the beautiful blooms. Who would send her flowers? The nurse handed her the card and left the flowers on top of her locker.

"Flowers aren't actually allowed on the ward," she said, "but since you are in this side ward on your own, they'll be permitted for the time being."

She glanced again at Neal and consulted her watch.

"Five minutes," she repeated, as she left them alone.

Stephanie opened the envelope and took out the little card which had been attached to the bouquet. She read the message through tear-filled eyes:

I'm sorry, Stephanie.
I have moved in with Sam for a while.
I will not enter our house again without letting you know first so you will be quite safe to return there.
I'm so sorry.
Richard.

Neal was relieved. At least she would still have her home without fear of another attack and he was freed from his rash promise. As he prepared to go now he softly kissed her bruised cheek and assured her once again that she was not alone in the world, that he cared for her.

"But it won't be like before," he said. "Think of me as a friend, a brother, not as a lover. I had no right to treat you as I did."

"I treated you the same way. I started it."

"You're too noble, Stephanie."

"But it's true."

He squeezed her hand and walked towards the door.

"Does your fiancée know about us?" she asked as he reached for the door knob.

"No," he replied, stopping in his tracks and hanging his head in shame.

Stephanie smiled.

"Then she never will. I have never uttered your name to a soul and I never shall. Your secret is safe."

Neal knelt by her bedside again and kissed her bruised and swollen lips.

"Oh Stephanie," he gasped, "you're wonderful. I'll make it up to you somehow."

With these parting words Neal hurried from the room before he would break down under the strain of so many mixed emotions.

Chapter 21

Neal and Charlotte were inseparable as their wedding plans began to take shape. Their love for each other was so intense, so overwhelming, so obvious to anyone who knew them. Susan was in a constant quandary as to what she should do regarding the possibility that they might actually be siblings. As the event grew closer, she found it increasingly difficult to sleep at night. Her tiredness and stress were obvious to her colleagues, several of whom had suggested that she make an appointment with her doctor. At last she decided to follow their advice.

"These tablets will help for a while," the doctor said, entering a key on his computer to print out a prescription, "but insomnia is usually caused by anxiety. If there is something on your mind, perhaps talking about it would help."

She hesitated.

"I can recommend a professional counsellor if it would help, Mrs Lovell, but please feel free to confide in me. I assure you that I will treat anything you tell me as strictly confidential. Sometimes people just need a sympathetic ear."

He had a very kindly manner and seemed to genuinely want to help. She had to talk to someone.

"My problem dates back over twenty years," Susan began. "I had a baby I didn't want. I mean it wasn't planned. I gave her away and thought nothing more about her for years but recently I came in contact again with her father, who never even knew of her birth, and I suddenly became obsessed with the idea of finding her."

She paused. The doctor adopted a very professional viewpoint.

"Do you think that would be wise after all this time? The girl may have been brought up in ignorance of her true identity. When you say you gave her away…"

"I left her on a doorstep."

"I see. So you have no idea where she is today?"

"I do know where she is. She's living about an hour away from here with a family called Jamison. They have five girls, all adopted."

Dr Matthews looked up, startled. Caught off his guard, he disclosed information he should have kept to himself.

"Yes, I know the family well. They are patients of mine, one of the families who remained on my books when I moved north to this practice. I started off down there in Hertfordshire."

Here was a sudden and unexpected ray of hope.

"You would have a record, then, of where each girl came from. You could tell me which one was found abandoned on the doorstep."

Dr Matthews looked uncomfortable.

"I'm sorry, Mrs Lovell, I probably would have a record of it but I cannot divulge that kind of information, not without the consent of Mr and Mrs Jamison."

"But I am the baby's mother!"

"Not in the eyes of the law, I'm afraid. What age would your daughter be now?"

"Twenty-one. It's either Melanie or Charlotte. It seems they have been brought up like twins."

"That's right. I remember the event quite clearly for it was during my first year there. It caused quite a stir in the neighbourhood. The Jamisons had signed all the adoption papers for one little girl when, out of the blue, another one was deposited on their doorstep."

He paused.

"What led you to do it, Mrs Lovell?"

He remained calm and spoke kindly with no hint of rebuke or recrimination for her actions.

"I wasn't married," she replied. "I lived in a small, rural community, where people were very self-righteous and narrow-minded; an illegitimate child and her mother would just not have been accepted."

"And you never told the child's father? Would he not have stood by you?"

"He would. I'm sure he would have, but he loved someone else whom he later married. He had told me about her before I realised that I was pregnant."

"So you didn't tell him? That was very magnanimous."

"Or very stupid!"

How easy it was to talk to this stranger. Susan recalled briefly the horrified reaction of Chris when she had made her confession to him. Of course the circumstances were not comparable.

"Dr Matthews," Susan now said, coming to the point, "I haven't told you the real reason for my recent state of mind. It's not just that I want to know which of the two girls is my child for my own sake. As I said, I came into contact again recently with the baby's father and, by sheer co-incidence, it turns out that his son is engaged to be married to Charlotte Jamison. There is a chance, therefore, that my daughter is going to marry her own brother."

"Ahh! This puts a different light on the matter altogether. Don't you think you should speak to Mrs Jamison or the girl's father?"

"I would do that if I knew for sure that Charlotte is my child. But it could be Melanie, in which case there would be no need for anyone ever to know. I don't want to go stirring up the past and upsetting people unnecessarily."

The doctor rose from his chair and paced about the room as he thought over all that had been said, weighing it all up in his mind. Susan held her breath, not daring to believe she would soon have her answer.

"In these very unusual circumstances," he said at last, "I feel that I would be justified in revealing to you which of the two girls was the abandoned baby."

Susan watched, tense and nervous, as he first interrogated his computer, clicking on various files and icons, and studying the information that appeared on the screen. Then he opened his filing cabinet and brought out the hand-written medical records of the Jamison family. The next minute felt more like an hour. Everything went very quite and still. She heard another patient enter the waiting room. The ticking of the clock on the wall seemed to get louder and louder. She watched the doctor's face as he fingered the relevant documents but his expression gave nothing away. It began to rain outside and Susan was aware of every drop as it hit the window behind her head. Her forehead broke out in a cold sweat.

"Here it is," he announced at last. "I have an entry dated 27th August, 1989. I examined the baby and found her to be in good health. I judged her to be twenty-one days old, but as the family had just adopted another child who was twenty-three days old, and wanted to keep this one as well, we decided that, if the second adoption was approved, two days would make little difference, so we agreed to keep the same birthday for both girls, unless any evidence of the true date was forthcoming. Every effort was made to trace the baby's natural parents."

"And the baby's name?" probed Susan.

He hesitated, then continued:

"They called the legally adopted child Melanie; the one they found on the doorstep, Charlotte."

Susan was just aware of Dr Matthews stammering an apology before everything began to spin in front of her eyes and she felt his arms reach out to support her. Her worst fears had been realised and she passed out.

Chapter 22

Music from an Enrique Iglesias CD flowed softly from the stereo as Neal entered the room and sat down in his customary armchair by the stone fire-place. Stephanie immediately mixed him his favourite drink, a gin and tonic with a dash of lemon, and brought it over to him before returning to the kitchen to check whether the meal was ready. An easy, friendly, platonic relationship had developed between them since the day he had visited her in hospital. Now he was happy to see that only the slightest physical trace of her ordeal remained in the form of a small scar on her forehead. She had changed her hairstyle, which was now much shorter with a fringe, in an attempt to hide it but he still noticed it every time he looked at her. Richard had kept his word. He had returned to the house several times to collect various belongings but always at a time when he knew that Stephanie would be out and after first telephoning to say that he would be coming and to explain what he wanted. He had touched nothing of hers, nor indeed anything that they owned jointly. Stephanie had not seen him since the attack.

Today, however, Neal was alarmed to see their wedding photograph prominently displayed on top of the television. He set his drink down and picked up the photograph to have a closer look. Stephanie looked radiant in her beautiful white dress, her black hair drawn away from her pretty, young face into a floral headband, from which hung a small, net veil. Beside her stood the handsome, smiling figure of Richard Walkington. Who would have believed it could all have turned so sour in two short years? Stephanie came back into the room.

"Why have you put this out?" he asked, accusingly.

"It's always sat there. I've just put it back in its normal position." Stephanie sounded defensive.

"But things are not normal. You're surely not going to take him back?"

"He has not suggested coming back."

"But even if he did, you would refuse, wouldn't you?"

She hesitated, looked again at the picture herself, as she replaced it.

"I don't know," she said. "Perhaps, in time… I just don't know."

"After what he did to you! You would be mad. Don't even think about it. Divorce him and find someone else. You deserve someone better. Sure you were never happy together."

Stephanie shook her head.

"No, that's not true," she said. "We were happy at first, very happy. And when I think of him now, when I hear his voice on the phone, I don't think of that awful night or the months leading up to it; I think of the times when we were first married. I think of our honeymoon in Devon. I'd give anything to have those times back again."

"But you can't live in the past, Stephanie."

He took her hand and smiled.

"You can't ever recapture those days. You have to move on."

"I know," she sighed.

There was a moment's reflective silence and then suddenly she changed her tone and brightened:

"Come on. Dinner's ready."

Neal enjoyed his meal. He had to admit he enjoyed being with Stephanie. He still thought about his past treatment of her with shame and embarrassment. Indeed it was uppermost in his thoughts now, as he ate the delicious chicken casserole she had prepared for him.

"You're very quiet," she said.

"I'm sorry. I…I…I was thinking about the times I came here before," he stammered. "Sometimes I didn't speak a single word to you. I was rough and selfish and I feel so ashamed of myself now that I know how nice you are."

"You forget who started it all. Stop blaming yourself."

"Tell me," he said after a moment, "why did you do it? Why me?"

"Bighead! Do you really want me to tell you how sexy you are? I did it because I enjoyed it. It was exciting."

"But you must have known it could never lead to anything but trouble."

"I didn't care. It was worth it."

In spite of all that had happened, Neal believed her and indeed shared her sentiments. He too enjoyed the excitement of his double life. He had two women devoted to him, one soon to be his wife, the other happy to accept that he was going to marry someone else. What more could he desire? But it could not go on much longer for he knew that he was not treating either of them fairly. Little did he know, however, as he made his way from Stephanie's house to meet Charlotte that very evening, that his double life was to end in just a few hours' time, without any decision whatsoever having to be made on his part. He was about to receive his second big shock.

★ ★ ★

The sound of the doorbell was just audible above the music on the television.

"I'll get it, Mum," said Melanie. She and her sisters, Erin and Yvonne, were watching a programme about Take That and heartily joining in with their own rendition of the old favourite, *Back for Good*. Jayne was out for the evening with Dean, and Charlotte was also out with Neal. Expecting the caller to be a friend of one of the girls, Janine Jamison continued reading her evening paper and looked up in surprise when Melanie led the visitor into the room.

"Mrs Lovell! This is a pleasant surprise. Do sit down," said Janine.

Erin politely turned off the television but soon wished that she had not because a prolonged silence ensued, during which they all felt rather awkward. Susan was trying desperately to find the right words to begin but her throat felt as dry as dust and the words just would not come. Somehow she had decided that it would be easier to speak to Mr and Mrs Jamison than to explain the situation to Jonathan at this late stage. Now she was not so sure.

"I wonder could I speak to you and your husband alone?" she said at last, her voice cracking up and betraying her nervous state.

Janine was immediately alarmed.

"Why, what's wrong?" she asked. "Has something happened to Charley or Neal?"

"No, no, nothing like that," Susan reassured her quickly, reluctant to say anything about the matter until the girls had gone.

Their curiosity aroused, they would have loved to stay but immediately all three excused themselves and withdrew to their rooms upstairs.

"Steven is out at present," said Janine pleasantly, "though I expect him back any minute. I presume this has something to do with Charley."

"Yes."

She hesitated and then managed to muster enough courage to begin.

"Is it true that Charlotte was found abandoned on your doorstep?"

Janine's attitude towards Susan changed at once and her face reddened with anger.

"Mrs Lovell," she said coldly, "I'll thank you to mind your own business. You are merely the landlady of my daughter's fiancée and, as such, I find such an enquiry improper and indeed quite insulting!"

"Forgive me," pleaded Susan, her heart breaking. "That must have sounded rude and presumptuous. What I want to say is that I ...I...I am that baby's mother. It was I who left her on your doorstep. Please tell me whether it really is Charlotte."

The colour drained from Janine's face as she stared at Susan in disbelief and anger. An ominous silence filled the air. For the first few years of Charlotte's life, Janine had imagined and dreaded a moment like this, had lived in fear of a stranger coming to claim the child she had grown to love so dearly. As the years had passed, however, such fears had gradually subsided until she had ceased to think about it at all. Charlotte was a young woman now.

Susan's voice broke in again on her thoughts:

"I can prove that what I have said is true. It was about seven o'clock in the morning on 27th August, 1989. I left my baby in a large basket on your doorstep and rang the bell. She was wrapped in a white shawl edged with pink."

There was no response so, thinking that Janine needed further convincing, Susan continued:

"The house had just been painted blue. There was a 'Wet Paint' sign by the gate. The big flower-bed in the centre of the lawn was full of pink roses."

Janine knew that she was correct in every detail.

"I still have that pink and white shawl," she whispered, almost inaudibly. She was trembling now.

"You don't need to go on. You obviously are who you say. But why are you making yourself known now, after all these years? Charley isn't yours any longer. She's had a happy life here. You are already on the guest list for her wedding. What more do you want?"

Susan recognised the anguish in Janine's voice and wished with all her heart that she did not have to reveal the rest but there was no avoiding it now.

"I want nothing more for myself," she went on. "I did a dreadful thing that day. I know I did wrong but I cannot turn the clock back and I'm sure you don't want to hear my reasons for doing it. Charlotte has had the best home possible and I thank you from the bottom of my heart for the way you took her in and cared for her. I'm not laying any claims on her now. As you said, she is not mine any longer."

Janine relaxed her guard just a little. She was still very agitated.

"I'm so sorry, Mrs Jamison, Janine. Can I call you Janine? I'm so very sorry. I can't keep this to myself. I had to speak up when I realised that Charlotte…that she…"

She could scarcely bring herself to say the fateful words:

"That she is about to be married to her own brother."

Now Janine grew angry again.

"You are trying to tell me that you're Neal's mother too!" she shouted. "That's ridiculous! I have met Mrs Ashby and Neal is the image of her. We all commented on it."

A door was heard opening and closing and footsteps approached them. Rusty came bounding in and licked Susan's hand. He looked at her with big, doleful eyes, reminding her momentarily of Chris and his beloved dog.

"I'm not claiming to be Neal's mother," answered Susan quietly, as Steven Jamison entered the room, "but Neal's father is also Charlotte's natural father."

Janine greeted her husband and hastily made the necessary introductions. He had not heard Susan's remark as he entered the room but straight away he sensed the tension in the atmosphere. His wife quickly explained the alleged relationship with Charlotte and then added, exasperated:

"Now she says that Jonathan Ashby is Charley's true father, in which case she is Neal's sister! I cannot believe it. Mr Ashby would never have allowed things to go so far if that were the case."

"He knows nothing about it. He never knew about Charlotte," put in Susan, apologetically. She turned to the newcomer, whilst stroking Rusty's soft, shiny fur, more to comfort herself than the dog. He rolled over, exposing his pale brown tummy for tickling.

"I'm sorry, Mr Jamison," she said. "I would never have interfered in Charlotte's life except for this blood relationship with Neal. I just could not stand idly by and watch her marry her own brother. I had to speak up."

Steven Jamison could see immediately that she was very distressed.

"You were right to come to us," he said, taking it all more calmly than his wife had done, "but it's a pity you left it so late. Could you not have foreseen this?"

"They were already engaged," she explained, "before I discovered that Charlotte was connected with this house or this family. It was only today that I knew for certain that she was my child. I came at once."

He didn't ask how she had come by that knowledge.

"Are you absolutely certain that Jonathan Ashby is the

father? You say he knows nothing about your baby. Could the father not have been someone else?"

Susan gave way to tears at last.

"Jonathan and I were lovers," she wept. "We had a relationship for almost three years. I was never unfaithful to him."

Steven apologised for his insensitive insinuation. There was no doubt about her sincerity.

They talked for a further half hour, discussing schemes for dealing with the situation. They were all most reluctant to tell the young couple the truth. They all suspected that they already shared a sexual relationship so the knowledge that they were actually siblings would be utterly repugnant to them. They were also unwilling to let the wedding go ahead as though no barrier existed because, although they discussed the possibility on the grounds that the two had not been brought up together and were unaware of the relationship, they all felt that they would be condoning something which they instinctively knew to be wrong, and that an even more disastrous situation could develop if the truth became known to them in the future. Somehow they had to find a way to separate the lovers.

No decisions had been taken when Susan excused herself and stood up to go home. She had done her duty in passing on the information but it was really not up to her to decide what should happen next. She had given up the right to make decisions about her daughter's life a long time ago. Steven saw her to the door.

"Thank you for coming," he said. "I can imagine it was not easy for you. You must try to excuse my wife; all this has been very upsetting for her. She'll come to see in time that the situation is not entirely your fault. You could not have foreseen such a coincidence."

Rusty licked her hand again. He seemed to sense that she needed a bit of tender loving care.

She went home, relieved that she now shared her burden with someone else but feeling desperately sorry for the young lovers. She had no idea how Janine and Steven would try to bring about a separation.

★ ★ ★

Jayne arrived home around midnight to find herself mysteriously beckoned by Erin into the room she shared with Melanie. Neither of them noticed Charlotte slipping into the house just as Jayne entered the bedroom and closed the door.

"What's going on?" asked Jayne, intrigued by the expressions on her sisters' faces.

"Shhh!" whispered Erin. "We're not supposed to know anything. Mrs Lovell was here tonight, you know, the woman Neal stays with. Well, she wanted to speak to Mum and Dad alone so Yvonne and I made ourselves scarce but Mel stood at the top of the stairs and heard it all. It turns out that she, Mrs Lovell, is Charley's real mother!"

It was at this point that Charlotte, having discovered Jayne missing from their room, and hearing the whispers from next door, decided to find out what was happening. She always enjoyed their joint powwows. Her outstretched hand was just about to turn the door knob when she heard her name mentioned from within. She halted and listened.

"How romantic!" It was Jayne's voice.

"It might be if that were all," whispered Erin, "but Mel heard her say that Mr Ashby is Charley's real father. She must have had an affair with him in the past."

"Neal's father!"

"So Neal is actually Charley's brother!" put in Melanie. "They're going to try to separate them somehow without telling them the truth. Mum and Dad thought it would be too awful for her to realise that she had been in love with her own brother."

Jayne's heart went out to her sister.

"Poor Charley," she said with genuine empathy. "If someone was to tell me that Dean was actually my brother …"

But Charlotte heard no more. At first she had stood stock still, as though fixed to the ground, refusing to believe what her ears were telling her. Now, hot tears blinding her, she went back downstairs and ran out into the night.

Chapter 23

"Charley! It's ten past eight!" Steven called from the bottom of the stairs.

The rest of the family were gathered around the breakfast table.

"It's not like her to be last up."

Whilst still employed part-time in the library, Charlotte was training to work with her dad in the family business. Today she was due to go on a course with him. She had never let him down before, had always been up on time and smartly dressed, ready for a punctual departure.

There was no response.

"She's not there, Dad," said Jayne, hesitantly. "She didn't come home last night."

"What? Not at all? Well why on earth didn't you say so sooner? There must be something wrong!"

While the girls muttered something about her probably staying over with Neal, Steven rushed to the telephone and called him. Neal confirmed that he had left Charlotte home around midnight. He had seen her enter the house, just a minute after Jayne had gone in. In fact he had spoken to Dean at the gate.

On hearing this, the girls immediately realised with horror what must have happened. They looked awkwardly at one another and at their parents, knowing that they would have to own up, for Charlotte's sake. God only knew where she might have gone in her distress or how she might be coping with such a shock. It was Melanie who spoke.

"It's my fault," she admitted, but before she could explain anything, she burst into tears. Jayne too began to cry. Being in a serious relationship herself, she was best able to understand how her sister must be feeling. Erin, remaining relatively calm, explained what had happened:

"Mel overheard your conversation with Mrs Lovell last night and, when Jayne came home, we told her about Mr Ashby being Charlotte's father." Her voice shook as she added, "She must have heard us."

"Oh no!" Janine sank down onto the nearest chair and covered her face with her hands. "Oh no!"

Steven was furious.

"You stupid girls," he yelled, banging the table with his clenched fist so that all the dishes rattled and hot tea spilled over into the saucers. Rusty yelped and ran to the kitchen, where he sat, quivering behind the recycling bin.

"How could you have been so bloody careless? And what were you doing eavesdropping on a private conversation in the first place? This is exactly what we didn't want to happen!"

Steven rarely swore. His daughters had never seen him so angry.

He wished now that he had not phoned Neal. No doubt he would be here any minute, wanting to help. Sure enough he arrived within half an hour, just as Steven finished a warning to the family that not another word about the whole affair was to be breathed to a living soul. They all gave their word. Neal was in a frantic state. How could his fiancée just have vanished from her own house? Thinking quickly, Steven apologised to Neal for having alarmed him and said that he had made a mistake. Charlotte had spent the night at home after all. She had gone out early that morning, leaving an explanatory note which he had only found after making the phone call. He said he had panicked when he found she was not in the house at breakfast time.

Neal relaxed.

"Where on earth has she gone so early in the day?" he asked bemused. "Was she not supposed to be going to some seminar with you this morning? What did she say in her note?"

"Oh, just that she wanted some time to herself," bluffed Steven. "She said she had some things to sort out."

The whole family was grateful when this explanation was accepted and a curious Neal left without actually requesting to see the non-existent note. But they were now faced with the real problem of deciding where Charlotte might have gone in the middle of the night and in a very distressed frame of mind.

Chapter 24

Susan was delighted to receive an unexpected visitor on Sunday evening.

"Dr Matthews!" she exclaimed, recognising him immediately.

"Good evening, Mrs Lovell. May I come in?"

"Yes, of course." She led him into the lounge where she had been preparing some documents and policies for the next day's staff meeting on assessment procedures.

"This is a surprise," she said.

"I have not been able to stop thinking about you since your visit to the surgery on Thursday," explained the doctor. "I thought I would come and see how things had developed. I only wish I could have given you better news."

For a fleeting moment Susan's mind had gone into overdrive, imagining that he had come to say he had made a mistake. It was Melanie, after all. Already she knew that this was not the case. He was only showing concern.

"Are you sleeping any better?" he now asked her.

"Yes, the tablets are helping, thank you, and even though my worst fears *were* realised, at least I now know the truth. I think it was the uncertainty that was giving me such dreadful nightmares and causing me so much stress. And, of course, it is always a help to be able to share a burden with someone else."

"Have you spoken to Mrs Jamison yet?"

"Yes, I went straight away, on Thursday evening."

Susan proceeded to give the doctor an account of the difficult interview, marvelling over the ease with which she could speak to this relative stranger.

"I don't know what plan they finally hatched to separate the two," she concluded, "but they told Neal the very next morning that Charlotte had gone out early, leaving them a note saying that she had things on her mind and wanted to be alone. He hasn't seen her since. Whether she is really away from home or not, I don't know."

Dr Matthews sighed and reflected for a few moments.

"I feel so sorry for the young couple," he said. "I have never met Neal but I have known Charlotte all her life and treated all her childhood ailments. She told me recently about her forthcoming marriage and I could tell that she was overflowing with happiness. I can't help reminiscing when I see a young couple so happy, ready to start a new life together. It reminds me of myself and Catherine at that stage. Anyone who would have tried to split us up would have had a hard job!"

He spoke her name softly and lovingly, yet hesitantly, as though it did not often pass his lips.

"I think you are right, however, to keep the truth from them," he continued. "To love someone as a lover, that is physically, sexually, and then to find out that she is your sister – well, it's just unthinkable."

Susan was grateful that he did not try to make light of the situation, that he freely admitted the tragic outcome of events. He helped her by sharing her burden, not by pretending it did not exist. Just knowing that she now had someone to talk to about her most private thoughts, someone who really cared, was already proving to be a great relief. She found herself wondering what kind of private life he led himself.

"Have you any children of your own, Dr Matthews?" she asked.

"Derrick. This is a social call, not a professional one."

"Derrick," she smiled. "Please call me Susan."

"To answer your question, Susan, no, I have no children. I did have a son once. Both he and Catherine, my wife, died of a virus we all picked up on holiday. He was just approaching his second birthday."

Susan's heart went out to him as his face was momentarily clouded by the saddest of expressions, portraying both love for those he had lost, and self-reproach, not only for being the only survivor, but also for having been so ill himself at the time that he had been unable to put his medical knowledge to use when it was most required.

"I'm so sorry," Susan stammered. "I had no idea."

"You too are a widow, I believe."

"Yes, Christopher was killed in a road accident five years ago."

Now it was his turn to feel for her. They each found great comfort in talking to one another.

Gradually the conversation turned to happier times and, for a while, their current problems and tragic memories were forgotten. Derrick was persuaded to stay for supper and took his leave soon afterwards, promising to call again and telling her not to hesitate in contacting him, even if she just needed a sympathetic ear. He handed her a small card bearing his private address, email address and telephone numbers. Gratefully, and with a lightness of heart she had not experienced for a long time, Susan accepted his offer.

★ ★ ★

Neal stirred his coffee for the fourth time and stared abstractedly at the bacon and eggs in front of him. He did not feel like eating. It was now Monday morning, three days since he had seen or heard from Charlotte. She had never before behaved so strangely and he felt instinctively that her sudden seclusion had something to do with himself, so once again casting his mind back to Thursday evening, he tried to figure out what he had done wrong. It was true that he had gone to meet her straight from the home of Stephanie Walkington, but how could she have discovered that? They had shared a wonderful evening, driving out of town to one of their favourite haunts in the countryside, where they had met some friends for a drink. Afterwards, in the privacy of his car, they had kissed passionately and had talked about the forthcoming weekend. She had agreed to travel north to Yorkshire with him and stay at his own flat for the first time. She had not appeared to be the least bit troubled about anything, quite the opposite. They had been deliriously happy. Now the weekend had passed and he had not even seen her. He had checked his phone and his computer over and over but there was not even a text message.

He buttered a piece of toast and ate a slice of bacon; it was cold. He sipped his coffee; it was barely lukewarm.

"Letter for you, Neal."

He looked up as Mrs Lovell handed him an envelope, written in Charlotte's distinctive hand. At last! His breakfast forgotten, he eagerly ripped it open to read the long-awaited explanation but, as he quickly scanned the page, his face grew pale, his first thought that someone was playing a cruel joke on him. But in his heart he already knew that he was indeed reading Charlotte's own words. But why? What could possibly have happened in so short a time to change her sentiments so entirely? Blinded by the first tears he had shed since he was a small child, he stumbled from the table and, averting his face from his landlady, groped his way upstairs to the privacy of his own room, where he slumped into a chair and re-read the fateful tidings.

Dearest Neal,

No matter how I break this news to you, I know it will come as a shock and be hurtful to you so I might as well come straight out with it. I'm sorry but I cannot marry you after all. There is no-one else involved — I have just realised that I don't want to get married. I know that saying sorry sounds totally inadequate but I have no other excuse. Please believe me when I say I have not willingly trifled with your emotions and I hope that, in time, you will come to forgive me.

I will be away from home for a while. Please don't try to contact me. My mind is made up and there can be no going back. A meeting would only make things worse.

I really am very sorry, Neal. I will always remember the good times we had.

Charlotte.

Neal was stupefied, totally overwhelmed by feelings of bewilderment, frustration, disbelief. His watch told him that it was already half past eight so, resolved to confront her right away at the library, he galloped back down the staircase, rushed outside and jumped into his car, slamming the door in anger. Usually a calm and patient driver, today he found the traffic jams irritating. He flashed his lights at other drivers and swore at them when his journey was delayed by even a few seconds, hurling a particular tirade of abuse at one woman driver, whom he considered to be overcautious in entering the main stream of traffic on the busy carriageway. He finally found a parking space and raced on foot to the library, only to be informed that Charlotte had not turned up for work so, rushing back to his car, he continued his hectic journey until he reached her home.

Yvonne was just coming through the gate, looking very young in her blue school uniform. As Neal jumped from the car, she appeared to quicken her pace, giving him the distinct feeling that she was trying to avoid him.

"Hi Neal. Must dash. I'm already late!" she called, and allowing him no opportunity to answer, she made off at a very rapid pace.

Only Janine was at home, everyone else having left for work. She was obviously embarrassed and was very evasive in response to Neal's enquiries, assuring him that she herself did not know where Charlotte was staying but that she had made contact to say that she needed some time to think about things and that she was taking an overdue break from work. Time, thought Neal bitterly, that she had been saving for her honeymoon. He was suspicious. Janine's welcome was not of the warm and hospitable nature he was accustomed to in this house and she appeared to be curiously calm and relaxed about the whole episode. *Surely*, thought Neal to himself, *if they really don't know where she is, Mrs Jamison should be pleading with me to help them find her.*

"Did she mention me?" he asked miserably.

Not knowing whether Neal had received any communication from Charlotte yet, Janine was again cautious.

"She said she would be writing to you herself," she said.

"Yes, I had a letter this morning. I don't understand it, Mrs Jamison. She says she doesn't want to marry me after all. Just out of the blue! There was no inkling of this a few days ago. Do you know what has made her change her mind?"

Neal's young face betrayed all the pain and suffering in his broken heart. Janine felt wretched.

"I'm sorry," she said. "She didn't discuss it with me."

Neal was sure that she knew more than she was willing to admit. She didn't even look surprised at what he had said. Sensing, however, that he would get no more information from her for the present, he apologised for having troubled her so early in the day and sadly took his leave.

Just as sadly, Janine watched him go, his head bent low, his gait totally lacking its usual brisk bounce as he shuffled his way slowly down the driveway and into the familiar yellow car. He had managed to keep the tears from his eyes but she knew that his heart was crying out for Charlotte's continued love. Janine had grown very fond of Neal over the past months. She sank into a chair and buried her face in her hands. This was all very distressing. She really did not know where her daughter had gone. But how bravely she had reacted to the dreadful news she had overheard that night. Janine and Steven, with the girls' help, had spent the whole weekend searching for her. Through discreet enquiries they were assured that she had not gone to either of her natural parents, nor to the homes of any of her close friends. She had sent one short text message on Saturday which at least let them know she was alive. Then, just an hour or so ago, a letter had arrived. Janine took it from her pocket and perused it once again.

Dear Mum and Dad,

Please don't worry about me. I just cannot come home for a while. You have probably guessed that I overheard my sisters talking on Thursday night and discovered the identity of my real father though even now I can hardly believe it to be true. Please don't be too hard on them – they didn't know I was there – but I wish to God that I had not heard what they said. I think you were right to try to shield us from the truth so please do something for me. Make sure that Neal never finds out. He has such a good relationship with his dad. I have written to him, breaking off our engagement, but I don't know how I will ever be able to face him again and already I am missing him so much. I am taking some time off work as I am too upset to see anybody. I'm sorry about missing the seminar. Don't worry about me. I will keep in touch.

Your loving daughter,
Charlotte.

She had given no address but the letter bore a local postmark. At least she was safe, and somewhere nearby.

"The engagement is off, at least," mused Janine. "Maybe Mel actually did us a favour."

Immediately she felt ashamed for having had such a thought as she looked again at Charlotte's tragic words:

"I wish to God that I had not heard what they said."

If only she knew where to find her. She wanted so badly to hold her in her arms and comfort her. Was the poor girl trying to cope with her distress alone? All plausible places of retreat had been eliminated one by one. She just did not know where else to look.

★ ★ ★

Susan was baffled. She could not comprehend how Charlotte had been persuaded to write such a letter. Utterly bewildered, she replaced it exactly where it had lain when she entered the room, glad that Neal had not taken it with him. She should not have gone into his room. She knew that and she felt guilty. But she couldn't help herself. She was the cause of the whole unhappy situation. She had to know. She left the room again, wondering how Neal would react. It was to be midnight before she would find out.

Somehow Susan had got through the day at work. Working in a busy school had its advantages during times of stress. She was so busy helping other people to cope with their problems that she often forgot about her own. Today, however, Neal's plight was never far from her mind. She hurried home as soon as she could get away, cutting short the scheduled staff meeting, much to the delight of her colleagues, who had no idea of the turmoil behind this decision. There was no sign of him. His room was exactly as he had left it that morning. She sat up quite late, anxiously awaiting his return. At last she heard a car pull up outside. Someone rang the doorbell. Thinking that Neal had left in such haste that morning that he had forgotten to lift his key, Susan walked over to the door to let him in. But it was not Neal. Through the glass panel in the door, she could just make out the distinctive uniform of a policeman. Nervously she opened the door.

"Is this the residence of Mr Neal Ashby?" asked the constable, consulting his notebook.

"Yes," answered Susan, her mind in a whirl of confusion, anxiety and curiosity. "What's happened? Where is he?"

"Are you his mother?"

"Oh no. He's just a lodger here."

"Oh, I see. In that case I am sorry for troubling you so late but this the only address we could find on his person. We thought he might have parents or a wife who would be worried about him not coming home."

Memories of the day Chris died flooded her brain. It couldn't be happening all over again. She couldn't go through that again.

"He's not really just a lodger," prompted Susan, sensing that the policeman felt he had done his duty and was going to offer her no more information. "I am very close to his family. Perhaps you could tell me what has happened."

"He's been arrested, Ma'am."

"Arrested!" Susan could not believe her ears. "But what has he done?"

"Drunken driving. He drove his car at speed straight into another vehicle. Luckily it was parked and unoccupied at the time. He had been drinking so heavily that he could not speak a single intelligible word. He sustained some moderate injuries and will be spending the night in hospital."

"Moderate?"

"He'll live. Nothing too serious."

Susan was speechless. This was so out of character for Neal. He had certainly taken Charlotte's news badly.

"Well, goodnight, Ma'am. Sorry for disturbing you. I just wanted to check in case there was someone waiting up for him."

"Goodnight, Constable," muttered Susan in reply and closed the door with feelings of relief that he had not killed himself or someone else mingled with a huge amount of self-reproach. This was all her fault.

Chapter 25

Charlotte sat down on the edge of her bed and surveyed the familiar room where she had been so happy, wishing that somehow the past week of her life would turn out to be nothing but a bad dream. She stared unseeingly at the pretty pink furnishings. Being back in the room she shared with Jayne, she relived that awful scene which had so suddenly shattered all her hopes and dreams for the future, heard again the hushed voices which had told her that her lover was her own brother. She had fled from the house that night, hot tears streaming down her face, and had run headlong into Aidan Quinn, a childhood friend who had long been one of her admirers. His parents lived just a few doors from the Jamisons but Aidan, who was now a successful businessman currently employed as manager of a popular gym and spa complex, had his own flat a few miles away and was just about to return there after an evening at home, when the rendezvous took place.

"Charley!" he cried, alarmed by her distraught appearance. "Whatever's the matter?"

She stared at him blindly and began to sob so loudly that he feared other neighbours would be aroused.

"Get into the car," he said gently, "and you can tell me all about it."

He held the door of his silver BMW open for her and obediently she climbed inside and sat down. He went round to the other side and got in beside her. She was still crying bitterly.

"Oh Aidan," she blurted out on an impulse. "I'm so sorry. All those times you asked me out and I refused. I should have said yes. I wish I had had never met Neal Ashby."

"Charley!" he exclaimed, completely unaware of her reasoning and quite out of tune with her state of mind. "It's not too late. I still feel the same way about you."

He edged up closer to her and gently patted her arm.

"Is your engagement off?" he asked cautiously. "Do you want to talk about it?"

"I can't," she sobbed, and then added: "I don't want to go home tonight. I need to think."

She continued to cry loudly as she said piteously, "I don't know what to do. I've nowhere to go."

"Come home with me," he suggested. "You'll not be disturbed there. I have a comfy sofa."

When Charlotte did not refuse his offer, Aidan started up the engine and drove off, wondering what Neal had done to upset her so much and glad to have another chance himself to win her affection. They had been good friends for years but he would very much like for them to be more than friends. What a strange end to his evening, which had started out as a simple visit to his mum and dad.

True to his word, Aidan made no attempt to seduce her. He took all he needed from his bedroom and made sure that she would be comfortable before leaving the room and making himself a bed on the sofa next door. All efforts to persuade her to talk about what was troubling her had been unsuccessful. She thanked him for his hospitality but appeared to be in a kind of trance, as though she did not really know where she was. She was very uncommunicative and withdrawn.

Once in bed and alone, the horror of what she had heard took on its full significance. The hushed voices now seemed to be screaming and reverberating in her ears:

"Neal's sister, Neal's sister!"

Suzannah, she thought to herself, *is Neal's sister*, and suddenly she had a vision of Neal making love to Suzannah, removing her clothes, fondling her naked breasts, touching her in the intimate places he had touched her, kissing her mouth, her neck, her breasts... The vision was so repugnant to her that she began to cry louder than ever until she became quite hysterical. Aidan came in and begged her to talk to him but her lips were sealed. This was such a dreadful and shameful episode in her life that she could discuss it with no-one.

Eventually she slept, but fitfully, disturbed at frequent intervals by the vision of Neal and Suzannah in bed together, naked, loving one another passionately, and telling herself that for him to have been in bed with her was exactly the same thing, and therefore no less repulsive.

By morning Charlotte was calm enough to ask Aidan to keep her whereabouts secret and to request refuge for another few days. He assented gladly but left for work reluctantly, anxious about leaving her alone in such an obvious state of distress. She spent the day writing to her parents and to Neal, hoping desperately that he would never discover the truth. What could have been a beautiful memory for her had been tarnished for ever by her present knowledge. It didn't need to be like that for Neal. There was no reason for it not to remain with him as a beautiful memory. Even though she now had to recognise the blood relationship between them, she had to admit that they had loved each other deeply and passionately and that, while it lasted, it had been a wonderful experience. She cried herself to sleep again that night, thinking of how they had intended spending the following day, secluded in their own private love-nest at his Yorkshire apartment. Heartbroken, she wondered how Neal would have reacted on finding that she had vanished.

Aidan posted her letters on Saturday, overcoming the urge to read them first. He had always been attracted to Charlotte and he felt that he just needed to be patient. She would eventually come to confide in him. It was some months now since he had asked her to accompany him to a party and she had refused on the grounds that she was already dating Neal Ashby. Now he had renewed hope. Whatever Neal had done must have been really dreadful for Charlotte to have reacted so violently.

Late that night Charlotte awoke, screaming hysterically, the vision of brother and sister engaging in sexual activity stronger than ever. Aidan rushed to her bedside and tried to comfort her, soothing her fevered brow with a damp sponge. The hysteria faded away.

"It would surely help if you talked about it, Charley. Don't bottle it up. Let me try to help you," he said.

"I can't tell you, Ade. I'm sorry. You've been so good to me but it's something I just can't talk about." "Can I do anything to help?"

She hesitated, and then whispered,

"Stay with me."

He was not sure whether he understood until she repeated it.

"Sleep with me. Make love to me."

He could scarcely believe she had really said it. There was nothing in the world he would like more but he couldn't. Could he? She was still so distraught, so vulnerable.

"Please Ade."

It was very tempting, so very tempting. His body was already aroused in anticipation, throbbing with excitement. She was no longer hysterical. She knew what she was doing. He climbed in beside her, turned off the light, and took her in his arms. Having no night clothes with her, she was completely naked. Aidan discarded his own pyjamas and began to make love to her. She shuddered with pleasure, or was it fear? He kissed her and she responded, but without passion. Aidan was puzzled. It was as though she was resigned to what was happening but did not really want it. He tried to stop but she held him closer, imploring him to continue and began to move with him with a sudden intensity of desire that alarmed him. It was all over very quickly.

"Oh Charley," he said, "I've wanted to do that for so long."

Charlotte said nothing. She closed her eyes tightly to stop the tears from coming. All she could think to herself was,

It was better with Neal, so much better with my own brother.

Charlotte had hoped that being with another man would help her to forget but the effect of Aidan's intimacy was quite the reverse. She spent the remainder of the night longing for Neal, crying out for him in her heart. Determined, however, to obliterate the memories which were at once so beautiful yet now so painful, she slept with Aidan again the following night. He treated her very lovingly and tenderly but when he became more amorous, she felt sullied and ashamed, repelled, disgusted with herself. She had always liked Aidan and she was so grateful to him for his kindness over this dreadful weekend. Why then did his love-making make her feel so indecent? With Neal it had been wonderful and exciting. Even now that she knew of the impediment to their relationship, she remembered their intimacy as a thing of beauty yet with Aidan it was ugly and repulsive. It should have been the other way round. She tried to hide these feelings but Aidan was not fooled.

"What's wrong, Charley?" he asked gently. "Did I hurt you?"

"No."

"It's Neal, isn't it? Are you going to go back to him?"

"I can't go back to him… Ever."

"But you still love him?"

He seemed to have accepted this and Charlotte had to come clean.

"Yes, I still love him. I'm so sorry, Ade. I didn't mean to use you and hurt you. I thought… I hoped that I could have loved you. I wanted to love you but I … I… I don't. I love Neal."

Slowly Aidan rolled away from her. He made no comment, kept his feelings to himself.

Soon after her avowal and believing Charlotte to be asleep, Aidan slipped back to his bed on the sofa. Gratefully she heard him go. She knew that it had been wrong of her to encourage him. He had only slept with her at her own request and she had treated him very badly in return for his kindness. Anyone else would have kicked her out and rightly so. What right did she have to be still lying in his comfortable bed while he made do with the sofa? She lay awake all night until, at six o'clock in the morning, she decided to tell him the truth. Wrapping herself in his dressing gown, which was hanging on the back of the door, she slipped into the living room. Aidan looked up in surprise as she entered.

"I see you haven't been able to sleep either," she said meekly. "I'm sorry."

He didn't answer so she continued:

"I owe you an explanation, Ade."

"That is somewhat of an understatement, Charley. You have humiliated me, you know. I've been thinking it over all night. I don't understand what is going on but I was only trying to help. What you did to me was very cruel. I would never have believed you could be such a bitch."

His words upset her but she knew that she deserved his wrath.

"I know it was cruel and I am mortified at my own behaviour," she said softly, in a conciliatory tone. "Will you please let me explain? You have every right to be angry with me."

She looked directly at him when he didn't answer her.

"Ade, I can only tell you why I have left Neal if you promise me never to repeat it to anyone."

Aidan was intrigued despite himself. He would at least hear her out.

"I promise," he said, sitting up to make room for her to sit on the sofa beside him.

Sadly Charlotte told him about the conversation she had overheard on Thursday night just before fleeing from the house and rushing into his arms. He listened, aghast, trying desperately to think of something he could say to console her but he could find no appropriate words.

"I didn't mean to use you, Ade," she concluded. "I was so confused, so ashamed, so desperately lonely. I wanted to love someone else. Please forgive me for treating you so badly. I'm really sorry."

Aidan squeezed her hand.

"Of course I forgive you," he said gently. "I understand now why you did it. I'm glad you confided in me, Charley. I won't tell anyone."

"Can we still be friends?" she asked tentatively.

"Always," whispered Aidan, kissing her on the cheek.

Charlotte had spent one more night under Aidan Quinn's roof but was now back in her own home to collect some items she needed. Thankfully she discarded the clothes she had been wearing for over five days, changing into a comfortable pair of jeans and a sweater. She ticked off the items on her prepared list as she packed them into a small suitcase. Then, checking that she had her credit card in her handbag, she took a final, wistful look at her room, went downstairs, and slipped out quietly, leaving a note for her mother on the hall table.

Chapter 26

Neal ordered another pint, then another ……and another. Never in his life had he felt so miserable, so confused, so angry. Charlotte had turned up at last. She refused to offer him any kind of explanation, refused to disclose where she had been, had heartlessly returned his ring with a few words of polite apology. He just could not comprehend what had happened. As he drank yet another beer, he involuntarily glanced around him, taking in his surroundings. Who was that man drinking alone, like himself, a few tables away? His mind and his vision were blurred with excess alcohol but that face was familiar. He did not want to meet anyone, had purposely chosen a strange bar, not frequented by his circle of friends, where he could drown his sorrows in peace. But he knew that face. Instinctively he knew it was the face of a man he loathed, a man he despised. Yes, he remembered now. It was Richard Walkington.

Neal stared at him. He looked pathetic, utterly wretched. Their eyes met and Richard nodded in recognition. His face was pale and expressionless. Neal rose on a sudden impulse and moved across to his table.

"You don't look too good," he said. "Can I get you another drink?"

Richard looked surprised.

"Haven't you heard about me?" he asked bitterly. "No-one else is speaking to me, let alone buying me drinks."

"I've heard what happened," Neal answered. "Do you want to talk about it?"

"No."

"You can't just forget it."

"Do I look as if I'm likely to forget?" he retorted coldly. "I have lost my wife, my very parents have disowned me, my 'friends' want nothing to do with me, parents are refusing to have their daughters in my class. I'll never forget, never till the day I die. I know what I did and I'm paying for it."

He shuddered. His voice was trembling. He had been drinking heavily, had consumed even more than Neal.

"You heard it from Susan, I suppose."

"Yes."

"What exactly did she say?"

"That she liked you. She hoped it wasn't true."

"And later? When she knew it was?"

"She has hardly spoken of it."

"But she told you what I did?"

Although Richard had said that he did not want to talk about it, he seemed to have a morbid desire to relive the incident, to recall the details of his actions. Neal thought of Stephanie and his blood boiled. He had not seen her since the day Charlotte disappeared and the vision he had now was of the evening he had visited her in hospital. He remembered her swollen face.

"I know what you did," he said. "Do you really want me to spell it out? I know how you attacked your wife like an animal and continued to beat her when she couldn't defend herself. I know how you killed her baby and nearly killed her too."

Richard flinched.

"Baby?" he said. "Who said anything about a baby?"

"Wasn't she pregnant?"

Richard hesitated a moment before admitting it.

"I didn't think they knew about that in school," he said.

"But surely that was the whole reason for your assault? You knew that she was expecting someone else's baby."

"It wasn't as simple as that, though that in itself would have been bad enough. How would you feel if your girlfriend suddenly conceived another man's child?"

"I haven't got a girlfriend," slurred Neal in reply to this. His head was beginning to spin. "She's left me."

"Oh, I'm sorry."

Richard looked again Neal's dishevelled appearance, so out of character for someone who usually looked so pristine, at the row of empty glasses on the table where he had been sitting.

"That explains a lot," he said. "I really am sorry."

"I love her," Neal now said miserably. "You ask me what I would have done in your shoes. I don't know. But I do know that I would not have harmed her. I could never do that. I love her."

Richard frowned and sighed loudly.

"You imply that I do not love my wife," he said.

Neal laughed scornfully.

"Can you deny it?"

"YES." He almost shouted it. "That's why it hurt me so much."

He lowered his voice again.

"Look," he said. "I'm not trying to make excuses but perhaps you will understand if I tell you the whole story. God, I'll go mad if I don't tell somebody. We had been going through a bad patch for some time, ever since a friend of Stephanie's died. She seemed to resent the fact that I still had my friends. Then I forgot her birthday and she never forgave me for that. I know that was a dreadful thing to do especially when she was so down but I really tried to make it up to her afterwards. She just wouldn't let it go. She had drifted into a state of acute depression and had withdrawn from me completely, refusing to let me even touch her. When I tried to get intimate she begged me to leave her alone so eventually I did. You see, Stephanie already had a nervous breakdown some years ago but she had made a full recovery or so I thought. This was the first time problems had recurred."

Neal was beginning to feel very uncomfortable.

Richard continued his story:

"Then everything suddenly changed again. For about a week leading up to the day, …the day it happened, she became more like her own self again. When I arrived home that day she had prepared a special meal, my favourite, and proceeded to serve it up in a nice, romantic atmosphere. Candlelight, soft music, the lot. We must have drunk a full bottle of wine each. She had had her hair done and was wearing a new, sexy dress. Afterwards I was just wondering whether I dared hope that we could resume relations when she stepped out of the dress, which was all she had been wearing, and *she* enticed *me* into bed."

Neal took a deep breath, remembering his own experience. This sounded authentic. He listened as Richard continued:

"The next hour was pure heaven. She more than made up for the months we had lost. It was wonderful. She said she was sorry, she was feeling quite well again. We had great sex. Then suddenly she said she would love to have a baby and we had sex again for good measure. I was over the moon."

Richard paused, took a long drink, shuddered at the memory of what came next. His voice wobbled:

"Then it happened. She was in the bathroom. I began to tidy up the clothes I had taken off and I found one of her earrings on the floor. I opened the drawer where she keeps her jewellery to put it in the box and there it was staring up at me…a pregnancy testing kit, already used, showing positive. Beside it was a letter from some doctor, not our regular one, confirming the positive result. She was already pregnant with some man's bastard!"

Richard's eyes showed the depth of his humiliation and his regret over his subsequent actions.

"I've misjudged you," said Neal humbly. "I'm sorry, mate."

"It wasn't just the fact that she was pregnant. It was all the scheming to trick me into believing that it was mine. Can you imagine how that felt? I really thought that she loved me again, that all our troubles were over.

God, she put on a good act. And it was all a sham, just to cover up some sordid affair she'd had. She didn't love me. She just wanted me to accept that child she was having, believe it was mine, give it love and affection all my life. I don't mean that I couldn't love someone else's child in different circumstances. It's the deceit that I couldn't stand. She tried to deceive me for my whole life! Just imagine if that child had survived. She would have pretended that she could see a likeness to me, pretended that it took after me in some way just to prolong the lie, when all the time she would have known the identity of its real father, would have seen his likeness in its face, its expressions. Do you call that love? If only she had confessed to me what she had done, I don't know, I'll never know, but I might have been able to forgive her, might have been able to accept the child. Can you understand what I'm saying? It was the deceit, the sham of her love-making that filled me with rage, that made me lose control of my senses. I struck her in anger, I admit that, and she fell awkwardly, hitting her face against the open drawer. I panicked. There was blood. For a moment my love turned to hate and I…I…I hit her, …I just went on hitting her. It was as if someone else had taken control of my hands. I wanted to stop but I couldn't. I regretted it immediately. I don't know what I should have done, but not that, not that, not that."

He looked earnestly at Neal: "What would you have done in my place?"

"I don't know. Maybe the same as you did. She certainly asked for trouble."

Neal thought of his own relationship with Stephanie. She had appeared to be totally honest with him but he knew now that she had not told him everything. He had no doubt that Richard was telling the truth. His distress was only too obvious, his remorse, his broken heart. Stephanie had even tried to imply that Richard had lost interest in her because he was gay. Neal could see now that this was not true either. Neal had several gay friends and acquaintances. Richard was not the least bit like them. He was in love with his wife. Richard's voice broke in again on his thoughts:

"I should have gone for her lover, of course, but would you believe it, she's protecting the bastard, she won't tell me who he is. Maybe it's just as well. I would kill him!"

Neal winced and felt very uncomfortable. Quickly he finished his drink and ordered yet another round. For a time nothing was said. They were both pretty drunk but Neal was still able to rationalise the situation in his head. Richard was no longer the despicable villain in his eyes, Stephanie no longer the sweet and innocent neglected wife. He was confused. He had never intended to become involved with her but he had let it happen. How could he not have seen that she was at least very depressed, if not indeed mentally ill? He could see it now. He was very much to blame for Richard's plight.

"Why don't you go to see her?" he said at last, remembering the photograph which Stephanie had replaced soon after her convalescence. "I'm sure you will find that she has forgiven you. She's probably as unhappy as you are about the separation. It will soon be in the past, forgotten."

"I wish I could believe that. I'll think about it. Maybe …"

"Don't waste any more time thinking. Go now, before you change your mind."

"I can't. I promised her that I would never come to the house without warning. I'll not break that promise. I don't want to frighten her."

He looked at Neal, as though weighing up something in his mind.

"Unless," he added, "unless I was accompanied. Would you come with me, just until she sees that I mean her no harm?"

"**NO!**"

The answer was so firm and abrupt that Neal realised it might arouse suspicion if he did not offer some kind of excuse but what could he say? Colour flooded into his cheeks and he began to perspire all over. Richard noticed his discomfort immediately but thankfully had drunk too much by now to pick up on the guilt-ridden panic.

"Sorry," he said. "I shouldn't have embarrassed you like that. Of course you don't want to mediate between a man and his wife, people you hardly know. I've said far too much already. You must be bored to death. It's the drink. It makes me talk. Would you believe I'm really very shy! And yet here I am telling you intimate details about my marriage."

Neal spoke hurriedly, before he would lose the courage:

"I'll go alone if you wish. I'll tell her that I've spoken to you and let her know how you feel, assure her that she has nothing to fear from you. I just couldn't be present when you are together. I'm sorry. I just couldn't."

Richard smiled for the first time.

"I'd appreciate that," he said.

"Tell me," said Neal, "why were you so surprised that I knew about the baby? Why should you have tried to keep that secret when it was the whole cause of what happened?"

Richard stared at the table as he experienced intense chagrin and an overwhelming desire to turn back the clock. He lifted a beer mat and turned it over and over in his hand.

"Partly shame that I killed it," he said, "partly humiliation that it existed, partly a desire to protect Stephanie. She'd been punished far more than she deserved already. I didn't want to be seen to be making excuses for myself."

"But these people who have disowned you, your own parents you said, what reason have you given them for your behaviour?"

"None really. They guessed that she had been unfaithful."

"Have you told anyone else what you told me here tonight?"

"No, nobody. I must admit I feel better for having spoken of it. You're a good bloke, Neal, a damn good bloke."

"If you've any sense, you'll go and make it up with your parents. Tell them what you told me and don't try to be so noble. Everyone makes mistakes and you were pushed beyond your limits. Have you any special message for Stephanie?"

Without further ado, Richard asked a passing barman for pen and paper and scribbled a note for Neal to deliver to his wife. He folded it over and added the address in case he would have forgotten where they lived. Then the two men parted company quite cordially, each somewhat intoxicated but at least in better spirits than when they had entered the bar. There is nothing like someone else's problems to take your mind off your own.

★ ★ ★

It was late when Neal arrived at Stephanie's house. She answered the door in a soft, pink negligee after looking out to see who could be calling at such an hour.

"Neal!" she exclaimed with undisguised pleasure. "I thought you had given me up altogether."

He stepped inside and slumped down into the nearest chair. It had been a long walk.

"You don't look well," she said.

No answer.

"Have you been out with Charlotte?"

Stephanie's innocent question merely served to magnify his intense loneliness.

"No," he answered sadly. She's left me. She's left me, Stephanie, and she won't even say why."

The heavy drinking and mental agony of the evening had been too much for him so that now he broke down altogether and wept. Stephanie touched him gently on the shoulder and knelt down beside him. She laid her head on his lap, very seductively, and waited until he was calm.

"Can I do anything?" she then asked, looking straight into his eyes.

Neal wished he had not drunk so much though he did feel better after his outburst. He put his hand into his pocket to give her Richard's note just as she, misunderstanding the reason for his visit, began to unbutton his shirt. His head swimming, he left the note untouched and gently pulled open the satin ribbon at the neck of her negligee. Underneath she was wearing a flimsy low-cut nightdress, through which he could clearly see the dark shadow of her nipples. He buried his face in her warm breast, breathing in the sweet fragrance of her body.

"Oh, Neal!" she sighed.

"This isn't what I came here for," he managed to say, his words somewhat slurred.

"But it's what you want."

He could not deny it, not while she knelt there in that provocative nightdress, speaking to him in those soft, sexy tones.

"Yes, it's want I want," he breathed.

Stephanie extinguished the light and together they entered the bedroom.

★ ★ ★

Neal slept late into the morning. When he did open his eyes he found himself alone and was glad of the opportunity to gather his thoughts, to examine his conscience. He was desperately ashamed of his own weakness. He had betrayed the trust of someone he really liked. Slowly he pulled on his clothes without even bothering to wash and then made his way to the kitchen, where he stood awkwardly at the door until Stephanie noticed him. He was reluctant to speak first yet anxious to get it over with. She was sitting at the table, drinking a cup of coffee. He cleared his throat. She jumped and turned to face him, smiling.

"Thank you for letting me sleep," he said. "I needed it."

Silence.

"Too much to drink last night," he added, as though a further explanation were necessary.

"I'll get you some breakfast," she now said. "Bacon and egg OK?"

"No, thank you," he said, walking towards her. "I don't want anything. I must get home."

She looked surprised. It was Saturday.

"I'll not be back," he added.

Now she looked alarmed.

"Why? Oh, don't leave me now, Neal, not after last night."

"Last night was nothing," he snapped, more sharply than he intended. "We were two hurt and lonely people who gave each other comfort. We used each other. I was very drunk. It meant nothing, nothing at all."

Stephanie opened her mouth to speak but no words came.

"I'm sorry about last night," Neal continued, more kindly. "I was distraught; I didn't know what I was doing."

At these words, Stephanie burst into tears.

"You knew what you were doing all right," she sobbed. "You made love to me, real love, not just sex like before. You were loving and gentle and passionate. You said you loved me…"

Here he interrupted her.

"I did not."

"You did."

"I did not." Neal was adamant.

"Well, you implied it. I thought you did. I love *you*, Neal."

She flung her arms around him and clung to him like a child clinging to its mother, still sobbing, her voice muffled:

"It was the best night of my life."

Gently, but firmly, Neal took a step back and pushed her away from him.

"Better than your wedding night?" he said. "Was I better than Richard?"

She stopped crying and stared at him, wiping the tears from her cheek with the back of her hand.

"Don't you love me at all, Neal?"

"In a way. I love you in that I care what happens to you and I want you to be happy, but not as a lover, a partner for life. That's the way I love Charlotte, even if she has left me. I'll always love her and I'm desperate to get her back. Last night was a mistake and I'm sorry for it, Stephanie."

A mistake? Her wonderful dreams shattered before they had hardly begun? A mere mirage in a waterless desert?

"So what am I supposed to do now?" she asked miserably.

Neal took a deep breath.

"Go back to Richard," he said. "He's a good man and he loves you very much."

Stephanie was appalled. How could he have become so callous?

"You've certainly changed your tune!" she retorted. "You were supposed to be protecting me from him."

"That was before I got to know him. You don't need my protection any more. You never did. He wouldn't harm a hair on your head again and well you know it."

Stephanie stared at him in total amazement.

"It would never have happened if you had been honest with him."

"I know," she sighed, covering her face with her hands as she realised that he knew the whole truth.

"Do you know why I came here last night?"

Neal took the hastily written, crumpled note from his pocket.

"I brought you this message from Richard."

Stephanie's heart began to thump wildly.

"He doesn't know about ……about us?" she asked, alarmed.

As Neal reassured her on that point, she glanced at the message in her hands. Her address was indeed formed in Richard's distinctive handwriting. Carefully she unfolded the note and silently read the words he had written. Her eyes filled up with tears. They rolled down her cheeks and unto the table. Neal was almost jealous as he watched her love for Richard return, love she had repressed, had been afraid to admit, even to herself. For a moment he was glad that he had slept with her. It should not have happened but it had been a very pleasant way to end their relationship, just so long as Richard never found out.

The telephone rang. Stephanie wiped her eyes again, letting the precious note fall from her hand as she went into the hall to answer it. Neal had at least reserved enough honour last night not to read the note he came to deliver but now, as it lay open in front of him on the kitchen table, he could not resist glancing at it.

My darling Stephanie,
    Do you remember Devon? It could be like that again.
Please give me another chance. Please. I love you so much.
    Your devoted husband,
    Richard.

It was just a few simple words but all that was needed to break down the wall she had built around her true feelings. Neal heard her lift the phone.

"Hello Richard," she said softly.

A pause.

"Yes, he was here. I've read your note."

Another pause.

"Oh Richard, I love you too. I've missed you so much. Of course you can come home."

Neal scribbled a note of his own.

Goodbye Stephanie and good luck.

Then, without a backwards glance, he slipped quietly out of the back door.

2012

Chapter 27

"The Horseshoe Inn. Good morning. You're through to Maxine. How can I help you?"

"Good morning, Maxine. Am I too late to make a reservation for this evening? A table for two, please."

"I'll just check for you now, sir. What time would you be arriving?"

"About eight. We would like to eat at about half past."

Maxine consulted the reservations chart and pencilled in the new booking.

"That will be fine, sir. Can I take your name and contact number, please?"

"Matthews. Dr and Mrs Matthews."

Derrick gave Maxine his contact number and put the phone back in his pocket, glad that they had been able to accept his booking at such short notice. He had intended to phone yesterday but two emergency cases had arisen so that it had completely slipped his mind. There were of course other equally good restaurants but, since it was their first wedding anniversary, he particularly wanted to take Susan back to the Horseshoe, where they had first eaten together. Indeed, it was during coffee at that first meal that he had proposed to her and had happily been accepted.

Since that memorable night his life had changed dramatically. His work in the surgery was as important to him as it always had been but it was no longer the sole focus of his existence. He now looked forward with pleasure to his free evenings, when his young partner, Damien Wells, was on call, evenings which used to seem so long and lonely ever since that far-off time when he had lost his first wife and baby son. For fifteen years he had believed implicitly that he would never find anyone to replace Catherine, that his days for romantic love were over. But then Susan Lovell had walked into his life. He had met her in such unhappy circumstances, and as a patient, that for some time, he did not dare to recognise the feelings he had for her as love. He pitied her and wanted to help her, just as he tried to help other patients who came to him with depression and other nervous complaints. He was a great believer in talking things over, in providing a confidential ear for those who had something worrying them, something they could not discuss with their own family members or friends. But he did not generally visit them at home, out of hours. With Susan he had felt a compulsive urge, right from the start, to share her troubles with her. He had started calling at the house regularly when he finally admitted to himself that he was in love. He had encouraged her to register with a different doctor to leave his way clear for the romantic involvement he craved. Now they had been married for a year and he wanted to give her a special treat – an evening to remember. He still had a few minutes before surgery was due to begin so he phoned her to relay the arrangements.

"That will be lovely, Darling," said Susan. "I'll be ready for seven-thirty. Have a good day in the meantime."

"You too, my dear. Bye for now."

"Bye."

Like Derrick, Susan also spent many happy hours that day, reminiscing over the past year and the changes it had brought about in her life. She now worked part-time so that she could be around when Derrick needed her. His work could not be confined to certain time limits. Quite often he was called out during the night or would have to work prolonged hours during the day. Patients did not always recover from serious illnesses and Susan felt that she could be a comfort to him on occasions when he had to deliver bad news or when someone he had cared for died in spite of his treatment or intervention. She had transformed his home, which had been sadly lacking a woman's touch for so long. While many modern men's homes may not require a woman's touch, Susan knew that Derrick had relied heavily on Catherine in the past and had never really been comfortable living on his own. He functioned best as part of a couple. So did she. And what an exciting year they had just enjoyed as a couple. The house had new colourful furnishings in every room and the bathroom had been completely overhauled with modern white and chrome fittings and dove-grey tiles. Plans were under way for an extension to include a large kitchen and conservatory, opening on to the garden which they both loved so much. Susan spent a good deal of her free time tending to the pansies, periwinkles, lavenders, heathers and various colourful alpine plants in the herbaceous borders beneath the pretty, flowering cherry, magnolia and lilac trees, which surrounded the lawn.

She would never forget the tragic circumstances which had led her to meet and get to know Derrick. In causing heartbreak to her own daughter, she herself had found happiness. She often wondered how Steven and Janine Jamison had persuaded Charlotte to break off her engagement to Neal. Charlotte had disappeared for almost four weeks and, on her return, was quite adamant that there was no point in discussing the situation. She had assured Neal that there was no-one else involved, had said that she simply did not want to be married. Poor Neal had taken it very badly. She remembered well the day he was discharged from hospital, covered in cuts and bruises to his face, and the day a few weeks later when he walked away from the law court, having been suspended from driving for eighteen months. His lovely yellow car, which had been his pride and joy, had to be towed to his parents' home in Yorkshire. She wasn't sure whether it had ever been repaired. Susan recalled how she had wished he were not still living under her roof because she had to witness daily the heartbreak that she had caused. Her worst moment of all came one evening at supper when, close to tears, he suddenly chose to confide in her, telling her how much he still loved Charlotte and how he could not face the future without her.

Susan recalled also the embarrassment Neal had caused her over the Richard Walkington affair. Richard had spoken to her privately one day after their other colleagues had gone home. She had discovered him lurking nervously around her door, just as Chris had done all those years ago, the day when he had first asked her for a date.

"Was there something you wanted to see me about, Richard?" she had asked.

It all came back to her, as though it had been yesterday…

Richard cleared his throat and came into the room. She sensed that he was trying to find the right words. Everyone was a bit wary of Richard since the alleged attack on his wife and he had become a bit of a recluse. No charges, however, had ever been preferred against him and the couple appeared to have settled their differences and were once more living together, had been for some time. Nevertheless, many people had been very unforgiving. Susan herself wasn't sure how she felt about him.

"Stephanie and I are going to have a baby," he said at last.

Susan looked up and smiled.

"Oh, that *is* good news, Richard. I'm glad things have worked out for you."

He stood there awkwardly. He obviously had something more to say.

"I do love Stephanie, you know. It'll be different this time."

Susan looked confused.

"Did Neal ever tell you what really happened the last time?"

"Neal?"

"Your lodger, Neal. He was very good to me. He helped us to get back together."

"That's strange," said Susan, bemused. "He has never mentioned it."

"Would you tell him my news? I think he'd be interested."

He paused for a moment.

"And tell him I said thanks for everything. He'll know what I mean."

"I'll tell him," Susan smiled. "I didn't even know he had kept in touch with you. But I'm glad you're friends. Neal is very special to me."

"He's a good bloke, Susan."

Susan was puzzled. Neal had never even shown particular interest or passed comment any time she had mentioned Richard in the house. She certainly hadn't been aware that they had become friends. Why had he not mentioned it? Come to think of it, he had appeared to deliberately change the subject several times when Richard's name was mentioned. She had put it down to boredom, had decided that Neal didn't really like him.

Richard was still hovering around, looking uncomfortable. His skin was twitching.

"Susan," he said at last, "do you mind if I ask you something?"

"Go ahead." She could see he was still bothered about something.

He looked embarrassed.

"I just wondered how you knew about the baby the last time."

"I'm sorry," Susan said, genuinely baffled. "You've lost me."

"The last time, when Stephanie lost the baby."

"I didn't know she'd lost a baby, Richard."

"But you told Neal about it."

"I assure you, Richard, I have no idea what you are talking about."

"The time I … the time I… I … "

He couldn't bring himself to say it. Susan left her desk and put a motherly arm around him.

"I didn't know she was pregnant then," she said, softly. "Don't torment yourself. It's all in the past now. If Stephanie can forgive you, so can I."

"But you don't understand, Susan."

He was fighting to hold back the tears.

"She *was* pregnant, but it wasn't mine."

"Oh, I see," Susan said, sympathetically.

"I'm not excusing what I did to Stephanie. I just can't understand how you knew about it, about the baby, I mean. No-one else on the staff seems to know about it."

"I *didn't* know. Honestly Richard, I didn't know. You don't seem to believe me. How could I have known about it? I don't even know Stephanie."

"Then how did Neal know?"

Susan shuddered even now as she remembered how the truth, the only possible explanation, had dawned on both Richard and herself at exactly the same moment. She relived the ugly scene that same evening when Neal arrived home. He called a greeting to her as usual, as he headed for his room. Susan waited until he was half-way up the stairs.

"Richard Walkington asked me to give you a message

today," she called, and watched with bated breath to observe his reaction.

He stopped dead and listened. Then realising that she was not going to shout the message upstairs, he came back down and entered the lounge, looking rather sheepishly towards his landlady.

Trying her best to sound casual, she said,

"He wanted you to know that his wife is expecting a baby."

"Oh, that's nice," replied Neal, relieved. "Tell him I said congratulations."

He turned round to go back upstairs, hoping to avoid a prolonged conversation about Richard.

"You hypocrite!" screamed Susan, showing her true feelings now, her blood suddenly boiling with rage. "Is that all you have to say to him?"

Neal realised with dismay that he had been found out. He felt like a schoolboy who had been caught cheating in an exam. He didn't know what to say.

Finally he blurted out, "I didn't think Stephanie would have betrayed me."

"She didn't." Susan turned away from him in disgust. "I did. Now get out of my sight, Neal."

Normally the motherly affection shown him by his landlady was something Neal valued but this prying into his private affairs struck him as being offensive.

"Surely my relationship with Richard and Stephanie is my concern. I'd prefer to keep it that way. My morals are none of your business."

"It *is* my business. Richard is a friend of mine. I introduced the two of you."

"You haven't let me explain. You don't understand the circumstances."

Susan ignored this remark.

"And what's more, if I remember correctly, this all happened while you were still engaged to Charlotte. No wonder she got out! I'm glad she left you now. She deserves better."

Neal paled visibly.

"This has nothing to do with Charlotte and it has nothing to do with you. But I *am* sorry if I have embarrassed you at work."

"Nothing to do with me!" She almost screamed it at him. "Charlotte is my…"

She stopped herself just in time.

"Charlotte is my… type. I liked her very much. And you abused her trust."

Neal hung his head in shame.

"Stephanie needed me," he said. "I know I made a mess of things but I've tried to make amends. I like Richard too. I really do."

"Stop trying to defend yourself. I'm disgusted with you."

She looked straight at him:

"Like father, like son," she said, her voice full of contempt.

Neal pulled a face.

"What does that mean? What has my father got to do with it?"

It had just slipped out. Susan thought quickly. How could she have been so careless?

"Oh, it's just an expression about men in general," she bluffed. "It's time they used their brains first before blighting the lives of women. It happens all the time."

"That's a very cynical view. Stephanie started it, not me, for your information. And Charlotte doesn't know what she wants. She has blighted *my* life."

Susan was exasperated. She was so disappointed in her 'adopted son'. She had idolised him and he had let her down so badly.

"Get out of my sight," she repeated, "and out of my house. You're not welcome here any more."

Neal obediently went to his room and began to pack his belongings. He had no idea where he was going to spend the night but he knew that he couldn't stay here. Mrs Lovell's strength of feeling on the matter had alarmed him and the knowledge that Richard himself now knew of his part in the whole sordid affair terrified him. His bags packed, he sat down on the bed to gather his thoughts. Ten or fifteen minutes passed.

"Neal?"

It was almost a whisper at the door.

"May I come in, please?"

Susan had composed herself and was now feeling quite calm again.

"You're right," she said simply, entering the room and sitting down beside him. "This is none of my business. Nobody's perfect, least of all me."

She hesitated.

"I once did something dreadful, something far worse than you have done. I've a nerve to criticize you."

Neal wondered what she meant. He still felt very uncomfortable.

"Please stay, Neal. I spoke in haste. I don't want you to leave."

He didn't want to leave either.

"Please, Neal. Don't take this the wrong way, but you're very special to me. I think of you as a son, you know."

"I know you do. I like having two mums. I promise I won't do anything to embarrass you like that again."

Relief was obvious in her expression.

"That's all it was," she agreed, "embarrassment – none of my business really. You sort it out with Richard. I'll keep out of it."

She came closer and patted him gently on the shoulder.

"I'm so sorry for bringing Charlotte into it," she said softly. "You say things you don't mean when you get worked up into a temper."

"Charlotte." He breathed her name softly and sighed, closing his eyes.

"You know, sometimes you remind me of Charlotte."

"I'll take that as a compliment," smiled Susan.

She was on the point of leaving him to unpack again, when she stopped on the threshold and looked him in the eye.

"I do understand how you feel, Neal. I know what it's like to lose someone you love," she said gently, a faraway look in her eyes, "to be left wondering why and trying to make sense of it all."

Neal's face reddened with embarrassment.

"Oh God, of course you do. I'm so sorry. I suppose it's

because you were already a widow when I first met you that I never really stopped to think what you must have been through. It must have been awful losing your husband like that. I suddenly feel very guilty for not being more understanding, for only thinking about myself."

Susan smiled.

"If there's anyone who should be feeling guilty, it's me. It wasn't actually my late husband I was thinking of," she admitted.

"No?"

Neal was intrigued.

"I loved someone else, years before I met him. He left me for another woman."

"But you got over it. You married someone else."

"It took a long time, Neal. I never really got over it completely because, like you, I couldn't understand why it had happened. It was so sudden."

She finally left him to rearrange his belongings, make the room his again.

"I'm just saying that I do understand how upset you are," she said as she left the room. "I've been there myself."

Whether Richard had ever confronted Neal over the affair with his wife, she did not know. She had kept her word and refrained from any further interference in his private business…

When Susan sold her house and married Derrick, Neal had been forced to seek alternative accommodation and it was over a year now since she had seen him, a year during which she had been very happy. The wedding itself had been a fairly low-key event but Kathleen had flown in from

Australia and had spent a fortnight with her daughter. It had been great to catch up with all that was happening in her life and fantastic to see that she was so happy with Brandon. It was wonderful having someone to care for again, someone who needed her just as she needed him. They had spent a fabulous holiday in Italy, exploring the Amalfi coastline and relaxing in the hot sunshine by a lovely pool surrounded by pink, white and red oleander trees in Sorrento. Susan often found herself comparing the three men in her life and concluded that she loved them all equally. She talked openly about her life with Chris and remembered him lovingly, just as her husband often spoke of Catherine and their life together before her untimely death. And even after all the distress she and those she loved so dearly had suffered on his account, she still retained fond memories of Jonathan, her first love.

It was after seven when Derrick arrived home, just in time to wash and change before setting off for the restaurant.

"You look lovely, Dear," he told his wife, as he fastened the gold necklace he had bought her round her neck and kissed her lovingly.

"Thank you," she replied happily. "You don't look too bad yourself!"

Indeed he was looking very much better than he had done when he lived alone. He now took much more notice of his dress and general appearance and was keeping to a much healthier diet. Many people had remarked that he looked ten years younger.

By half past eight they were sitting at an attractively laid table and had ordered their first courses. Susan was glad that her husband had brought her back to the place where he had proposed to her. They were sitting at the very same table. She thought it was a lovely room. Cream and beige chintz curtains hung by the windows, toning in perfectly with the rich carpet which was patterned in various shades of yellow and gold. Soft music playing in the background, lively but not intrusive, and subdued lighting provided by pretty lanterns on the walls and candles on the tables all added to the romantic atmosphere. The napery in the form of fresh, lemon and beige tablecloths and napkins gave the room a smart appearance and an air of cleanliness. Delicious aromas wafted from the open kitchen.

Susan regarded the other people in the restaurant, mainly couples like themselves. There was one large group of about ten at the far end of the room, sitting at a table festooned with pink and purple balloons, one of which had the number 40 on it, and Maxine was showing four young people, who had just arrived, to a circular table in the corner. Susan gave a start as she recognised the two girls in the group. They were Charlotte and Melanie Jamison. Charlotte looked lovely. She was dressed in a long, very elegant, pale green dress with short bell-shaped sleeves. Melanie also looked very pretty in her soft pink but of course it was Charlotte who caught Susan's attention, Charlotte, her own daughter. She looked happy and one of the young men was being very attentive to her. Susan thought they must be celebrating something special; they all looked so smart.

She was so absorbed in what she saw that she did not notice the waitress setting down her carrot and ginger soup. Derrick spoke to her but didn't get a response. He glanced across to the corner where her interest seemed to be focused and he too recognised the two sisters. He reached out and squeezed his wife's hand, wishing now that they had not been able to accept the late booking after all. They could have gone somewhere else.

"I'm sorry, Darling."

"No, I'm all right. She looks happy."

She returned her attention to her husband and said, smiling,

"Sorry, Dear. I'm neglecting you."

She sipped her soup and commented on the delicious flavour, determined that nothing would spoil this special evening for Derrick, who had given her a whole new lease of life since she had married him a year ago today. She ate a slice of homemade rustic bread, fresh from the oven. It complemented the soup perfectly. The aroma from Derrick's garlic prawns was heavenly. She couldn't resist having one. It was scrumptious.

Soon the main course was being served to them. Derrick had ordered a steak, coated in a highly spiced and colourful sauce containing mushrooms, tomatoes and peppers; Susan had chosen a grilled salmon steak, served with a generous helping of hollandaise sauce. When the boiled baby potatoes and freshly prepared green vegetables had been added, their plates were piled high and smelt delicious.

"I never know where to begin with a plateful like this," said Susan, her mouth watering. "I'm always afraid of knocking something off the edge of the plate."

As she spoke, one of Derrick's mushrooms rolled onto the tablecloth and they both laughed. He shifted his plate along a bit to hide the small stain.

"Maybe we should have chosen one of those gourmet restaurants where you get much smaller portions," he remarked.

"You don't get food any tastier than this," Susan said. "You made the right choice. This is perfect."

They didn't converse much while they ate and presently Susan found her gaze once again wandering to the table in the corner, where the four young people were seated. They were all laughing. She focused on Charlotte's radiant face and her heart filled with joy at the thought that she had finally got over her love affair with Neal and had found another boyfriend. She turned her attention to the man sitting next to her. He had a smart, pleasing appearance and a nice smile. Happily Susan took another mouthful of succulent salmon. It was hard to believe that the elegant young lady she had been watching was her very own flesh and blood. She knew of course that she could take no credit for the way she had turned out but secretly prided herself in the knowledge that she had at least given her that pretty face.

"I enjoyed that," said Derrick, setting down his knife and fork.

"It was delicious," agreed Susan.

A young waitress, smartly dressed in black and white and with her long hair neatly tied back in a pony tail, came to clear away their plates, handing them another menu to choose a dessert. Susan could never resist fresh strawberries when in season so she settled for the strawberry flan while Derrick chose the Zabaglione. Yet again both choices proved to be extremely palatable.

While they waited for coffee to be served, Susan excused herself and went to the powder room to freshen up. During her absence Derrick sat absorbed in his own thoughts, reflecting on the happy year he had just spent, until suddenly a voice interrupted him:

"Why, hello there, Dr Matthews."

He looked up at the girl who had stopped by his table.

"Hello, Melanie," he said. "I noticed you and your sister earlier on. You're both looking very well. Are you celebrating something special?"

"My engagement," she announced, proudly holding out her hand so that he could admire her sapphire and diamond ring.

"Well congratulations. I hope you will be very happy. Which is the lucky young man?"

He looked across to where her three companions were still seated.

"Ricky's the one with the blond hair, in the blue and grey shirt, sitting beside the window."

"And the other young man? Is he Charlotte's boyfriend?"

"Not really," Melanie replied, just as Susan, unnoticed, came up behind her.

"She sees a lot of Aidan and likes him very much, but not really as a boyfriend, if you know what I mean. Actually I feel rather sorry for him because he has been in love with her for years but she will never commit to him, or anyone else for that matter; not that she's leading him on – she has told him that it can never lead anywhere, that she will never agree to marry him. You see, as you probably remember, Charlotte was engaged to be married nearly two years ago. Well, she had a terrible shock at that time and she has never got over it. She won't go near a man now, except for Aidan. I've tried to persuade her to go and talk it over with you. You could put her in touch with the right professionals, someone who could …"

Melanie suddenly sensed the presence of someone behind her and, swinging round, she came face to face with Susan.

"Susan, my dear, I think you know Melanie Jamison, one of my patients," said Derrick.

"Yes, indeed."

She tried to smile but her evening had been ruined by what she had just heard.

"Hello, Melanie."

The young girl's face had turned quite pale and she stared, stupefied, at the newcomer.

"Mrs Lovell!" she blurted out at last.

"Matthews," corrected Derrick. "Susan and I have been married for a year today."

"Oh! Congratulations! We all heard that you had got married after a whirlwind romance but I didn't realise it was to someone we knew. Wait till I tell Mum!"

The colour was slowly returning to her cheeks and Susan, completely unaware that she knew of Charlotte's relationship to herself, wondered why she had been so shocked to see her. She concluded that Melanie probably thought that her association with Neal might upset Charlotte, were she to be seen.

"Melanie is out celebrating her engagement to that young fair-haired gentleman in the corner," said Derrick with some trepidation. "We had better not keep her from him any longer."

Susan now offered her congratulations and best wishes and Melanie moved away from their table in the direction of the ladies' room.

Susan and Derrick drank their coffee quickly. They did not feel like prolonging their evening out now. They were almost finished when Melanie, on her way back to rejoin her friends, stopped again at their table. She was close to tears.

"Mrs Lovell, I mean Matthews," she said, "I'm so sorry you overheard what I said. Me and my big mouth again!"

Then, lowering her voice to almost a whisper, she added conspiratorially:

"You see, I know about you being Charlotte's mother. I overheard you talking to Mum and Dad that night."

Susan just looked at her in a daze.

"I'll come and explain everything to you tomorrow," Melanie said gently, as she moved on towards her own table.

"Who was that you were speaking to, Mel?" asked her fiancé, as she retook her place at the table.

"Oh, nobody you know. He's our family doctor."

"Dr Matthews!" exclaimed Charlotte, trying to bring him into focus. "Is that his new wife with him? What's she like?"

"She seems very nice," said Melanie, glad that Charlotte, who was a little short-sighted, could not see the pair clearly.

"Why don't you go and have a good look at her," joked Aidan, laughing at the way she was squinting towards them.

Melanie kicked him under the table but it was too late. Charlotte was already out of her seat.

"I think I will," she said.

She noticed, as she approached their table, that they were just preparing to leave.

"Hello, Doctor," she said. And then she noticed Susan.

"Mrs Lovell! You're not the new Mrs Matthews are you? Gosh! It's a small world!"

Susan wished she could tell her just how true those words were.

"Hello, Charlotte," she said. "It's lovely to see you. How are you?"

It was so formal. If only she could greet her properly with a big hug.

"Not too bad, thank you. Mel mustn't have recognised you."

She hesitated and then faltered:

"I suppose you never see Neal now."

"No, it's been over a year."

"We had some good times in your house."

"Yes, I know."

"I know he was upset when we split up but, believe me, there was a good reason."

Susan felt the colour rise to her cheeks.

"I'm sure there was. Are you happy now?"

"Sometimes."

She smiled wistfully. As mother and daughter said goodbye, each was quite unaware that the other knew at least part of the truth.

Chapter 28

"I felt awful," explained Melanie, "when I realised that you had overheard me last night. You looked devastated. And there was me nearly blurting it all out to your husband of all people!"

True to her word, she had come to Susan's home, choosing a time when she knew that evening surgery would be in progress so that Dr Matthews himself would not be there. Melanie had never been inside the doctor's house before so she wasn't aware of the transformation but she was still very impressed by the fresh, bright, modern furnishings.

"Derrick and I have no secrets," answered Susan, "but I had hoped that Charlotte would have got over Neal by now. She looked cheerful last night."

She hesitated, then added,

"You said that you knew about me being Charlotte's mother. What else do you know?"

"Everything. I'm sorry, Mrs Matthews, but the whole drastic situation is my fault. If I hadn't listened to your conversation that night, Mum and Dad would have thought of some way of persuading her to break with Neal, like you suggested. They never even had the time to think about it. When it all went wrong, I tried to get them to contact you but Mum was against it. I don't think it was right for them to leave you in the dark all this time. I keep thinking how angry I would have been if I thought they had met my real mother and treated her like that."

"It all went wrong? What do you mean?"

Susan dreaded hearing the answer to her question but she had to know.

"I overheard most of what you said that night. I didn't mean to listen at first, honestly, but when I heard the strained voices I couldn't resist the temptation to find out what all the mystery was about. I know I shouldn't have done this and I'm so sorry but later on I was telling my other sisters what I had heard when Charlotte arrived home and overheard us. None of us realised she was there."

Susan paled visibly. She felt quite faint.

"You mean Charlotte has known about me all this time! She knew who I was last night!"

"No, it seems that she didn't hear everything we said. She doesn't know who the visitor to the house was that night, has no idea that you are involved at all. Mum and Dad made us swear not to speak to her about it again and we haven't. But she knows about …"

Melanie looked embarrassed and hesitated:

"She knows about Mr Ashby being her real father."

There was a shocked silence as Susan absorbed the full horror of the information she had just received.

"Charlotte knows!" she stammered at last. "She has known for over a year that Neal is actually her half-brother!"

"Yes."

"And Neal? Does he know too?"

"No. Charlotte insisted that he should never find out."

"How did she react to the news?"

"She took it very badly. She disappeared that night before any of us discovered her; we still don't know where she went. It was nearly a week before she came home for clean clothes and money while everyone was out, and then she went away again for nearly three weeks. She said she just couldn't face people and had to be alone for a while. I don't know where she was but she sent us the odd text message to at least let us know she was safe."

Susan recalled the letter Neal had received. She had wondered how Charlotte had been persuaded to write it. Never had she dreamt that the poor girl knew the truth.

"How has she been since?" Susan now asked Melanie.

"She gets very depressed. She won't talk about it but you can tell it's always on her mind. She avoids Neal like the plague but still talks about him in her sleep. For a long time he tried to make her change her mind. He phoned her every night and saw her every day but she just kept telling him that she didn't want them to get back together until he finally gave up. Then she became more upset than ever. One of her friends told me that she burst into tears one day because Neal walked past her with another girl and didn't speak."

"Has she had no other boyfriends?"

"Just Aidan, the one she was with last night. It seems that he was a comfort to her at the beginning and she confided in him, although I don't understand why she chose him and not one of her girlfriends. It's a very strange relationship. I feel really sorry for him because she is determined that she will never settle down with him even though he is crazy about her. She won't have anything to do with other men. She seems to feel dirty or defiled because of her association with Neal, and yet she's still madly in love with him."

"That's just what I feared," said Susan, miserably.

"I know. I'm sorry. If only I had been out that night … "

"You don't need to keep apologising, Melanie. Don't blame yourself. It was good of you to come and tell me all this. I just wish I had known sooner."

Susan then asked after the rest of the family and discovered that Jayne was now living with Dean and Melanie herself was just about to move in with her fiancé. They planned to get married in a few months' time.

"I don't believe in long engagements," she said happily, while Susan admired her ring and expressed once again her congratulations and best wishes.

Susan was saddened by the news about Charlotte but she did not attach any blame to her sister. She accepted that she would have acted no differently in her place. It was just unfortunate timing. The real fault was her own. There was no getting away from that. Melanie was a lovely girl, so genuine and unpretentious. What a great pity it was Charlotte who had turned out to be the baby she gave up all those years ago, and not her 'twin' sister. If only it had been Melanie.

Chapter 29

The library was very busy. Charlotte, who by now had started working in Steven's company, having successfully achieved her business studies qualifications with flying colours, had received a phone-call asking if she could help out. She still did the odd shift in her former workplace. The examination season was drawing near and students were flocking in to do some last minute revision. Silence reigned in the individual study cubicles, disturbed only by the footsteps of those arriving and leaving, the turning of pages, the tapping of computer keys and the occasional clearing of throats. In the hallway, where Charlotte was on duty, there were repeated requests for the same books, books which formed the basis of various courses and which the more conscientious students would have bought, downloaded or borrowed and digested months ago. Long queues of undergraduates waited impatiently for the photocopying machines and printers to obtain their own copies of articles which were available for reference only. A steady flow of students went in and out of the adjoining coffee bar for a welcome break from their studies.

Charlotte was kept busy most of the time but, when things became slack for a few minutes, she found her thoughts reverting to the previous evening. She had enjoyed herself and was genuinely happy for her sister but she was feeling increasingly guilty for seeing so much of Aidan Quinn. She felt safe with him. He understood her fluctuating moods and had been a tower of strength to her when she most needed someone, helping her to come to terms with her unhappy situation. Her parents and sisters had avoided talking about it, afraid of hurting her still further or at least prolonging the agony. But she had to talk about it and Aidan had provided a sympathetic ear and an abundance of good advice. It was he who eventually convinced her that she had not done anything indecent or shameful in sleeping with her brother, when the relationship was totally unknown to her. It was solely due to his comforting words that her dreadful nightmares had ceased and the times she had spent with Neal were remembered once more as times of joy and beauty.

All this she admitted freely yet she could not bring herself to love Aidan as he loved her. The spark just wasn't there. She still remembered those two nights they had spent together and how she had been repulsed by his touch. Even taking into account her distressed state of mind at the time, she remained quite sure that he could never excite and satisfy her the way Neal had done and that, therefore, he was not right for her. At least, however, thanks to him she was beginning to think in terms of loving someone again. The worst must surely be over. She resolved there and then that she must stop using Aidan as a crutch. She must let him go and find someone who could return his love. She would be forever grateful to him but she had to be fair.

Her thoughts were interrupted by a final-year geography student looking for one of the books in popular demand.

"I'm sorry," she told him, consulting the computerised catalogue, "but all six copies available for loan are already out."

Things were becoming quite hectic again after the lull but, glancing at her watch, she saw thankfully that she had just another fifteen minutes to go before her friend, Christine, took over for the final session of the evening. The time passed quickly and, just as she cheerfully said goodnight to Christine, she heard a familiar voice at her shoulder:

"Hello Charlotte."

Turning round, Charlotte looked straight into the eyes of the man she still loved to distraction. He too was just leaving.

"Hi Neal," she said, smiling.

He registered that she had just lifted her coat and handbag.

"Have you finished for the night? he asked. "Why don't you come and have a drink with me?"

She hesitated. She had refused such offers time and time again during the first few months of their separation, when she knew that she could not cope with such a situation, but now …

She wasn't sure …

"Just for old times' sake?" he persisted.

It had been so long now since he had even spoken to her. Why not have a drink with him? What harm could it do? The temptation was too strong.

"Yes, I'd like that. Thank you," she said.

Neal had expected another rebuff. He was both delighted and surprised. His face shining with joyful anticipation, he walked with her to the nearby Yellow Door, a favourite haunt of many of the students. They sat down at a secluded table in the corner. Charlotte ordered a martini and was surprised when Neal ordered a tomato juice for himself.

"That's not like you," she laughed.

"A new resolution," he declared. "I've only just got my driving licence back and I intend to keep it. I don't drink at all now, when I'm driving."

"But you never did drink heavily. Did you have an accident or something?"

Neal related how, under the influence of alcohol, he had crashed his car and, exaggerating a little, had nearly killed himself. His injuries had resulted in his withdrawal from the tennis tournament at his club, he told her. He had been in a potential winning position at the time.

"It was the day I received your letter," he concluded.

Charlotte's face turned a deathly shade of white and she felt her eyes sting with unshed tears.

"I'd no idea," she stammered. "I'm sorry."

"Why did you do it, Charlotte? Why did you change your mind so suddenly and disappear like that?"

"I can't tell you."

"Was it because of that tall, dark-haired chap I've seen you with?"

"Aidan? No, he's just a good friend."

"Well, was there something I did that night to offend you? You seemed to be so happy. I just couldn't believe it when you said you were leaving me."

Charlotte realised now that it had been a mistake to accept his invitation.

"No, you didn't offend me, she said. "I'll keep saying sorry until I am blue in the face but I just changed my mind."

"And you still feel the same way?"

"Yes."

Nothing more was said until Charlotte, trying to change the subject, revealed that she had been speaking to his former landlady the previous evening and Neal replied that he had been intending to pay her a visit for some time now.

"She was so good to me while I was lodging with her," he said. "I really miss her."

"Yes," agreed Charlotte. "She's very nice. It's a real shame that she never had any family. I'm sure she would have made a perfect mother. She has done Dr Matthews the world of good. Everybody is talking about how well he looks."

"There's something about her always reminded me of you. You're two of a kind. Don't you think you too would make a perfect mother?"

She stared at the table, saying nothing. So much for changing the subject!

"You don't really mean that you never intend to settle down with someone, surely, never have children of your own? From what I remember, you are not the type of person who could live a fulfilled life without a physical relationship."

He lowered his voice:

"Can you honestly tell me that the times we made love meant nothing to you?"

Still she stared at the table, refusing to allow her face to be seen.

"Look at me, Charlotte."

His voice was a mere whisper.

"Look at me and tell me straight that you do not love me."

When she didn't answer, Neal stretched out one hand and gently raised her chin. Her eyes were wet with tears and her expression a mixture of anguish and ... yes, it was unmistakeable ..., anguish and love.

"Say it, Charlotte. Tell me that you don't love me and I'll leave you alone."

"I can't," she stammered at last, the tears now trickling down her cheeks.

His heart filled with renewed hope, Neal gently persisted:

"I still love you, Charlotte. These past two years have been pure hell! Come back to me. Let's try again. If it's marriage that scares you, I won't mention it for the present. We're still very young. There's no rush. Let's just be together and enjoy ourselves again."

He paused.

"If you cannot say that you don't love me, can you not tell me that you do?"

Something inside her snapped. She looked straight into his eyes and, finding that she could not tell him a lie, she quietly said,

"Yes, I love you, Neal. I have always loved you and I always will but I'm sorry, things can never be as they were. Please don't press me to say any more."

Neal was more confused than ever. He implored her to tell him what it was that stood in the way of their happiness, begged her to be straight with him.

"Were you unfaithful to me? Is that was it was? I don't care. It doesn't matter anymore. Forget the past. We love each other now. Isn't that all that matters? Trust me…, tell me the truth…, *please*."

"I can't."

"Was there someone else? Were you unfaithful to me?" he persisted.

She shook her head, sadly.

Neal sighed loudly.

"Then it was me," he said. "You found out about Stephanie and me, didn't you? Oh, Charlotte, I'm so sorry. I never meant to hurt you. She didn't mean anything to me, not the way you do, and I … "

Charlotte interrupted his tirade and eyed him suspiciously.

"Who is Stephanie?" she asked. "I don't know what you're talking about."

"You don't?"

Neal felt his face go very red. It was now his turn to stare at the table, unable to look her in the eye.

There was an uneasy silence.

Then, momentarily forgetting her present relationship with Neal, Charlotte allowed feelings of intense anger and jealousy to well up inside her, until her whole being almost exploded in passionate rage and she spat the words at him:

"You slept with another woman, while you were engaged to me! How could you, Neal? I trusted you. I would have done anything for you. We were perfect together, so much in love. Was that not enough for you? I loved you, Neal. I loved you. I trusted you."

Neal did not even notice that people were staring at them. Unwittingly he had aroused an animated response at last, rekindled the fiery passion which had never been extinguished.

"Can't we try again?" he said, gently. "I promise I'll never look at another woman."

He paused, then added, bewildered as ever,

"But if you didn't know about Stephanie, what on earth is it that has been keeping you away from me all this time? You've just admitted that we were perfect together. Why, then, did you decide that it was over? You said you trusted me. Then prove it and tell me. *Please*."

Charlotte's mind was in a whirl of total confusion, her self-control irretrievably broken down. Once again she looked straight into the eyes of her former lover and experienced an intense longing to be with him again, to be loved by him. Her whole body ached for physical contact with his and the thought of someone else sharing his bed was torturous. Neal read her thoughts as accurately as if she had uttered them aloud. She looked lovelier than ever, though sad and pale. He moved closer to her, drinking in the delicious fragrance of her hair and her body, and he gently slipped his arm around her waist. Instinctively she recoiled, rejecting his advance. The moment of weakness had passed.

Neal was exasperated:

"I don't understand, Charlotte. For God's sake, what's wrong with you?"

Her equilibrium not quite restored, she spoke suddenly, throwing all her fine resolutions to the wind:

"Ask your father!" she blurted out. "Ask your rotten two-timing father! It's all his fault."

As Neal stared at her in utter disbelief, Charlotte rose from the table and ran outside, already regretting her words. She could have bitten her tongue out. Neal followed her, demanding an explanation, but her lips were tightly sealed. She had said too much already. She would say no more.

Chapter 30

It was well after midnight when Neal arrived at his family home in Yorkshire, his blood boiling with rage. The house was in total darkness. Jumping out of the car, he strode up the driveway and hammered loudly on the heavy, wooden door with his fist. There was no response. He pummelled on the door again, even more loudly than before and pressed the button for the door bell, keeping his finger on it so that it kept ringing non-stop. This time a light went on in his parents' bedroom and his mother's face appeared at the window. Releasing his finger he stood back from the door and signalled, so that Helen could see him. Recognising him at once, she rushed downstairs, alarmed by his unexpected visit at such a late hour. She opened the door.

"Neal!" she breathed. "What's wrong? What are you doing here in the middle of the night?"

"I need to talk to Dad. I'm sorry it's so late. I didn't have time to go back for my key."

"Back from where? Where have you come from? Your father is asleep. Can't this wait until the morning? Is it something urgent?"

Somehow Jonathan had slept through the initial commotion.

"It's urgent, all right," Neal replied. "In fact it's nearly two years overdue!"

He bounded up the stairs, two at a time, and stormed into his parents' bedroom, where Jonathan was already out of bed, aroused by the raised voices downstairs.

"Why did Charlotte leave me?" Neal demanded angrily.

Jonathan stared at him blankly, utterly speechless.

"What happened between you and Charlotte?" he screamed.

Jonathan now grew cross at his sleep being disturbed in such a manner.

"You've been drinking again, Son. I'm disappointed in you. Go to bed and we'll talk in the morning."

"We'll talk now," shouted Neal. "I'm as sober as a judge. I've been talking to Charlotte and she says she left me because of you! Now I want to know why. What did you do to her?"

"Go to bed."

"I did not drive here in the middle of the night just to go to bed! I want an answer!"

"We'll talk in the morning."

"We'll bloody well talk now!" he screamed. "What did you do to Charlotte?"

Jonathan was becoming increasingly impatient. He was not going to attempt a rational conversation while his son was so obviously drunk, or so he thought. His silence, however, only seemed to confirm Neal's growing suspicions.

"God!" he cried scornfully. "You read about these things in the newspapers! But my own father! You, who taught me right from wrong! If you've defiled that girl, I'm warning you, Dad, you may be my father but I'll see that you pay for it. You've ruined our chance of a life together. You selfish bastard! You bloody selfish bastard! How could you do it to her? To me? I ... "

Jonathan hit him hard, landing a heavy blow on his jaw, stemming the flow of obscenities and sending him reeling against the bed. Blood began to trickle down his cheek. Jonathan was very shaken. Never before had his son spoken to him with such disrespect.

"Look, Son," said the older man, visibly shaken by the encounter and realising now that Neal was not drunk, "I haven't seen the girl since the weekend she spent here with us. How dare you suggest that anything improper took place! What on earth has got into you? The girl has concocted some story to get you off her back. It's been well over a year now. Can't you just accept that she doesn't want you? Move on and find someone else!"

"I don't want anyone else. I want Charlotte."

He sank down unto the bed and covered his face.

"She says she still loves me," he said, speaking slowly now, enunciating every word carefully in an effort to remain calm, "she still loves me but she cannot be with me because of you. She is very unhappy. You must have done something, Dad, or said something. She wouldn't just make it up."

"Are you calling me a liar now? I think you've said quite enough for tonight. There is no substance whatsoever to her allegations and I'm shocked that you could have believed there was. Now get out of my room! And don't ever disturb me or your mother like this again in the middle of the night."

Neal didn't move. Instinctively he knew that his father was telling the truth, that he should never have doubted him. Their relationship must surely be in tatters, beyond redemption. The blood dripping slowly from his left eye bore testimony to that. Jonathan was not a violent man, had never hit him before. What had he done? How would he ever be able to look his father in the face again?

"I told you to get out, Neal."

Still he stayed where he was.

Helen stood trembling at the doorway in her dressing gown, appalled by the scene she had just witnessed and anxious to avoid further violence.

"Please go to bed, Neal," she said softly, but firmly.

The younger man rose at last, revealing his face which was red and swollen. Slowly he walked over to his father and touched him lightly on the shoulder.

"I'm sorry, Dad," he said simply. "I'm sorry."

Very much confused, but ashamed of his own behaviour, Neal was relieved to reach the privacy of his own childhood bedroom, which was still the way he left it when he moved out. He almost wished that his father had hit him harder. He had said some terrible things to him. As he looked in the mirror and began to wash off the dripping blood, he was suddenly reminded of another face covered in blood and, inadvertently, he began to contemplate his strange affair with Stephanie Walkington. How she had deceived both Richard and himself, and most of all herself. How confused that poor girl had been. Of course! That was it! Why hadn't he recognised it sooner? What sort of a psychologist was he? Was not his beloved Charlotte displaying similar symptoms? He must get her to see a doctor.

Chapter 31

Alannah Lovell was fascinated by the atmosphere around her. Now fourteen, she had been to a big, international airport quite a few times but she still found it all very exciting. She felt so grown-up today, travelling alone for the first time. Alan had been with her on the way over but, after handing her over to Susan, he had continued on his way to his business conference. There had been just the one overnight stay in England for him so he was already back home. It had been very nostalgic seeing Alan again. It had brought back some happy memories. Chris had been very close to his brother and Susan had always liked his wife, Doreen. The four of them had often gone out for an evening together. Susan accompanied her niece to the check-in desk, where she showed the boarding pass they had printed out that morning and handed over her small pink suitcase. There was just fifteen minutes to go before the allocated gate was due to open.

"I won't be allowed to go through security with you, Anna, so I'll have to leave you soon. Are you sure you'll be OK?"

Susan was amazed by her level of maturity for one so young.

"I'll be fine. Mum and Dad will be waiting for me in Belfast. And they've asked the airline people to look after me. I just have to show them my boarding pass and they'll make sure I don't get lost."

They went into one of the busy shops, where Alannah bought some sweets and a magazine for the short flight and then they checked one of the large electronic screens. The Belfast flight was now open for boarding. Susan walked with her as far as she was allowed.

"It's been lovely having you for the week," she said, giving her a big hug and a kiss on the cheek.

"I've had a great time, Auntie Susan," she answered. "Thanks for everything. And thank Uncle Derrick for me again for taking me to so many interesting places. He's nice."

"I'm glad you liked him. What did you enjoy the most?"

"I loved going up on the London Eye and seeing Buckingham Palace and Downing Street. And the trip to the theatre was fun. And the shopping, of course! Seeing all those designer boutiques you read about in magazines! Cambridge was nice too but you're so lucky to live near London. You'll be able to see the Queen at the Diamond Jubilee."

"Yes, I'm looking forward to that. There's going to be a special flotilla of boats on the Thames. It's going to be something really special. I'll try to get a good view from one of the bridges."

"I'll be watching it on television. Hopefully they'll get a nice, sunny day."

"Don't forget to tell your mum and dad and little Chris that I was asking for them all."

"I will. Mum says you're to bring Uncle Derrick over to meet them soon. He's quite like Uncle Chris in some ways."

"Yes, I think so too."

They embraced again and she was gone.

Susan went back into the shop and bought herself a newspaper. She sat down on a spare seat and started to read, not wanting to leave the airport until she was sure that Alannah's flight had taken off safely. The daily codeword completed, she was soon engrossed in an article about the forthcoming Jubilee celebrations and when she next looked at the screen, she realised that the flight had just departed. She would miss Alannah this week. She had grown into a lovely young lady and had been great company. She was making her way towards the exit when suddenly she was halted by a familiar voice at her elbow: "Why, Mrs Lovell, I mean Matthews! How lovely to see you. How are you?"

It was Neal Ashby.

"Neal! I'm very well, thank you. What are you doing with yourself now? Still studying?"

"Yes. Actually I've just finished. Waiting for results. That's the worst part!"

He grinned.

"Where are you living now?" asked Susan.

"Still the same place – a flat in Hope Street. It's not bad but I'm still not used to looking after myself after the way you spoiled me! Actually I'll soon be moving back to my own place up north. I think I've a good chance of a job up there. I should know for sure in a day or two."

"Good for you. I hope that works out for you."

"Me too."

He paused and then continued:

"I always meet somebody I know in a place like this. Are you waiting for a flight or have you just come from somewhere?"

"Neither. I've just been saying goodbye to my niece. She was over from Belfast for a short holiday. Her plane has just taken off."

"You're free now then? Why don't you join me for a coffee?"

When Susan said she would love a cup of coffee, she was totally unaware of the impact that decision would have on the lives of the people she loved, totally oblivious to the fact that this was the day that would change their lives for ever.

They made their way through the throngs of business men in suits, carrying briefcases and laptops, and holiday-makers trundling large suitcases, golf clubs and surfboards, to one of the many snack bars, where Neal ordered coffee and blueberry muffins.

"My treat," he said, as they sat down.

"Thanks, Neal. So how are things? Are the family all well?"

She was, of course, thinking affectionately of Jonathan.

"They're very well, thanks. My sister, Suzannah, was married last week, which explains what I'm doing here in the airport. An uncle came over from Canada for the wedding and I've just been seeing him off again. He has been in Ulster for the past few weeks, visiting old friends, and then came over here for the wedding and spent a few days with us."

They chatted happily for a few minutes about Susan's new life as a doctor's wife and Neal's prospective new job opportunity in Yorkshire. Then, during a lull in the conversation, Neal took her by surprise:

"I believe you were talking to Charlotte recently."

"Yes." This was awkward. "How did you know?"

"She told me."

"Oh! Are you seeing her again?"

She knew he wasn't but what else could she say?

"No." A look of sadness crossed his face.

"Did she seem a bit strange to you?"

"Strange?" Susan was cautious.

Neal sighed.

"I have a feeling that she's not well. You know, she never gave me a good reason for breaking our engagement. Then, a couple of weeks ago, she came out with me for a drink and, when I pressed her for a reason, she suddenly blamed my father! He swears that he doesn't know what she means and, when I tackled her again, she would hardly speak to me."

Susan's heart sank. Maybe, she thought, it would have been better for everyone to have known the truth from the start. Somehow the matter was now coming to a head.

"I'm sorry," said Neal. "I'm embarrassing you."

The gloomy silence which followed was broken by Neal again, changing the subject.

"Tell me, Susan," he said apprehensively, "do you ever see Richard or Stephanie?"

She smiled, remembering the only time she had ever been angry with Neal.

"You don't mind me calling you Susan?"

"Good heavens, no, I wish you would. Mrs Matthews sounds so formal."

She hadn't answered his question.

"Richard wrote to me, you know."

"Oh?"

She was both curious and surprised.

"I was sure he would come after me, terrified of what he might do to me. I waited almost a month, on tenterhooks. Then this letter arrived. I was still living at your place at the time but I didn't say anything. He called me a bastard in no uncertain terms and warned me to stay away from his wife but then went on to say that I had 'opened his eyes to Stephanie's vulnerability' and had probably saved their marriage in the end. He even referred to his attack on Stephanie and said he regretted causing the miscarriage of my child! That scared me. I had never thought of it as my child, probably because it was already dead before I even knew of its existence and because of the way Stephanie suffered. I only thought of her at the time. It gave me a very funny feeling to think of what might have been if he had never found out. I could have been a father without even knowing it."

"I always wondered how he had reacted towards you," said Susan. "I didn't dare ask you after the rollicking I gave you that night!"

"And I told you to mind your own business! Sorry."

He repeated his question:

"Do you ever see them now? I know you're working in a different school."

"Yes, I did see them both recently," Susan revealed. "There was a special function at my former school to mark the Jubilee. The children had put on a brilliant exhibition. I was invited to attend along with several other former members of staff. Derrick came too."

"And Richard still works there, in the same school?"

"Yes, he was there with Stephanie. He introduced her to me. It was the first time I ever met her. She was very friendly."

"I'd love to see them both," sighed Neal. "I really like them both but I don't think I'd be welcome and I don't blame them. Richard has been more forgiving than I could have been."

"Actually, Neal, they did both mention you," she admitted. "Richard said he should have 'given you a hiding' and probably would if he ever caught up with you. Stephanie laughed and said that he would do 'nothing of the sort' or he would have her to deal with! It was weird and I must say I was mystified. They didn't mention any letter, probably assumed that I knew more than I did."

"So they seemed quite happy?"

"Oh, definitely, no doubt about it. And they have a little boy now."

"Good. Thank God it's Richard's own this time. I'm sorry, Susan, I should have tried to explain it all to you, but to be honest, I didn't even understand my own feelings. I never loved her, you know, not the way I love Charlotte. I … I felt sorry for her, …but I did like her, …very much… and Richard too."

"You don't have to explain. It's all in the past."

"But I betrayed Charlotte's trust. I don't know how I could have done that. No matter how much I liked Stephanie or felt sorry for her, it was not worth jeopardising my relationship with Charlotte. She won't admit it but she must have found out."

Susan felt awkward again. She sipped her coffee and stared at the table, hoping against hope that he would not labour the point.

"My dad hasn't been himself since I accused him of… of…, well, I didn't make a specific accusation, but I made allegations, insinuations. I thought he must have molested her in some way or asked her for some sort of favour, something inappropriate. Dad was quite ill the next day and my mother was furious with me, said I could have given him a heart attack, saying things like that. He has hardly spoken to me since. It spoiled the whole atmosphere for Suzy's wedding. I know now that there was no substance to it; at least I think I do, but I can't understand what made Charlotte say it. She's not usually malicious or vindictive, anything but, but she definitely said she blamed him. It's crazy; it just doesn't make any sense."

Neal felt close to Susan, having lived under her roof, felt quite at home discussing intimate matters with her. After all, Susan knew Charlotte better than his own parents did. They had only met her a few times, whereas Charlotte had once been a regular visitor in Susan's house. It was indeed in her house that he and Charlotte had made love with such loving tenderness and passion. Neal also recalled how Susan had confided in him about her own experience of loneliness and rejection.

"Your husband is still Charlotte's doctor, isn't he?" Neal said thoughtfully after a moment. "Would you ask him to talk to her, maybe recommend someone who could give her some counselling? I'm worried about her."

He sighed and concluded, sadly:

"Even if she refuses to have anything more to do with me, I still care about her. I don't like to think that she may be ill."

Susan nodded and smiled sympathetically at her daughter's former boyfriend.

"I'll see what I can do," she said hurriedly, making no promises and trying to think of another topic of conversation that would be less stressful for them both.

"I didn't know you had relations in Canada," she said at last.

"Just the one uncle," answered Neal. "I'd never met him before. He went out to Canada over twenty years ago. When he heard that I was getting married, he thought it was a great excuse to come over and see all his old friends. Then, when my wedding was called off, he was so disappointed that Mum invited him to Suzy's, even though he's not actually related to her at all."

It took Susan a moment to register the incongruity of this last statement.

"I don't understand," she said, puzzled. "If he's your uncle, he must surely be her uncle also."

"No. You see my mother was married twice. Her first husband, Uncle Joe's brother, was my real father, though he died in 1988 when I was just a baby and I never actually think of him as my father. He was only twenty-five. Mum was married again before I was two and I was brought up as Jonathan Ashby's son. They did tell me all about it years ago but I never took much interest or talked about it to anyone. As far as I was concerned, he was the only father I'd ever known and he has always treated me as well as any real father could. I must admit though, now that I've met Uncle Joe and heard him talk about my real dad, I'm beginning to take more interest in him."

Susan jumped to her feet, her mind a whirl of confusion, her heart palpitating wildly, her eyes shining with tears of joy. He wasn't Jonathan's son! He wasn't Charlotte's brother after all! Neal's photograph album jumped into her mind. She saw again that lovely photo of Neal as a baby with Helen and a man she had assumed to be her brother. No wonder it was such a lovely photograph, unmistakeably exuding bounteous love! It depicted a complete family unit, a young couple, madly in love, with their newborn infant son. If only she could tell him here and now, but no, that wouldn't be right. She had to see Jonathan first. After all these years, she would have to tell Jonathan the truth after all. Why had she never realised that Neal was older than Charlotte? It had never occurred to her to enquire about his age. Jonathan didn't marry Helen until the autumn of 89, a few months after Charlotte was born. Susan had always assumed that he was born after that.

"Are you all right?"

Neal was bewildered by the sudden change in her demeanour.

"Yes, fine! I must dash," she said, consulting her watch, though she had no more interest in the time than he had. "Thanks for the coffee, Neal. It was lovely. I'll be in touch."

She beamed at him, unable to conceal her obvious happiness and excitement. Then, bustling through the crowd of tourists and foreign businessmen, she hurried outside to her car, leaving Neal quite baffled as to what had caused her sudden exuberance and haste.

★ ★ ★

"Derrick! **DERRICK**!"

There was no answer so Susan jumped back into the car, thinking he must have been delayed at the surgery, and was about to drive off again, when he appeared at the open window of their bedroom, where he had been dozing.

"What's the matter?" he called. "Did Alannah get away safely?"

"Yes. The plane left exactly on time."

She ran back into the house and rushed up the stairs, two at a time, like an athlete half her age.

"Oh, Derrick," she cried, flinging her arms round him, "I have heard the most wonderful news. I can hardly believe it."

Breathlessly, she proceeded to tell him what she had just learnt.

"He's not related to Charlotte at all," she concluded,

unable to contain her excitement. "There's no impediment to their relationship, nothing to stop them being together."

Derrick was less enthusiastic.

"It's nearly two years now, Darling," he reasoned. "Maybe it would be better to just let things work themselves out in their own good time. Their feelings for one another might have changed. We don't know who else might be involved."

Susan reminded him of her recent meeting with Melanie and told him what Neal had said to her that very day. There was no change in their emotional commitment to each other; she was certain of it.

Susan's overwhelming excitement was infectious and very soon Derrick was admitting that it was indeed splendid news. Together they decided that there was no longer any point in hiding anything from anyone. The truth was going to come out, and the sooner the better.

Chapter 32

Helen Ashby heard the doorbell ringing. She glanced out of the window and saw a woman she didn't recognise, a strikingly beautiful woman about her own age. She opened the door.

"Mrs Ashby?"

"Yes. How can I help you?"

Helen spoke softly and smiled. She had lovely, blue eyes, thought Susan, Neal's eyes. She hadn't noticed that so much from the photographs but in the flesh it was so obvious.

"My name is Susan Matthews. I'm Neal's former landlady." Susan explained. "My name was Lovell at that time."

"Yes indeed, I know the name. Neal loved living in your house. It's lovely to meet you at last," she said warmly, "but I'm afraid Neal is away from home tonight, although he has been staying with us recently. He'll be sorry to have missed you."

"Actually, I was talking to him this morning," revealed Susan. "I met him at the airport. It's you and Jonathan I want to talk to, Mrs Ashby."

Helen was surprised to hear her refer to her husband by his first name. She led Susan into a tastefully decorated sitting room. There was a distinct air of opulence. Susan couldn't help thinking what a level-headed and down-to-earth young man Neal was, to have grown up in such obvious luxury. The chandelier alone, in the middle of the room, must have cost a fortune and the paintings on the wall looked like David Hockney originals. Those same bright hues and distinctive swirls. They couldn't be, surely. Helen had been watching a tennis match on the biggest television screen Susan had ever seen. She turned it off.

"Jonny is not at home at present," she said, "but I expect him back shortly."

"That's good," continued Susan. "I would prefer to speak to you privately first."

Helen was mystified, a little alarmed.

"I really don't know where to begin," faltered Susan, nervously. "What I have to say may be hurtful to you but I want you to understand from the start that I am speaking out only for the sake of Neal's happiness."

The mystery deepened.

Susan took a deep breath.

"Does the name Susan Summers mean anything to you?"

Immediately Helen's mind drifted back to the time when, as a young widow with a baby just a few months old, she had rekindled her love for Jonathan, her childhood sweetheart. Her rival then had been a girl called Susan Summers and she knew that, although Jonathan had thankfully chosen her, he had never quite forgotten Susan. Even today, a little bit of his heart belonged to her.

"Yes," she said, cautiously. "I remember the name."

"I am Susan Summers."

Rivals in love they may have been but there was no animosity between the two women at that moment. Helen smiled to think that her son had been living under Susan's roof.

"And Neal has found out about you and his dad? Is that it?"

"No," Susan said. "There's more to it than that. Neal doesn't know anything yet. There is something I have kept secret even from Jonathan, solely on your account and his, but which, for Neal's sake, he will now have to be told. Maybe I should have spoken up before but, please believe me, I thought I was doing the right thing."

Helen could not imagine what all this could have to do with Neal but begged her to continue.

"Shortly after Jonathan and I split up," said Susan quietly, "I discovered that I was pregnant. Jonathan has a daughter he never knew about."

Helen started, as though she had touched a live wire. She stared at her visitor, her feelings a confused mixture of anger, disbelief, guilt and gratitude, most of all, on reflection, gratitude that this woman had not used her condition at the time as an excuse to claim Jonathan for herself, and guilt, an overwhelming sense of guilt. She had always known that Jonathan and Susan Summers had been intimate, that he had loved her physically, but she too had loved another man, Neal's father. She had never felt jealousy towards Susan for she knew that, once Jonathan had made up his mind to break with her, he had never afterwards been unfaithful. But if he had known what she had just learnt, his decision would surely have favoured her rival. Yes, she felt very guilty. She had stolen Jonathan from Susan Summers. Where would she have been today without Jonathan? She shuddered at the thought.

"Why did you not tell him at the time?" Helen asked Susan at last.

"I knew he loved you more," Susan answered simply. "I didn't want him to stay with me for the wrong reasons, just because of the baby, and maybe come to resent me in the future."

"But you loved him! I remember him telling me how hurt you were and how guilty he felt when he broke with you. You must have been so lonely."

Susan was amazed. She had been apprehensive about coming, had not been sure what kind of reaction she should expect, but Helen was actually concerned about her own feelings!

"I cannot deny that I was desperately lonely at the time," she said, "but since then I have had two wonderful husbands. I don't regret anything."

Helen got up from the sumptuous, brown, leather sofa and, offering Susan a drink, poured herself a large brandy from a crystal decanter on the mahogany sideboard. Susan said she would have the same. This had all been a great shock.

"What has this to do with Neal?" she asked, sitting down again.

Susan took another deep breath.

"Well that brings me to the crux of the matter, the reason I have decided that I have to speak out. By the strangest co-incidence, Neal fell in love with my daughter, Jonathan's daughter."

"Charlotte!" breathed Helen, in a whisper.

"Yes."

Helen took a moment to digest this news.

"No wonder they were so alike. I once looked at a photograph of Charlotte and could have sworn that it was my own daughter, Suzannah. So they are actually half-sisters!"

Susan went on to explain that it was only that very morning that she had discovered that Jonathan was not actually Neal's natural father. She told Helen about the conversation Charlotte had overheard and how, believing herself to be in love with her own brother, she had broken off her engagement and had lived in a state of mental turmoil ever since. Helen felt her heart go out to the young girl, as Susan explained why she had concealed from Neal the true reason for leaving him. She recalled the night, not so long ago, when Neal had arrived home after midnight in a frantic rage and had launched a verbal attack on his father. Jonathan had ended up hitting him, quite hard, on the jaw. It all made sense now. In her torment that night, his former fiancée had almost been tempted to tell him the truth. If only he had told her about his real parentage from the start. Helen was annoyed and surprised that he had not. After all, he had been engaged to marry the girl.

Panic suddenly gripped Helen's heart and she felt quite distraught as the situation gradually became clear to her and she realised that she too would have to make a confession. She couldn't let Neal suffer even more needless heartbreak. But she couldn't tell Susan *her* secret, she just couldn't. How would she break the news to Jonathan? Maybe she could persuade Susan to leave now, before Jonny got back, persuade her to keep quiet about Charlotte. Jonny didn't need to know about all this. She could talk to Neal herself, tell him in some indirect way that he should have told Charlotte about his real dad, make sure that she found out. No, it was hopeless. Charlotte would be sure to tackle Jonny about it sooner or later. There was no escape. She would have to tell him.

The front door opened and clicked shut again and footsteps could be heard on the polished wooden floor in the hallway. Helen hurried from the room and embraced her husband, holding him long and close. He sensed her agitation, felt her heart thumping wildly in her breast.

"We have a visitor, Dear," she said at last, wondering whether he would recognise her at once.

He did, of course, but not sure whether she had come in the guise of Neal's landlady or as an old friend of his, he was not sure how to address her.

"Hello Jonathan," she said.

He continued to look at her awkwardly until Helen said quietly,

"Susan has something she wants to tell you. I'll go and make some tea."

Nervously she embraced her husband again, then hurried from the room. How remarkably well she had accepted the situation, thought Susan gratefully, at least the revelations about Charlotte's birth. She did, however, appear to be more anxious concerning Neal's involvement.

"Helen knows who you are?"

Jonathan was surprised.

"Yes."

He was a bit annoyed that Susan had intruded, uninvited, into his family home. He spoke rather coldly:

"Well, what is it you want to tell me?"

"It's about Charlotte Jamison."

He frowned and sighed loudly. What had that girl been saying now? She was lucky he hadn't taken her allegations to the police. But he knew from the experience of others that such a manoeuvre could backfire against him. An unsubstantiated rumour had caused the downfall of Simon Moffatt, one of his work colleagues. Once people have got the slightest whiff of suspicion, real trust goes out the window. He gritted his teeth.

"Yes?"

Susan decided to come straight out with it.

"I'm her mother, her birth mother."

Jonathan looked at her in disbelief. He had no idea what he had expected her to say, but certainly not that.

"She was born long before I was married. The Jamisons have brought her up since she was a few days old."

Jonathan felt exasperated. This was such a strange encounter. Charlotte Jamison had brought him nothing but grief, had ruined his relationship with his son. He really didn't need Susan Summers of all people, or whatever she called herself these days, butting in to plead her case. This wasn't the Susan he knew and loved.

"Why are you telling me about this? She and Neal parted company a long time ago. In fact I think the girl is somewhat deranged. Neal's besotted with her but recently she has caused a lot of friction between us. She's been making ridiculous accusations about me being responsible for ending their relationship."

"You are."

"I beg your pardon?"

"You are her father."

Jonathan went as white as a sheet and stared at her dumbfounded whilst she continued:

"Neal never told Charlotte that you weren't his natural father so she thinks that he is her half-brother. That is why she broke off the engagement. She was devastated when she found out and has been through hell these past two years."

Jonathan hadn't yet grasped the full significance of what she was saying.

"You had a baby, our baby, and never told me! Why?"

He took her hand and squeezed it.

"You should have told me. I wouldn't have let you go through that alone."

"You love Helen," Susan whispered, "and I love Derrick. Everything has turned out for the best."

"I can't believe this, Susan."

He held her close now and gave her a light kiss. She closed her eyes, for one short moment revelling in the glorious sensation she had longed for ever since that far-off time when they were lovers. She did love Derrick very much. But Jonathan had been her first love and his touch was different, special. Only he had that electrifying effect which made her whole body tingle with intense pleasure. For that one short moment she relived the best days of her life and then, reluctantly, lest her secret lust be revealed, she gently pushed him away and he released her.

"Just for old times' sake," smiled Jonathan, alarmed by the feelings she had evoked in him, yet again. He would happily have prolonged that kiss, would have done, had she not stopped him. Quickly he moved away from her, shaking off the urge to kiss her again.

"I could hardly believe it when Neal told me this morning that you were not his real father. I had never even considered such a possibility. I thought that there was no escaping the fact that they were brother and sister."

Susan could not conceal her obvious delight.

"Did you say anything about this to Neal?"

Jonathan looked anxious, less enthusiastic.

"Oh no, I came to see you first. It wouldn't be my place to tell him. But it's wonderful news."

"What have you told Helen?"

"The truth. I had to come clean. You do understand that, don't you? I hope I haven't caused any trouble between you."

Jonathan was puzzled.

"Did she not tell you anything?" he asked.

"What do you mean? Tell me what?"

"About Neal. Oh, Susan, I don't know how to tell you this… I don't know why Helen didn't tell you in the circumstances."

Susan felt uneasy.

"Tell me what?" she repeated.

"Neal *is* my son," said Jonathan, simply. "It is true that he was born while she was married to Daniel and no-one suspected anything was amiss until Daniel suddenly died very young. Helen and I had been friends for years and we had slept together once, just once, during her marriage. It shouldn't have happened. It was a mistake. We were both a bit drunk after a party. Neal was the result of that one night of passion. It was the only time I was ever unfaithful to you, I swear it, Susan. It was only after Daniel died that she told me her baby was actually mine."

He paused, trying to remember.

"Did I not tell you about it at the time? It was because of Neal that I broke with you and went back to Helen. I loved you, Susan. I wouldn't have left you otherwise. I had been somewhat grieved when Helen left me for Daniel but then I fell in love with you and, for a time, I had forgotten all about her until that stupid night. We came across each other at a function and had far too much to drink. It was snowing and I kind of got stranded. We ended up in bed together but it meant nothing to either of us. She was still madly in love with Daniel at the time and I was missing you so much. He had told her he was at a redundancy meeting or something. Turned out his 'meeting' was with a hospital consultant. He had been worried about his health for some time but had said nothing to Helen at that stage. His brother had gone with him for moral support. It was that very day he found out that his prognosis was not good. I'm so ashamed when I think about that and it was even worse for Helen. Of course we knew nothing about his illness at the time. We were both just lonely. I was furious with her the next morning when we woke up and it dawned on me what we had done but I had to admit it was my fault as much as hers. I'm still ashamed to think that Neal was conceived in that way, that his birth was all a big mistake, the result of stupid drunken sex I don't even remember in a hotel room. I told Helen that morning that I never wanted to see her again but I didn't know what fate had in store for her, for all of us. I called to pay my respects when I heard that Daniel had died and she told me then about Neal."

Jonathan scratched his head, again searching his memory.

"I thought I had told you, Susan. I couldn't just leave her to bring up my son alone. It was around his first birthday when I found out and just coming up to Christmas. He needed his daddy. I was sure I had told you all this at the time, Susan!"

"I don't know what you told me, Jonathan. I don't remember."

They looked at each other forlornly, sharing each other's torment.

"Charlotte is my daughter!" sighed Jonathan. "It's incredible."

"So she and Neal are brother and sister, after all."

It was too much to bear after the joyful anticipation she had felt since speaking to Neal that morning and the despair showed on her face.

"Why did Neal say his father was dead?" she asked. "I still don't understand."

"We never told Neal that he was born out of wedlock," Jonathan explained. "He knows his mother was married to

Daniel at the time. But we never talked to him much about Daniel either, since he wasn't really his father, at least I didn't …which probably explains why he never even mentioned him to Charlotte. What a mess!"

"So you are actually Neal's real father but you've never told him? You let him believe it was Daniel?"

"That's right. Only Helen and I know. I hinted to him once that he really was mine but he was very young. I don't think he understood."

"I feel so stupid now for coming here," declared Susan, visibly upset. "I only came because I thought there was a real chance of happiness for Charlotte and Neal. I love them both so much."

"You were right to come," Jonathan replied, kindly. "You should have come years ago. How does Charlotte know about me? Did you tell her?"

"No, no, she doesn't even know about me. She overheard a private conversation, by mistake."

There was no point hiding anything now. Sadly Susan gave her former lover a brief résumé of her life since their parting all those years ago and an account of what she knew of Charlotte's life to date.

Jonathan listened to her story, aghast.

"I'll make it up to both of you, somehow, Susan. I'm just so confused at the moment."

They shared a hug and a quiet moment of reflection, both thinking how life could have turned out very differently.

"What's keeping Helen with that tea?" Jonathan then said as a distraction.

He called for his wife to come and join in the discussion but several minutes passed and she had neither appeared nor made any response.

"Helen!" he called again. "We're ready for that tea now."

Again she failed to respond.

Recalling Helen's agitated state when he arrived home, Jonathan suddenly realised that she may have been more upset about Susan's revelations than even he himself was. He shouldn't have left her alone for so long.

"Excuse me a moment, Susan," he said, and went out to the kitchen to comfort her. She wasn't there. He sensed an uncanny stillness. As he turned to go out again, a piece of notepaper on the table caught his eye. He went over and picked it up.

I LIED TO YOU, JONNY. DANIEL WAS NEAL'S FATHER. THERE WAS NEVER ANY DOUBT ABOUT IT. ALL WE DID THAT NIGHT IN THE HOTEL WAS SLEEP. I'M SORRY.

Immediately Jonathan feared the worst. He raced upstairs and found the bedroom empty too but her handbag and car keys were sitting on the bed. She wouldn't go far without those. He ran from the room, calling her name, and tried the bathroom door. It was locked!

"Helen! Open the door!" he screamed, but there was no response.

The unmistakeable sense of foreboding, of impending disaster, overwhelmed him. He knew what she had done, he just knew.

"Oh my God! Susan! **SUSAN!** Call an ambulance!"

He banged on the bathroom door and called her name again and again:

"Open the door, Helen. It doesn't matter about Daniel. It's in the past. I don't care."

Whether she heard him or not, he never knew. She was already dead when the ambulance arrived.

Chapter 33

It was a hot, cloudless summer's day, the peaceful silence broken only by sounds equally restful to the soul. Industrious honey bees buzzed from one gaily-coloured flower to another, whilst the leaves of the beech trees rustled gently overhead in the soft, warm breeze. A solitary chaffinch claimed his territory in an occasional burst of the melodious notes which make up his distinctive song and, far off in the distance, one could faintly distinguish the sound of a neighbour mowing his lawn and the happy voices of children at play. The scent of fragrant honeysuckle filled the air.

Charlotte Jamison sat in a shady nook of the garden, re-reading a brilliant book called The *Vanishing Act of Esme Lennox*. She had turned back to the start of the book as soon as she finished the last chapter, this time looking for any clues she had missed first time round. The story had fascinated her. On the patio, Erin and Yvonne lay stretched out on colourful sun-loungers, basking in the glorious sunshine, every now and then raising themselves sleepily and comparing their skins to see who was achieving the better tan. Erin was currently busy texting and receiving messages on her phone, Yvonne lazily skimming though the latest edition of *Hello* magazine.

"What a pity it rained," commented Yvonne, looking at the pictures of the recent Jubilee celebrations, "especially since the weather was so nice the week before."

Charlotte, engrossed in her book, made no response.

"Quinnie says 'hello', Charley." This came from Erin.

Charlotte was aroused this time, on hearing her name.

"Is that who you're texting? Why?"

"Well, if you don't want him, I don't see why I can't have him. He's gorgeous!"

Charlotte smiled. Erin and Ade would actually make a good team.

"Well, good luck with that then."

"You wouldn't mind?"

"No, of course not."

She went back to reading her book.

After some time a car was heard to pull up at the front of the house, where Janine and Steven were both engaging in their favourite pastime of gardening. Rusty could be heard barking excitedly. Greetings were exchanged and all three girls, curious to know who had arrived, strained their ears for a familiar voice. It was too early to be Jayne and Dean or Melanie and Ricky, all of whom had been invited for an impromptu barbecue later. Sunny Sundays were not to be wasted in Steven's eyes; they were always seen as the perfect opportunity to chill out with a bottle of wine and let loose the caveman instinct. As soon as the shops had opened he had joined the scramble for sausages and baps.

Janine had prepared some kebabs with chunks of succulent chicken along with red peppers and onions. The girls had been put in charge of the salads. They would do that later. It had gone quiet now but the car hadn't driven off. They all wondered who it was. Nothing more was audible, however, and they were all too comfortable to move, so they temporarily forgot about the incident. Another fifteen or twenty minutes passed before Yvonne, on the pretext of wanting a drink, decided to go and investigate. When she still had not returned after five or ten minutes, Charlotte, having come to the end of a chapter, turned off her Kindle and joined Erin on the patio. She was pensive as she lay down on her back, exposing her face to the sun.

"Do you really fancy Aidan?" she asked her cousin.

"Yes, so you can't have him back!" teased Erin.

"I don't want him back. But just make sure you treat him well. He deserves more than I was able to give him. I don't want to see him get hurt again."

Charlotte had done the honourable thing and had broken up with Aidan. Living just a few doors away, the whole family knew him very well. He had often played in their garden when they were growing up, and he in theirs. They had had a swing and a paddling pool; he had had a trampoline and football nets. Even before Erin had lived with them, she had been a frequent visitor with her parents. Where had those carefree days gone? In some ways it seemed like yesterday; in other ways it was a lifetime away. Erin was remarkably well-adjusted in the circumstances but she still had her moments, when she became overwhelmed by a great sadness and a sense of terrible divine injustice.

"Do you remember the time we raided his mum's supplies and bandaged up Fiona's arm?" Erin now said, chuckling. We told Aunt Janine that she had fallen off his trampoline and broken her arm. We pretended that she'd been to hospital!"

Aidan's mum was a nurse.

Charlotte laughed, then looked thoughtful:

"I must give Fiona a ring," she said. "I haven't seen her for ages."

"He was always playing practical jokes," said Erin, still thinking fondly of Aidan. "And Fiona was such a gamine!"

Becoming drowsy now, Charlotte turned over to let the sun at her back, lying face down into the foam cushion Yvonne had left behind. The soft breeze lifted her silky chestnut hair and dropped it gently again on her shoulders. The sounds of nature around her receded still further into the distance as she almost slept, so that she was just vaguely aware of a door opening and her mother's voice calling,

"Erin! Phone call for you!"

Erin, who had also been on the threshold of sleep, slowly roused herself and made her way into the house. Who on earth was calling her on a Sunday afternoon on the landline? All her friends used her mobile number. She did not return either. Charlotte lay on.

Presently footsteps could be heard approaching and some-one addressed her amicably:

"Hello, Charlotte."

The voice was familiar, yet she could not immediately place it. Turning over quickly, she looked up into the still handsome face of Jonathan Ashby. Her heart sank.

He's come to confess and plead with me not to tell Neal any more, she thought to herself. *I never meant to say anything, I wish I hadn't, but he pressed me too hard.*

As these thoughts flashed through her mind, she suddenly realised that he was not alone. He was carrying over the wooden bench where she had sat reading, but still standing beside her were the sandaled feet of a woman. Straightening herself up now, she discovered his companion to be Susan Matthews. Her hostility towards Jonathan did not extend to Susan. She had always liked Susan Matthews.

Confused, Charlotte murmured a greeting, as they both seated themselves on the bench, facing her. Knowing Susan as an acquaintance of the Ashbys in her own right, she did not think to make the connection, assumed it had something to do with Mrs Ashby's sudden death. She had heard that Helen had died. It was Jonathan who broke the silence:

"Charlotte, there is a great deal to be explained between us, and I am not going to attempt to say it all now."

He paused.

Why did he have to come today? she asked herself. *Why did he have to spoil such a lovely afternoon?*

She looked at him with sudden loathing and indignation.

He disowned me all these years while he was married, ignored me so that his wife would not find out about some sordid affair that he'd had. He needn't think he can just walk into my life now because she's dead. It's disgusting, the very thought of it. She's hardly cold yet in her grave and he comes waltzing in here, expecting me to accept him! Well, I won't. It's too late for apologies and excuses, far too late. I don't want anything to do with him. Mum and Dad shouldn't even have let him in. What were they thinking about? Sure he didn't even have the decency to come himself and explain about Neal that time – he sent some woman, his mistress, I suppose, someone we didn't even know. She may have given birth to me but he's the one we know. He should have had the decency to speak to Mum and Dad himself. In fact he should have done it far sooner, before Neal and I ever got so serious about each other in the first place. He's a real jerk!

Aloud, she said nothing.

Jonathan spoke again:

"Can you believe that I only discovered something very recently, which I believe you have known for some time?"

He looked embarrassed as he went on:

"…that you are my natural daughter."

So it was definitely true. *But he didn't know?* How could she have been so stupid to lose her control that night and blurt it out to Neal?

"It's a long story, Charlotte," continued Jonathan, "but I didn't even know you existed until Susan here gave me the greatest shock of my life. You see, we were lovers many years ago, before either of us was married."

Charlotte gaped open-mouthed at Susan:

"YOU? You are my mother? she stammered.

"Yes," Susan admitted, her lip trembling, "though I did not realise it when I first met you, or for a long time afterwards. It was I who was talking to your parents that night, when your sisters overheard us. I'm so sorry, Charlotte. I know how you have suffered since."

As though he could read his daughter's thoughts, Jonathan again took up the story:

"We haven't just come to set the record straight. In the circumstances, I know that such a meeting would only have served to make things worse. As I said, I only found out about our relationship recently."

He paused again and his face clouded over.

"It was the day Helen died."

They all observed a strained but respectful silence for a moment before he continued:

"Well, there is something else which Susan only discovered that same day, when she met Neal at the airport, something which prompted her to come and tell me about you after all these years of secrecy, something which Neal himself should have told you when you were engaged to be married."

Charlotte winced at the mention of Neal's name. As she stared at the ground, consciously fighting to keep the tears at bay, a brightly-coloured butterfly rested for a moment on her dress and she asked herself again why they had deemed it necessary to mar her enjoyment of such a perfect day. She had been quite relaxed, having some fun with her family. What did it matter now, what Neal had or had not told her? They were only making excuses for themselves.

"I think you should see this, Charlotte," Jonathan said gently.

He took an envelope from his pocket and removed a folded document. He opened it up to its full A4 size and held it out towards her.

"What is it?"

"It's Neal's birth certificate."

Neal's birth certificate? She could not believe it! That must be the last thing on earth she wanted to see! How could they be so insensitive, so cruel? She knew only too well about the impediment to their relationship. There was no need to rub salt in the wounds. Nevertheless, she had to get this over with. She took it from his hand and glanced at it involuntarily, almost casually. She recognised the date immediately, 17th November, 1987, Neal's birthday. But surely this could not be his birth certificate. This was for some other Neal, the son of Daniel and Helen Collington, another Neal, born the same day. In spite of her resentment, she was curious.

"Neal was nearly two years old when I married Helen."

It was Jonathan's voice, offering the explanation she sought. He spoke softly, kindly.

"Daniel Collington was his father."

Charlotte's heart gave a flutter as she looked again at the precious document in her hand and the wonderful truth became evident to her.

"You are not Neal's father?" she whispered. "You're my father but not his?"

"There's no blood relationship between you and Neal whatsoever," confirmed Jonathan, "nor have you been brought up together as members of one family. There is nothing to prevent you resuming your relationship, if that's what you want."

The totally unexpected and undreamed of news came as a bolt from the blue, energized her brain like electricity being restored following the longest ever power cut. She was no longer staring at the ground, wishing they had not come, could no longer stem the flow of tears which were now streaming down her face; but they were tears of relief and joy, through which she managed to smile at her new-found parents. She could scarcely believe it. She felt as though her heart would explode with the intensity of so many mixed emotions. Once more she scanned the information on Neal's birth certificate and handed it back to Jonathan. She was quite speechless, simply could not express in words the heartfelt relief and renewed hope she was experiencing with the knowledge that her love for Neal was legitimate after all. She closed her eyes and drank in the warm summer air and sweet scents of nature, trying desperately to gather her thoughts.

"I always knew there was something special about you," she said at last, opening her eyes and turning to face Susan. "I just felt it instinctively from the very first time we met."

At these words Susan too was choked with emotion and could not answer but merely smiled at her daughter through a haze of unshed tears. Jonathan realised at once the significance of what Charlotte had just said, was so happy that she had said it, that her first thought had been for the mother she had just discovered, that her feelings were so obviously genuine. That would mean so much to Susan.

"We had to tell Neal everything," said Jonathan, calmly. "There have been too many secrets already."

Charlotte took a moment to digest this information.

"So he knows why I broke off our engagement?"

"Yes."

"And my parents? How did they react?"

"They are both happy for you," Susan took up the story. "We spoke to them first, of course, and gained their permission to talk to you. Derrick is still in the house now, chatting to them."

"I'll always think of them as my parents, you know."

"Of course you will! We wouldn't have it any other way. We both assured them of that."

Charlotte smiled and dried her eyes.

"And you really didn't know about me? You didn't just ignore me on purpose?"

She felt a bit guilty now for having had such unkind thoughts when she first saw them arriving.

"I assure you, I knew nothing," said Jonathan. "And Susan only discovered who you were when it was already too late. She didn't know about Daniel. Susan's had an awful time worrying about you."

"I'm so glad to know that my real parents loved each other," Charlotte said. "I always worried that I might have been the result of someone being raped or something equally awful."

"We have a lot of explaining to do, Charlotte, but you don't have to worry on that score," said Susan. "We were very much in love when you were conceived."

Jonathan took hold of Susan's hand and squeezed it gently. It was not withdrawn.

"We love each other still," he said, "in a different way. Susan has always been very special to me."

A warm glow of contentment was gradually filling Charlotte's whole being. It was incredulous that things could have turned out like this.

"What does Neal think about it all?"

Charlotte spoke his name softly, tentatively, as though she were afraid of what the answer might be.

"He feels very stupid and guilty for not being straight with you but also very angry towards Helen and me for not being totally honest with him. He is very confused at the moment."

Charlotte tried to assimilate this, to make sense of Jonathan's words:

"Do you mean he lied to me deliberately or he didn't know himself? I don't understand."

"Officially," said Jonathan," Neal is Daniel Collington's son. We've never tried to hide that from him. He has always known that Collington was the name on his birth certificate. But I never encouraged Neal to take any interest in his Collington roots and I even told him once, years ago, that he wasn't Daniel's son at all. I told him he was my own son but that he should not let on to his mother that I had told him because she didn't want anyone to know that he had been born out of wedlock. At the time I believed this to be true. That is probably why he never mentioned Daniel to you or to anyone else. He had no interest in him at all until he met Daniel's brother recently and found that they had several things in common. In fact there was an uncanny family resemblance which should have alerted me to the truth, as it did with Neal. I was surprised when Helen even suggested sending Joe Collington an invitation to Suzy's wedding but I didn't raise any real objection. I accepted that she had once loved Daniel and wanted to maintain some contact with his family. But I was shocked when Joe arrived from Canada to spend a few days with us and brought with him a scrapbook he has been keeping over the years, a scrapbook full of photographs, school magazine articles and newspaper clippings concerning Neal. Unknown to me, Helen had been sending him these items on a regular basis, keeping him informed about Neal's progress, interests, achievements – everything – he even had a photograph of you and Neal together."

"But why were you so shocked that Helen had kept in touch with him? asked Charlotte. "Was it not a natural thing to do in the circumstances? He was her brother-in-law."

Despite the trauma he had been through over the past few weeks, Jonathan remained relatively calm.

"Helen deceived me, Charlotte," he said. "She told me that Neal was my son when she knew all the time that he was not. I am finding it very hard to forgive her for that. She sent all these things across the world without ever consulting me. It was all so furtive. There was even a copy of a doctor's letter in the book, confirming that Neal had been tested to make sure he had not inherited any of the medical problems which had caused Daniel's death. Thankfully the tests were all negative but Helen had never even told me he had had those tests or needed them."

Charlotte suddenly remembered the phone-call she had overheard in the restaurant the day she retuned from Portugal. Jonathan's friend, Jack, had been quite dismissive of Helen. Seems he had been right to mistrust her.

"So you thought you were Neal's father until you saw this scrapbook?"

"Even then she denied that Daniel was his father, convinced me that she had just kept in touch for the sake of keeping up appearances because Daniel was his official father. I was suspicious… I could not understand why she had been so secretive… but I believed her in the end. Helen could be very persuasive. Subconsciously, I probably knew the truth some time ago but I didn't let myself think about it."

Charlotte pondered over these revelations, somewhat confused, but fascinated, still intoxicated with happiness and relief that she was not related to her former lover.

"I think I understand," she said. "Neal never mentioned Daniel to me because he believed himself to be Daniel's son in name only, a name he didn't even use, but in fact, it turns out that he really is Daniel's son."

"Yes, that's it in a nutshell."

"But why did Helen not tell you the truth? It's not as if she was unfaithful to you during your marriage. You said Neal was already born before you married her."

Jonathan exhaled loudly.

"That's right, Charlotte, he was. Helen was a widow."

He cleared his throat and continued in a broken voice, choked now with the mixed emotions of his recent bereavement along with the knowledge of Helen's past indiscretions.

"Helen deprived the three of us of the life we should have had together. She prevented me from marrying your mother by telling me that her baby son was actually mine.

There was only the remotest possibility of her claim being true, none actually as it turns out, but I was naïve and gullible and I believed her. So I left Susan, my true love, the person I really wanted to be with, unaware that she was pregnant, and I married Helen."

"And she never changed her story? How can you be sure then that she wasn't telling the truth?"

"For all her faults, she truly loved Neal and she knew how Neal felt about you, how cut up he was by your separation. She told the truth in the end for his sake but she knew it was too late for Susan and me. She died of a guilty conscience. She just couldn't live with the truth, the shame of what she had done."

"You mean…?"

Charlotte didn't want to say it.

"Yes, it was suicide. She's back with Daniel now, together again, where they belong."

Now there was a hint of bitterness in his voice.

"I'm sorry," said Charlotte. "I didn't know. I heard that she had died suddenly but I didn't know how."

A sombre mood now prevailed as all three contemplated Helen's tragic end.

"Neal must be devastated," Charlotte said, thinking aloud.

"Suzy is devastated more so than Neal. Neal is confused and upset," explained Jonathan, "but he's also very angry. He feels he has been manipulated and his very identity distorted."

"But he understands now why you acted as you did," put in Susan, who had been sitting very quietly though

Neal's disclosure. "He has been lost without you, Charlotte. He loves you very much."

"Did he say that?"

Charlotte felt the need for reassurance.

"He doesn't need to. It's so obvious. But yes, he has said it, many times."

"But I rejected him so many times."

She still wondered whether they could really forget the trauma of their prolonged separation and get back together, rekindle the magic.

"He understands now why you did it," Susan repeated.

"But it's well over a month since his mother died and you say this all came to light that day. He has made no attempt to contact me or let me know that he understands."

"Don't blame him for that, Charlotte. We asked him not to come. He wanted to, desperately, but we all needed some time to come to terms with what has happened," Jonathan said, gently. "Helen *was* Neal and Suzy's mother and they loved her."

As he spoke, he was suddenly reminded of Susan as she had been when he had known her in the past, just by a quick flick of her hair, a distinctive look in her eyes. This was her daughter all right.

"Susan and I felt that we wanted to talk to you ourselves, directly, not let you find out about us through Neal's eyes."

That made sense. It was quite reasonable.

"So he does want to see me?"

Susan and Jonathan exchanged glances and smiled, knowingly.

"Yes, he does," Susan said. "But what about you? Are you ready to see him? Maybe you need time to think about it."

Charlotte shook her head, happily.

"I've had all the time I need," she said. "I just feel that the longest nightmare ever has ended at last."

As she spoke, she was just aware of another glance, another smile, a nod from Jonathan. She noticed that their hands were still locked together, lovingly.

"He's in the house now, waiting for you," Susan whispered in a broken voice, emotion getting the better of her. "He's hoping you'll go with him after the barbecue. He has a room booked for tonight."

"In Paris!" added Jonathan. "Steven has agreed that you're due a week's paid leave."

Charlotte leapt to her feet and looked expectantly towards the house. Her heart missed a beat. There he was, standing at the window, waiting for some sign that she was ready to see him. She returned his friendly wave, then swung round again to face Susan and Jonathan and spontaneously embraced them both.

The patio door opened and Neal emerged from the house into the hot sunshine. Charlotte looked towards him nervously, momentarily rooted to the spot, feeling awkward and shy, until Neal flashed that familiar lop-sided smile and called a friendly greeting. Instantly all her inhibitions vanished and she started to run. The nightmare really was over. Her parents were now standing at the door, her mum looking a little forlorn. Derrick Matthews was there too with Erin and Yvonne. He went straight over to

Susan and they embraced. Jonathan took a step backwards, gave them space. Rusty seemed to sense that he was on his own and sat down at his feet, snuggling against his leg. Jonathan gave him a pat on the head. Melanie and Ricky had just arrived for the barbecue. Ricky had a bottle of wine and some crisps in a Marks and Spencer's carrier bag.

"Isn't it wonderful!" Charlotte called to them all, not worried at all about the audience that had gathered to witness her reunion with Neal. She was so happy she could have screamed it from the rooftops for the whole world to hear. She ran over to Janine and hugged her so tightly that it took her breath away.

"You'll always be my mum," she said, reassuringly, hugging her still more tightly. "No-one can ever take that away from me. Be happy for me, Mum. You know how much I love Neal."

Janine was too choked up with emotion to answer but Charlotte knew she had her blessing.

Steven gave her a hug.

"Enjoy your holiday, Sweetheart," he said, kindly. "You deserve it."

She shouted jubilantly to Melanie, who was now walking towards the group, looking quite mystified and puzzled by Neal's presence in the garden, even more so when she caught sight of Susan Matthews and her husband, who were standing alongside another man she didn't recognise. Rusty was now running around the garden in circles, excited by what he obviously perceived as a developing carnival atmosphere.

"Oh, Mel, it's just incredible! Mum will tell you what's happened. You won't believe it!"

Melanie wasn't just her sister; she was her best friend, her confidante.

Jayne and Dean were suddenly making their way along the driveway with a big bag of charcoal and who was that walking behind them, going over now to stand beside Erin? It was Ade! Maybe it really would work out for those two. She hoped that Aidan would be happy for her. She hoped they could remain friends. Ade would understand. She just knew instinctively that Ade would understand. He had too. She realised now that she did love Aidan Quinn in a special sort of way. She was going to miss him.

But Neal? Neal was the man she truly loved in every way. He had that one unique quality that brightened her world, made her heart sing with joy, and ultimately gave meaning to her life. She loved his wit and humour, his common sense and intelligence, his well-groomed handsome looks, his little quirky mannerisms. She loved his twinkling, blue eyes, his seductive lips, his electrifying touch, his loving kiss, everything about him…and his persistence, his refusal to let her go, no matter how often she had rejected him. She remembered with renewed joy the ecstatic pleasure that she had experienced when they made love. She could allow herself to think about that again. It wasn't taboo after all. She looked at Neal now and his eyes were full of love and longing for her.

One more glance at her parents, one more smile for her bewildered sister, one fleeting nod towards Aidan… Then, releasing at last all the passion she had repressed for two long years, Charlotte took that final step and melted into the outstretched arms of the man she loved.

A personal note from the author:

Thank you for reading *A Voice from the Past*. I hope you enjoyed it. I would love some feedback from readers so please feel free to contact me through my website or via Facebook or Twitter. You may be interested to know that I am currently working on my second book; *In the Greater Scheme of Things*. If you enjoyed *A Voice from the Past*, I think you will relish this spin-off/sequel too. I am certainly taking pleasure in writing it. Read on for a preview of the first chapter.
Many thanks, Heather.

Website: www.heathermacquarrie.com

Facebook: facebook.com/heather.macquarrie.novelist

Twitter: @h_macq_novelist

In the Greater Scheme of Things

Heather MacQuarrie

Chapter 1

She heard the front door gently click shut and watched sadly from a chink in the dove-grey and cream striped curtains, which were drawn across their small bedroom window, as her husband ambled out through the rusty, wrought-iron gate, got into his silver Audi, and drove off down the road without a backwards glance. A huge sigh of relief escaped from her taut body. Thank God to be alone for a while. She would make sure she was asleep before he returned. In the meantime she had work to do. The time had come for her to flee, once and for all, from this miserable sham of a life which had become so unbearable.

Turning her phone off, lest her father or anyone else should make another attempt to reason with her, she started up her computer and checked the same websites yet again to see if anything new had been added. First things first; if she was to begin a new life on her own, away from all that was familiar to her, the number one priority was finding a new job. She couldn't live without money. Thankfully she still had her own bank account which was in a healthy state due to that gift from her late grandparents. They hadn't got round to opening a joint one yet. After all, they had only been married for three months and she had liked retaining that bit of financial independence. Her husband had been perfectly happy with the arrangement. She certainly hadn't expected to have to rely on it so soon. The fairly substantial sum she had saved would be enough to get her started in a new home with a new job and a new identity but it wouldn't go very far after that. She had to have her own funds. She was leaving her family for good. She didn't want to see them or hear from them ever again. The sense of rejection and humiliation had been too complete, too overwhelming. She just couldn't contemplate being part of their pathetic lives any longer.

Nothing on the screen jumped out at her. What now? Turning it off, she lifted the newspaper she had bought earlier in the day and turned directly to the 'situations vacant' page. As she had done every night that week, she scanned the list of job opportunities for something that would interest her. It was quite amazing that, even in the present economic climate with so many people out of work, there were still a fair number of jobs being advertised. Tonight there were two full pages of them but she hardly read any of the entries. Her eyes were drawn immediately to the bold, black type in the lower, left-hand corner of the second page, where she saw the phrase **'French-speaking nanny'**. Instinctively she knew that this was the job for her. Not only would she change her identity, but she would even invent a new nationality. She was a fluent French speaker. She could easily pass herself off as a French citizen. It could even be fun and it would certainly be an extra safeguard against anyone finding her out. Her heart was gripped with excitement as she copied down the details. She didn't cut it out. That would have been inviting Matthew to check it out and follow her. She mustn't leave any clues. Nor did she hide the newspaper or throw it away. Its very absence could raise his suspicions. He knew they had bought a paper, as usual. She just copied down the details on a scrap of paper and put it into her handbag.

An exhilarating thrill at the prospect of beginning her new life so soon prevented her from sleeping so that she did hear Matthew return just before midnight. For a moment her heart thumped wildly and she held her breath, hoping that he would come to bed straight away and make love to her, that they could recapture the magic they had lost. If he had, the future course of her life might have taken a totally different direction. But he did not. He went into the tiny kitchen and made himself some coffee, then took it into the lounge, where he sat down and turned on the television. He sat there for a long time, listening to one of the music channels. Or maybe it was the sound track to a film. Although he kept the volume low, it was just audible in the bedroom above. It was a very small house but they were only renting. Their accommodation here was supposed to be a very temporary phase. They had been saving hard before the wedding and almost had enough for the deposit on their dream home. But they would never live there now. If Matthew had only known that she was experiencing that one short moment of weakness, or was it strength, when she would have welcomed him with open arms, he would have been upstairs in a flash. But he feared another rejection and he preferred to listen to his music and let her sleep. She would come round in the end. She just needed time. She had suffered a very traumatic experience.

By the time he did go to bed she had fallen asleep but not before writing Matthew a short letter and making some plans for her new life. For the past three hours she had let her imagination run riot. Already she was beginning to believe that the person she had been no longer existed. She was now Francine Martin, a French student taking a year out in England. Her parents, Guy and Thérèse, were still living in Malasherbes, a little town not far from Paris. She had no brothers or sisters, no husband or steady boyfriend patiently waiting for her return. She was quite free to do as she pleased.

Who, then, was this other person lying beside her in the bed? She was half-awake now but still living in the fantasy world she had created. This must be Mathieu, another French student she had met on her travels. They would part company and go their separate ways in the morning but what was he doing here, in her room? Maybe she had invited him to spend the night with her. Yes, that was it. She 'remembered' now. He was going back to

France tomorrow while she was to go job-hunting. They would probably never see each other again and she had invited him to spend his last night with her. She had fancied him for ages.

"Mathieu," she murmured, as she reached out and touched him gently.

"Sorry, love. I didn't mean to disturb you," he replied. "Go back to sleep."

"Non, mon cheri. Tu ne veux pas faire l'amour?"

Matthew hardly spoke a word of French but he had no difficulty understanding her meaning when she rolled towards him and began to stroke his body with loving tenderness. Tentatively at first, he too reached out and touched her intimately, somewhat bemused by her use of a foreign language. She didn't recoil as of late but pulled him closer, indicating that she wanted to make love. Fully aroused now, he did not hesitate to gratify. It was all over very quickly the first time but her intense passion was not spent. Desire for physical contact still radiated from her lithe and warm body, made so obvious by her breathless kisses and sensuous movements. They made love again and then again for a third time. Matthew felt a surge of happiness. Maybe now things could return to some kind of normality. But he sensed he should take it slowly. There was no need for conversation tonight. She was saying it all through her body language, telling him all he needed to know. They could talk in the morning.

He hadn't spotted the small, white envelope, partially hidden under a book, on her bedside table…